GRADING
ON A CURVE

GRADING ON A CURVE

ANDREA WICKBERG

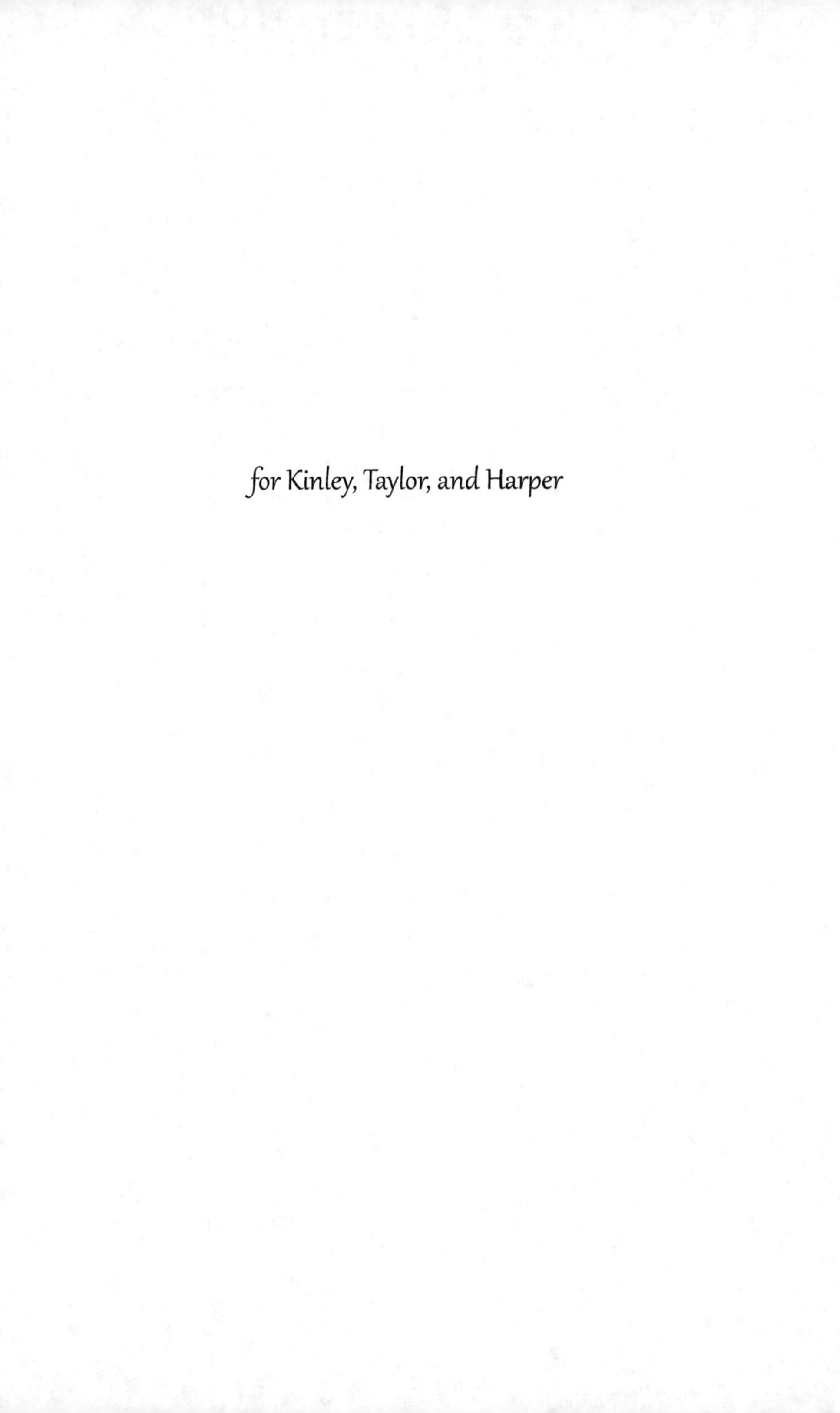

for Kinley, Taylor, and Harper

GRADING ON A CURVE

part one

winter

Chapter One

JACKIE | *DAVID*

Trying to sleep last night was about as effective as trying to run between raindrops, and somehow I convince myself that a cup of coffee can substitute for actual rest. Since I can't stand coffee, I drop a few ice cubes in to make it lukewarm and basically chug it down.

A few minutes later, I'm cursing my stupidity. What the hell was I thinking? Just because David drinks this ridiculous stuff by the gallon doesn't mean it's going to save me. My head feels every bit as heavy and clouded as it did before, except now my hands are shaking.

He's been texting me all morning, and he keeps telling me not to worry, but I can't help it and I don't know how he can either. If that kid saw us together, he's screwed. *We're* screwed.

I've been trying to get a grip on myself all morning but I'm a nervous wreck and lousy at keeping my face in check. When it's finally time to go to his class, I start running until I realize that I look insane and settle for a fast walk instead. I'm in high school, not kindergarten.

I almost went there this morning, before school. To his classroom. I used to do that kind of thing all the time last year, so I don't think it would be too weird. But I knew he wouldn't like it, so I didn't. Instead, I drank the coffee and told myself all morning that I only had to hold out until third period. Then I'd see him. Then everything would be okay.

I try to slow my racing heart as I approach the door, act like this is any other class on any normal day. As I walk in, I feel relief flood my body as though I'm sliding into a hot tub on a freezing night.

He's there. Sitting at his desk and looking the way he always does. Looking at *me* the way he always does, the way that turns me into someone else. Someone better.

"Hey, Jackie." His greeting is as casual as it needs to be, always, but I don't mind. He says other things to me with his eyes and the curve of his mouth, things I play to myself at night when I can't sleep.

"Hi, Mr. Harrison." I sit down at my own desk in the front row and pull out my iPad so I have something to do with my hands. But I never take my eyes off him. I'm not sure if I actually can, since I'm not in the habit of trying.

"Good morning, everyone," he says a few minutes later when the bell rings. He holds up a batch of papers in one hand and a DVD case in the other. "I'm going to pass these back and then we're going to watch this movie to kick off our next classic. Don't let the fact that it's in black and white put you off. That's a significant artistic choice by the director."

"I thought you hated book movies," Beth comments with a grin. She sits next to me, and she's nice enough, but I hate the way she flirts with David. Which is idiotic. I waste enough energy being jealous of Alicia as it is – I don't need to be obsessing about the other girls in David's classes.

He smiles back at her, and I try not to scowl. "I do. Except for this one. It's the only movie I'm going to let you watch in class all year, so enjoy it. *To Kill A Mockingbird* comes across very differently depending on whether you're reading the story or watching it. I want you thinking about why that is."

He presses Play and hits the lights in the back of the room, then starts passing back our papers, face down. All of my other teachers do these things online, but David's old school. He insists that we print our papers because he likes to handwrite his comments.

I don't bother turning mine over to see how I did. English was my best subject even before I became the ultimate teacher's pet. Instead, I wait until most of my classmates are watching the screen and David's back at his desk, then slink over to him.

"What's up?" he whispers.

His composure is super annoying. I've spent the last two days and three nights in a grip of anxiety so extreme I can barely get through a conversation, and David looks about as calm and relaxed as his golden retriever Maggie does when she's getting her belly rubbed.

"You tell me," I reply, so quietly you can't even call it a whisper. "Is everything okay?"

"Why wouldn't it be?"

"No one said anything to you?"

"About what?"

"David, come on. No one's listening."

He leans in closer and his friendly expression dissolves.

"First, it's Mr. Harrison in here."

I roll my eyes.

"And second, we can't talk about anything right now. You know that."

I do know that. I'm not sure what I'm trying to achieve. This isn't the right day for clear thinking of any kind.

I change course. "After school then."

"Jackie…"

"The usual place, okay?"

"Fine. But I need you to go sit down before someone wonders what you're doing up here." It's not like anyone's even looking our way. Everyone is either watching the opening credits or texting their friends behind their iPads. Like that ever fools anybody.

But I square my shoulders and go back to my seat, accepting temporary defeat. As soon as I sit down, my exhaustion overwhelms me and I let my head sink to the desk. I can barely keep my eyes open.

How did this become my life? If I were smart, I would cut this whole thing out and start sleeping with someone my own age.

Or at least someone who's not married.

Less than a minute later, my eyes find him again. I can't help it. And when they do, he's already looking at me. Talking to me again with that tiny private smile.

I'm kidding myself. I might as well try to quit breathing.

Chapter Two

I don't need a lecture. I already know I'm a bastard. I teach high school, so getting involved with one of my students practically makes me a cartoon villain, all the more depraved for being real. The whole thing is such a cliché. But like I tell the freshmen, lots of things are clichés for a reason.

The important thing to understand is that *Jackie* chose this. Chose me. This has always been her decision, every part of it. She wanted me from the moment we first met, though it took her a long time to understand that about herself, and even longer to admit it.

Alicia says I'm charismatic. She's a little biased, being my wife. But it's true that I know how to make people feel good, women and girls especially, and I admit I've been using that to my advantage all my life. Jackie's not the first student I've ever had fall for me, far from it.

She's important to me, though.

It's not like I have a great explanation, at least not one that anyone else would accept. I can't readily elucidate what makes her worth the risks I'm taking. All I can say with certainty is that I enjoy her company. I like talking to her, making her laugh. And yes, I'm also deeply attracted to her, although that one snuck up on me. We'd known each other for almost a year before I saw her as anything other than a particularly bright student.

When that changed, I was equally reluctant to acknowledge it. Nothing good lies down that road. I should know.

But it refused to go away, and here we are. Sometimes it doesn't pay to look too closely at these things. Once in a while, people are drawn to each other across all kinds of barriers and for no reason at all, as I explained to Jackie once. She takes my word on things like that. Probably due to the isolation and neglect she experienced growing up, she doesn't relate all that well to her peers and she's never had a boyfriend. I still can't decide whether I qualify or not.

What I know is this – we have a special connection, something she's never known before, and I like being the first one to share it with her. It's not going to last forever, possibly not even very much longer, but I'm determined to make our experience together a good one. Something that she can look back on with nostalgia for the rest of her life.

They're never going to be normal memories. For obvious reasons I can't take her to dinner, I can't kiss her in public. That kind of thing will never be an option for us. I'm not about to get caught, not only because of the personal backlash for me but because I have no intention of letting Alicia get hurt. And as long as she doesn't know, she never will.

But Jackie doesn't want normal. She's not a normal fifteen year old in the first place. Too much of her youth is gone for that, was stolen long before I even met her. And there's plenty I can give her that she wouldn't get from any boy her age, as I remind her from time to time.

To her credit, she's very good at focusing on that.

***

I do go meet her at the bookstore after school, of course I do. She should have known I would be there – I would never let her stay this upset. Ordinarily she has more sense than to approach me in class like that, so I chalk it up to the fact that she's had a rough few days.

I don't like to linger anywhere we might be seen, so I talk fast and finally get her calmed down enough to come for a drive with me. When I stop about halfway to our normal spot and pull over to the side of the road, she looks at me questioningly.

"What are you doing?"

"Want to drive?"

She smiles at me for the first time all day. "Sure."

We switch places and she slides in behind the wheel. I only started teaching her a week ago, but she's picking it up fast. The road to the out-of-the-way location where we spend time together is a perfect place to practice, because there's very little traffic on it.

"Get in the habit of looking all around you," I remind her. "Usually the danger will be ahead of you, especially on the highway, and that's where most people focus. But occasionally it sneaks up behind you."

She nods. I smile at the expression of concentration on her face, and reach over to play with her dark blonde hair.

"David, don't," she says, barely glancing at me. "You'll distract me."

"You should get used to driving with distractions."

"How about I get used to driving first?"

"Point taken," I reply, moving my hand away. We reach our spot less than ten minutes later, and she carefully pulls over.

"Good job."

She smiles again. "I'm learning."

"You'll be ready for your test in no time."

She leans over the seat to kiss me. "Thank you."

"My pleasure." We reach for our respective door handles. A few moments later, settled semi-comfortably in the backseat, we've seamlessly re-entered the private world we created. The place no one else even suspects, let alone has reason to investigate.

I'll never be able to sell anyone else on this, I get that, but I don't think of what we have as wrong. At least not for the reasons other people would. It's wrong of me to be with someone besides my wife without her consent, I acknowledge that, although I still maintain it's not an issue for her if she doesn't know. Jackie's no threat to Alicia.

But it's not nothing, the way I feel about her – even if it's not the way she loves me, not quite the same way I love Alicia.

I'm careful. I'm considerate. I let her initiate things between us over half the time, put her in the driver's seat figuratively as well as literally. I even gave her space to make the first move, once she was ready. I try to give her control whenever I can, to make up for the various inequities between us which mostly favor me.

Afterward, she's pressed up against me with her eyes closed. I love the look of contentment on her face, love being the one to bring that out in her. It's the only time she really looks relaxed to me.

"How was your day?" I ask her, tracing the pattern of her cheekbone.

"Stressful."

"Just the Friday thing? Or something else?"

"That was enough."

"I'm sorry."

She opens her eyes to look at me. "I'm surprised you weren't more worried."

"I'm not the worrying type, Jackie. You know that." Though I probably should be, if I'm going to start doing phenomenally stupid things like that on a regular basis. Last Friday, I drove to the school during a football game to see her and parked in the darkest spot I could find on the lot. She came out to meet me, and she thought one of her fellow students saw her leaving my car to go back to the game. She was in a panic about it all weekend.

"Yeah, but still. If he had seen something, and told someone, I would have lost you. And you would have lost everything."

If that had happened, I would know it by now. But it certainly wasn't out of the realm of possibility. I'm not normally so reckless, and I don't have any excuse except I was home by myself and I wanted her desperately. Not that I'm going to tell her that.

"Which is why I wouldn't have let that happen."

"I know. It scared me, though." She rests a hand on my chest. "I can't stand the thought of losing you. Even though I don't really have you."

"You do have me." I cover her hand with my own. "I love you."

Her breathing changes, grows heavy and slow. The sleepless nights are catching up with her.

"We better go," I say, squeezing her hand gently.

"Okay."

She gets back in the passenger seat, leaning against my shoulder until we get close to the main road again. Then she sits up, reaching over to hold my hand instead. I never have to tell her to do things like that.

"Feeling better?" I ask as she stifles a yawn.

"Yeah, actually. I think I'll be able to sleep tonight."

"Good."

"I wish you could be there with me. I like falling asleep with you."

"I know you do. I like it too." I've only ever managed to spend one whole night with Jackie, which is a shame, but that kind of thing is too high-risk to be a part of our normal routine.

I drive her home, craning my neck for Isabel's car. Jackie's grandmother is approximately as dependable as the sunrise, so it's not like she would ever come home from work early for any reason short of a dire emergency. Still, you never know. I have a couple of stories ready in case she should ever see me driving Jackie home, but any of them would only work once.

I pull over next to her house, which is much too conveniently isolated, and turn to Jackie.

"I'll see you tomorrow." She looks solemn. "What's the matter?"

"Nothing," she says. "I'm relieved everything worked out, that's all." She pushes an errant lock of hair behind her ear.

"Me too." I brush her cheek with the palm of my hand. Jackie has a few freckles, but they're so light that you can't see them unless you're right next to her face. "Get some sleep. I love you." I don't normally make a point of telling her that, let alone twice in one day, but I sense that she needs it today.

"I love you too." She reaches down for her backpack and goes into the house without looking back at me.

Chapter Three

JACKIE | DAVID

I wander back into the house and try to settle down enough to do my homework. It's useless. After staring at a page for five minutes without taking in a single word, it's all I can do to make it into my bedroom and collapse. Normally I have this ecstatic, buzzy energy after spending the afternoon with David but this isn't a normal day.

I guess I didn't need to stress myself out so much about what happened at the game, since he clearly didn't.

That whole thing started when he texted me on Friday night. I was over at my friend Nicki's house getting ready for the game. She's always bugging me about going out more, and I decided it would be good for me to spend one night being a regular teenager.

So much for that.

Nicki tried to talk me into taking a hit or two on her vape pen but I hate the way pot makes me feel all dizzy and paranoid, so I just had some of the wine we snuck upstairs. I don't usually drink either but I figured if I was going to do this football thing, I might as well go all out.

She smirked at me when I took a sizable gulp in between putting on mascara. "Take it all, why don't you?"

I grinned at her. "I'm just following your lead."

"About frigging time. You're going to the dance next week too."

"Oh God, you're back on that again?"

"Yes. You have to start having fun like a regular person. You act like a forty year old."

"Thanks, bitch," I said with a laugh, shoving her a little with my shoulder. But I didn't really take offense, since what she said was true. I didn't have much in common with other teenagers to begin with, and being with David definitely killed any interest I might have had in dating high school guys. My social life would be pretty nonexistent if it weren't for Nicki.

I'm not even sure how she and I became friends, actually. She's popular and notorious throughout the school for her daring side. In other words, she's cool. Much cooler than I'll ever be. But we've known each other since middle school, and Nicki is nothing if not loyal.

"So it's decided then. Game tonight, dance next week."

"I'm not going to get out of this, am I?"

"Nope. Maybe I'll even find you a date."

"Literally zero need for that."

"There has to be someone in the school who doesn't repulse you." She eyed me in the mirror. Nicks considers my lack of interest in boys extremely suspicious. She semi-regularly accuses me of being a lesbian. Sometimes I wonder what she'd think if she knew the truth. Nicki's done a ton of things I haven't, but even she's never been into anything as risky as what I've got going with David.

My phone buzzed in my pocket right then — not my regular phone, my secret David phone. I always keep it with me, even though he usually only texts me during the day. My heart leapt into my throat and I quickly went to the bathroom so I could read it in private.

The phone is kind of a joke to me. It's not like we need it. Gran doesn't even know my lock code. But David's got it in his head that a separate flip phone is safer for us and there's no talking him out of it.

What are you doing?

I forced myself to drink some water and wait for a couple of minutes before I answered him.

Getting ready to go to the football game. You?

The phone beeped with a response almost immediately.

Oh sure, same here.

I laughed. David hates football. While I was trying to think of a witty response, he texted me again.

Who are you going with?

Nicki. I texted again before I could think about it too much. *Why? Want to meet me? :)*

A moment passed before the phone beeped again.

Sure. I'll meet you in the parking lot at 7:30.

I hadn't expected him to say yes. Part of me wanted to play it cool and say no, show him I'm not at his beck and call, but I couldn't resist the excitement of seeing him at night for the first time since Alicia was out of town.

Besides, I pretty much *am* at his beck and call, at least for the moment. We both know it.

The game was crowded and Nicki immediately started passing an edible back and forth with some junior and senior guys, all of whom ignored me. It was easy to slip away.

David flicked his lights when he saw me so that I could find his car, way on the outer edge of the lot. I got into his familiar backseat, momentarily overwhelmed by the faint smell of his cologne. He has this fresh spicy scent that's entirely unique to him. I adore it.

"Hi," I said, glancing at him in the rearview mirror.

"Hi, yourself."

"You going to join me or what?"

David has this very graceful, deliberate way of moving that I love to watch. He always reminds me of a dancer, which could also be because he's built like one. He's very thin and barely an inch taller than me, and his features are so delicate they're almost pretty.

Alicia is taller than he is, which I thought looked a little funny the first time I saw them. Now I just try never to picture them together. At all.

He got into the backseat and I immediately pulled him toward me. A month ago, I would have waited for him to start but I was getting braver.

"How's the game going?" he asked me as he nudged my coat off. I could feel his breath on my neck and it made me shiver in anticipation.

"Who cares?" I asked. That was the last thing either of us said for a long time.

Before David, I hadn't gone much beyond kissing. He took it slow with me at first, so slow I started begging him for more. It didn't take me long at all to go from fixating on David himself to developing an obsession with his body, and the things he does to mine.

We've only been having sex for a few weeks now, but it's practically all I ever think about. The rest of my life is starting to fade into a series of irritating distractions standing between me and the next time I can get him alone.

I still can't believe this is happening. I can't believe he loves me, and I can't believe he *lets* himself love me.

His hand tightened around my wrist, hard enough to hurt, and I felt him gasp. I love that so much. The moment at the end when he loses control to *me* for a change makes me feel so powerful. It's almost the best part.

He kind of collapsed on top of me, and I had to push him up after a minute so I could breathe. As I was trying to find my pants, I saw him carefully removing the condom and stashing it in a plastic bag he had ready. David's so meticulous about everything, it cracks me up sometimes.

The strapless top I'd been wearing was all twisted in the back. David straightened it for me, then pulled me against him.

"Why'd you text me tonight?" I asked him. I turned my head so I could look at him.

"Because I missed you. You have a problem with that?" he asked as he kissed me.

"Not at all. I missed you too." I resumed my position against his chest and ran my hand down his leg. I love being able to touch him like that. "Where did you say you were going?"

"Alicia's out. She was already gone when I left."

"Oh." I didn't even know why I was asking. I don't like talking about Alicia.

"What are you going to tell Nicki?"

"She's so stoned, she won't even notice I'm gone," I said. "She always gets trashed on game nights."

"Why?"

"I don't know. It's what Nicki does. She likes to party."

"You haven't been smoking, have you?" His fingers drew a path along the edge of my ear.

"No. I hate pot."

"Drinking?"

"Only a little. Not much."

"Did we just break my rule?"

I laughed. "For someone who's breaking the law, you have a lot of rules."

"I'm entitled to them." He turned me around to face him again, suddenly serious. "You're not drunk, right?"

"No, I swear. I had a couple sips of wine, that's all." I paused. "Why do you care, anyway? Are you going to lecture me about underage drinking?"

He didn't take the bait. "I don't want you to get drunk to be with someone. Especially me."

"Why?"

"Mainly because I don't want you to regret anything we do."

"That's not going to happen."

He kissed me again, for longer this time. "You should probably get back."

"I don't want to," I murmured against his mouth. "I want to stay with you. This sucks."

He nodded. "It does." I felt his finger graze over the tiny gold stud in my ear, a present from Gran. All of a sudden, I felt a strong urge to bail before I said or did something stupid.

"Okay. I'm going." I pulled on my coat and got out of the car, then started running for some reason. But I'd only made it about halfway across the parking lot when I heard a voice call out to me.

"Hey! Jackie! What are you doing out here?" I looked over and saw a boy I vaguely remembered from my Spanish class last year. I stared at him in horror, wondering if he'd seen me get out of David's car.

"You okay?"

I didn't stop to answer him. I just took off running again, which was dumb. What I should have done was say something halfway normal to him first. He must have thought I was nuts.

I hope he didn't see David driving off.

But if he did, I guess he didn't say anything. That's what matters.

Chapter Four

JACKIE | **DAVID**

Alicia's still at work when I get home, since there's a school board meeting tonight. I would hate doing things like that, but she actually seems to enjoy all the bureaucratic nonsense that goes with being vice-principal. I start making dinner, knowing she'll be starving by the time she gets back.

When she gets in around seven, she looks happy.

"How was the meeting?" I ask her.

"Fine." I'm standing by the stove, stirring a sauce. She comes over and motions to my workout clothes. "Did you go for a run?"

"Not yet. I was thinking of taking Maggie –" Alicia is directly behind me, and without warning her hand is sliding inside my shorts. I chuckle. "Hey, it's nice to see you too."

"Can you stop without burning that?"

"It's done. I'm just stirring to make sure it doesn't…" I pull in my breath abruptly as her second hand joins the party. "…stick."

She proceeds to tell me what she was thinking about during her meeting, in vivid detail. Those budget discussions must get awfully boring.

Normally I try not to do this with both Jackie and Alicia in the same day – for some reason, it feels disrespectful to both of them – but I can see I'm not going to have much say in it this time.

We don't even make it to the bedroom. She pulls me over to the couch instead.

Alicia and I have always had a great sex life. It's one of the best parts of our relationship, and hasn't even suffered unduly from the inevitable boredom of routine. Ever since I started seeing Jackie, it's gotten better and if anything, more frequent. Whether it's from guilt or just the extra energy Jackie brings out in me, Alicia's reaping the benefits. So she gets something out of this too.

Or so I like to think.

When we're done, I give her an exaggerated wink. She laughs and kisses me.

"Better?"

"Absolutely."

"Want some dinner?"

"Yes. Just let me go take a quick shower first."

I watch her go, feeling unearned pride in her body. Alicia's a stunner, there's no question about that. She's tall and voluptuous, and has this fiery red hair I've always loved.

She looks nothing like Jackie, who's all narrow lines and straight edges. Like me.

I tell myself it's none of Jackie's business, what goes on between me and my wife. And it isn't. She's known the score from the very beginning; I've never once lied to her.

But sometimes I can't help feeling like she's the one I'm cheating on. Like I'm letting her down in some way.

Having an affair is all about compartmentalizing. The more I can separate the two of them in my mind, see them as two completely separate relationships with me as the only bridge, the better things are for everyone. But it's easier said than done.

Occasionally I delude myself that Alicia could almost understand about Jackie. After all, she dated one of her own professors in college. Sometimes I tease her that she only married me so I could fulfill her leftover student-teacher fantasies on a regular basis. Which I do, although that feels a little twisted these days.

But deep down, I know it's bullshit. By the time she got to the "understanding and acceptance" phase, Alicia would have long since ripped me to shreds not so much for the cheating, but because I'm cheating with a student. It's definitely less about the injury and more about the insult with her.

***

Bookstore today? I text Jackie over lunch.

A brief answer comes back about twenty minutes later.

Bad time :(

I smile at her euphemism, which is as direct as she ever gets when it comes to things like that. Jackie's still shy sometimes, even with me. I text her back.

I don't mind. Still want to see you.

The phone beeps again.

Okay :)

We go for our usual drive, head for our normal place and immediately switch to the backseat once we're there. Force of habit goes a long way. She lays her head back in my lap and I tilt my head down, then immediately pull it back up.

"Ow."

"What's the matter?"

"I slept on my neck wrong, and it's been aching all day. That kind of thing happens when you get old."

Jackie frowns slightly – she doesn't love being reminded of my age. I'm not actually old at all, but I remember how impossibly distant thirty-something seemed when I was fifteen. "Want me to give you a massage?"

"I won't say no to that."

She sits up and repositions herself behind me. Then she hesitates. "I don't really know how to do this. Even though you do it to me all the time."

I place her hands on my neck where it's bothering me most. "Just rub here, as hard as you want. I'll tell you if it's too much."

She does, and she's pretty good at it. She keeps up an intense, steady pressure that feels better than anything has all day.

"Mm. That's great, Jackie."

"Really?"

"Yeah. You're a natural."

"Good." Her voice is light and happy, the way she always sounds when I compliment her. She continues, working her way down. "It's hard to do this through your shirt. Can you take it off?"

I smirk and comply. The girl loves to get my clothes off. Any way she can.

"I never noticed this before," she says a moment later.

"What's that?"

"This scar here, on your shoulder blade." She runs a finger over it, lightly. "Looks deep. That must have hurt."

"It did."

"What happened?"

I pause, trying to decide whether to tell her this story. But I don't have the energy to make something up. Anyway, she can handle it.

"I was maybe ten, and my dad was drunk and furious about something. He hit me and I fell backward onto our glass coffee table. When it broke, a piece caught me in the shoulder." I didn't have the greatest childhood, not that it matters to me anymore.

Jackie winces. "Ouch. That's awful."

I shrug. "Not the first, last, or only time something like that happened. My mom was just as bad."

"So what happened?"

"Sam came in —"

"Your brother?"

"Yeah. He's eight years older than me, so he was big enough

by then to stand up to my dad without getting hurt. Mostly. He was outside mowing the lawn, that's why he hadn't come in sooner. Anyway, he started screaming at my dad and trying to get me cleaned up at the same time."

"Did you get stitches?"

"No. I probably needed them but I'd just been to the ER for something else, and Sam didn't want to risk me getting handed to CPS. That happened to one of his friends and he was afraid it would be even worse for me. So we made do with superglue and duct tape."

"Are you serious?"

"That's why the scar looks ugly." I laugh. "Sam's not exactly a doctor."

"Wow." Jackie continues rubbing, but she stays away from the scar.

"It's okay. You can touch. It's not like it still hurts."

"My dad never did anything like that," she remarks. "He never hit me. He wasn't a mean drunk like yours, at least."

"I'm glad." I reach behind me and lay my hand on her knee. "Doesn't mean the way he treated you was okay, though."

"I know. But still." She keeps massaging me, moving to my lower back. "So that's why you never drink, huh?"

"Pretty much. Yeah."

"I don't blame you."

Chapter Five

JACKIE | *DAVID*

Hearing David's grisly anecdote depressed me and I can't get that hideous scar out of my mind. I'm not sure how I missed seeing it before. He's mentioned to me that his parents used to drink, but he sounded so casual about it. I didn't know it was that bad.

After he drives me home, I start catching up on my homework. I'm still at it a couple of hours later when it starts sleeting.

I like Oregon weather. It's fun to actually have seasons. I didn't think so at first, but that was mostly because of the reason I was here to see fall come around in the first place.

My mom took off on us when I was barely six. It's getting hard to remember what she looked like, because my dad threw out all the pictures he could find of her one night when he was wasted. I still have a few left, but I don't ever look at them. I tell myself it's easier that way.

My dad and I were never exactly close, but he got me through the next few years all right. Even then, he sent me to my grandma's house every summer so he wouldn't have to pay for daycare in California. I was fine with that, though. I liked Gran's little, cozy house in the woods and I always had fun with her.

Gran's been on her own ever since my grandpa died, but she has so many friends that she never seems to get lonely. Everyone loves her, especially me. Even when I was a kid, she always listened to me and took my opinions seriously. I didn't get that at home.

My dad's drinking didn't get really bad until I was about twelve and he started staying out until all hours at night, usually without bothering to tell me. It was like I didn't exist. He'd stumble in hours after I'd fallen asleep in the living room with the TV on, since I was too scared to sleep in my room.

That was the summer he decided to leave me up in Oregon, which he didn't even have the balls to tell me himself.

"Sit down, dear," Gran said to me when I asked her if my dad was coming to get me soon. "I talked to your dad last night, and he asked me if I would consider having you live here for this school year." No beating around the bush. That's not Gran's style.

"You mean, he doesn't want me to come home?"

Gran frowned and patted her short-cropped, silver hair. She's tiny, almost birdlike, but I know from experience that her fragile appearance doesn't reflect the inside of her. "It's not you he doesn't want. The problem is him. He doesn't feel like he can be a good father to you right now."

"Well, at least he admits it," I said quietly. "He's never around anymore. He's always at work or off drinking somewhere." It had been good to get away that summer. I couldn't have put it in words back then, but a big part of what I love about Gran is her stability. I craved it when I was little.

"Perhaps this is for the best then."

"Is it… okay with you?" I couldn't quite look at her.

"Of course it's okay. You know you're always welcome. It's nice having you here."

I wanted to believe her but if my own parents didn't want me, it was hard to accept that anyone else could. "I can help you out," I said, still staring at the table. "You know. With shopping and stuff."

"You don't have to sell me on this," Gran said firmly. "I'm not thrilled with my son's choices right now, but I'm happy to have you staying with me. And the middle school here isn't bad." I nodded, but my eyes started filling with tears. "Oh, darling. Come here." Gran held out her arms, but I shook my head. I don't like to cry in front of anyone, even her.

"I'm okay. Really." I stood up to go to my room. "I want to be alone for a while."

She let me go. Gran's always respected my space. By the time she came to check on me a few hours later, I'd pulled myself together.

"This is fine. Really," I told her. "I *want* to stay here. It's just that he's my dad. He's the only parent I have left."

She nodded. "I know, Jackie. I'm sorry this is happening to you. It's not right. And I know I can't take the place of your parents." She placed a hand on mine. "That being said, you do have me. And as long as I'm here, you will never be alone."

***

My dad never asked me to come home. I doubt he ever will. The only time I hear from him these days is an occasional drunk dial, when he remembers he has a daughter.

I've been happier here in Gran's house, mostly. It was a new experience to have someone around who cared about my schoolwork and made sure I went to the dentist. Sometimes it got annoying, and we had our rough patches, but we got through them.

I've always hated hurting or disappointing Gran. Concealing my real relationship with David from her is one of the hardest things about it, but I have no choice. Apart from the obvious reasons she can't ever know, Gran is friends with David's wife. I met Alicia before I even started high school. Before I met him.

David took an interest in me from the time I wrote my first paper for him. He said I was a talented writer, and he wanted to help me get even better. I loved knowing that he considered me important enough to challenge. He wasn't shy about telling me when he thought I was slacking, but when I did well he was just as generous with his praise.

Like Gran, he treated me with respect. He gave me more of his undivided attention than I felt I deserved, usually before school or at lunch. At first we mostly talked about books, but eventually I started to confide in him because he made it so easy. I can't remember him ever blowing me off or making me feel silly.

I love him for that.

I pretended to see him as a mentor, which was more or less true last year. It was over the summer that I started missing him like crazy. I thought about him constantly, and lived for his emails. Gran invited him and Alicia to a fundraiser she threw, and that night was the highlight of my summer.

A few days into my sophomore year, I came to a realization that was actually more about Alicia than him. As much as I liked her – and I really did – thinking about her in David's presence was starting to make me uncomfortable.

That was around the time he told me about the essay contest.

I'd entered the previous year at David's urging and pretty much forgot about it after that. It was a statewide contest, so it wasn't like I was going to win. But one day, I walked into his classroom before school to find him sitting on his desk, beaming. I almost didn't believe him when he told me.

Alicia made a huge deal about this at school, even calling an assembly over it. David was the one who presented the award, and he gave me a hug in front of everyone when he did.

"You deserve this completely," he murmured in my ear, making me glow. "I'm so proud of you."

Alicia took a photo of me and David in the auditorium afterward, which she posted on the school website. I saved it to my phone, of course. It's the only picture I have of us together.

It's weird to look at now, because it's also the last picture of me before everything changed.

The following day, he asked if he could take me to get a cup of coffee after school. To celebrate. I said yes and spent the rest of the day in a state of frantic anticipation. I'd been alone with him before, and I'd seen him outside of school, but never both of those things together. I kept telling myself I was crazy, he was just being the same nice guy that he always had been, but I couldn't shake the thought that getting coffee with him sounded almost like a date.

Maybe that's what gave me the courage to blurt out what I did almost as soon as we sat down.

"I wish you weren't my teacher," I'd said suddenly, surprising myself. David smiled.

"Why? I enjoy being your teacher."

"I don't mean it like that," I said. "You're an amazing teacher. I just wish we had met some other way sometimes."

"And why is that?" He'd leaned forward a little bit and my pulse tripled. It felt like his eyes were prying me open, skimming over my thoughts. And I got the definite feeling he didn't mind what he found there. The secret I hadn't even been willing to tell myself.

"I don't know if I should say," I said at last. What I really meant was that I wasn't sure if I could.

"Go ahead." He took a sip of his coffee. "You can say it."

"Okay," I said, gripping my cup as hard as I could without making hot chocolate spill out over the edges. David waited while I took a deep breath and finally said it. "I care about you." A peal of panicky laughter flew out of me. "In a way I… shouldn't. I know you probably don't want to hear that from me." He was still silent, so I kept talking. "I'm sorry. Forget I said anything."

"Your hands are shaking," he observed with a hint of amusement in his voice. But I didn't feel like he was laughing at me. His expression was serious, but kind. "You don't need to be sorry. If it helps, I already knew."

"You *knew?* How?"

"I could tell by the way you act around me. But I wanted to hear you say it. Relax." He reached out and put a hand on my arm. "Just because nothing can happen between us doesn't mean I'm not flattered, Jackie."

I nodded furiously. Most of what I remember feeling in that moment is relief that he wasn't mad, with some embarrassment mixed in. I said the first thing I could think of that wasn't about me.

"I guess this happens to you all the time, huh?"

"Why do you say that?"

"Well… you're *you*." I couldn't imagine anyone not loving him.

"No, this doesn't happen all the time." Now he did look amused. I totally didn't believe him, and it must have shown on my face. "Really, it doesn't. I don't put myself in this position."

"What, you don't take all of your students out for coffee?"

"Never. This is actually the first time. It's not a great look for a high school teacher. People could get the wrong idea."

"So why are you doing it now?"

"Because it's a special occasion," he said. "And I trust you."

We must have talked more after that, but all I remember is him driving me home. He pulled up to Gran's house, which is in the middle of nowhere. I walk a half mile to the bus stop every morning and pass our two neighbors on the way.

Gran wasn't home. For the first time, we were genuinely alone.

"Here we are," I said, unclicking my seat belt. "Thanks for the coffee, and the ride." But I didn't get out. Something kept me rooted where I was and when I looked at his face, I realized it was him.

He didn't want me to go.

The tension felt like it was crushing the air from my lungs but I made myself sit there and wait. And the next thing I knew, he was reaching over to caress my face.

I couldn't believe he was actually going to kiss me, not even as he started doing it. His lips touched mine so gently that it could have almost been something I was dreaming, not that I cared if I was. I didn't care about anything except the explosion of pleasure that echoed through me.

When he pulled away, I stared at him in shock.

"Did… that really just happen?" I asked him, trying in vain to catch my breath.

He shook his head. "Not officially. Unless you want me to lose my job."

As soon as he said that, Alicia's face flashed in front of me and my stomach clenched painfully.

"I'm not going to say anything," I said. "But… why?"

He reached across the seat and wove his fingers between mine, which felt almost as good as his kiss had. "I wanted to give you something," he said. "I wanted you to know that it's not wrong to tell someone how you feel about them. You never know what might come of it." Before I could absorb that, he was kissing me again.

I never thought for a second this scene was going to repeat itself. I thought I knew better than that. But he'd awakened this crazy desire in me, a hunger. Nothing any boy had ever made me feel came close. It overpowered me immediately as I half-stumbled into the empty house, already desperate to hang on to the memories of his face so close to mine. The way he smelled.

I started to touch myself, imagining David doing it, and I came before a full minute had passed. It was the first time I'd ever done that with him in mind. I sprawled out on my bed, breathing hard, and brought up the photo Alicia had taken the day before.

I kissed Mr. Harrison. I kissed my teacher.

I kept staring at the photo for what must have been an hour. When Gran came home that night, I barely spoke to her. I was too afraid I'd say the wrong thing and she'd know.

I would have been floating on air, except that Alicia would not leave my mind. A guilty little cancer was already starting to form in my chest.

All we did was kiss, I told myself over and over. *It's no big deal.*

But it was to me. It was everything.

I wondered if he regretted kissing me. If he would start treating me differently. And he did, but not in the way I expected.

Two days later, David astonished me by showing up in my favorite bookstore after I mentioned that I would be there. He gave me a ride home again. Before long, we were meeting there on a regular basis so no one would see us leaving school together.

I started to call him David when we were alone.

Every fantasy I'd ever had about him, and plenty I hadn't, began to collect sound and texture and living color.

Chapter Six

Alicia and our principal, Kathryn, hold several assemblies throughout the year for sophomore and junior classes about preparing for college. On the day of this month's assembly, I walk over to the library with Jackie's class. As everyone's getting settled, I feel a soft touch on my shoulder that lasts a beat or two longer than simply getting my attention would require. I turn to one of Jackie's classmates, a girl named Beth.

"Can I come see you after this, Mr. Harrison?" Beth asks me.

"Sure, if there's time. Sometimes this presentation goes the whole period. What's up?"

"I need to ask a couple of questions about the paper you assigned."

"Okay, no problem."

When I glance up, I find Jackie and Alicia both glaring daggers at me from their respective positions in the room and I have to stifle a laugh at how identical their expressions are. They're both too far away to hear what Beth is saying, but it's not what we're talking about that's bugging them. It's the way Beth is looking at me.

Beth is a very pretty girl, in a hugely stereotypical way. She looks like every cheerleader in every teenage movie. And she loves to flirt. With everyone. Constantly.

"You better go sit down," I say to her. Beth nods and accidentally-on-purpose brushes my forearm with her breast as she turns, which makes me want to laugh even more.

Jackie looks away, crossing her arms in front of her. Alicia still looks annoyed, but quickly turns the room's attention to the topic at hand and all is forgotten. For the moment.

At the end of the period, Jackie hangs back near the computers as Alicia and Kathryn come over to say hi. What she gets out of eavesdropping on our small talk is anyone's guess.

I chat with them for a few minutes before glancing toward the door where Beth is waiting near the front desk. Alicia follows my gaze and the exasperated look is back.

"I better get going." I give Alicia my most charming, guileless look and she shakes her head. "I'll see you at lunch, Alicia. Bye, Kathryn."

"See you, David."

Beth walks over to me as I head for the door.

"Follow me," I say. "We can talk on my way back to class."

I peek over my shoulder as we leave. Jackie is determinedly facing the computer.

***

"You looked pretty pissed earlier," I inform her later, as we're driving.

"What are you talking about? When?" Her voice is carefully neutral.

"In the library." Her mouth forms a thin line and she stares out the window. It's so rare to see her rattled about anything, I can't resist teasing her a little. "What, are you jealous?"

She sighs. "Don't make fun of me, David."

"I wouldn't do that, Jackie. I'm kidding." I pull over and the car falls into silence. "Did it really upset you? The way Beth was talking to me?"

"No." She's not turning toward me.

"Jackie. Look at me."

She takes her time doing so. To my dismay, she actually looks hurt.

"You *are* jealous." She still doesn't respond. "You don't really have a right to be."

"You think I don't know that?" Her voice sounds a little bit choked.

"Why does it bother you?"

"I don't know. Maybe because she obviously likes you and she's about a million times prettier than me."

It's my turn to sigh. "Jackie, girls like Beth flirt with their teachers the way they flirt with baristas at Starbucks. It means less than nothing to me. It doesn't even mean anything to *them*. It's a game they play." I soften my tone and stroke her hair. "And she's not prettier than you."

She pulls away, looking uncomfortable.

"What are you thinking?"

She doesn't answer for a while, and her gaze drifts out the window again.

"Do you think this is wrong?" she says at last.

"What, you and me?" She nods. "There's no good answer to that question. What brought this on?" Jackie had frequent stabs of conscience when we first got together, but lately she seems to have adjusted. I thought she'd accepted our situation for what it is and let go of the guilt.

"I don't mean only because of… her." Jackie tends to avoid using Alicia's name. "If you weren't married, would it be wrong? What we're doing?"

"Do you think it would be?"

"I don't know. That's why I'm asking you. Can't exactly ask anyone else."

"It totally depends on the culture, Jackie. In a lot of parts of the world, maybe even most, our age difference wouldn't raise an eyebrow."

"But here, it could get you arrested."

"True. But a lot of things that aren't particularly immoral are still against the law, like speeding. And on the other side of the coin, there are a lot of unethical things that aren't illegal. The law isn't a great metric for what's right or wrong."

"I don't like knowing that you could get in trouble for being with me. It makes me feel like *I'm* doing something wrong."

"I'm an adult. It's my choice to be here. You didn't make me do anything." I reach for her hand and pull her toward me. "You have to understand, I'm not worried about getting in trouble. That's not likely to happen unless you were to tell someone. And I know you love me too much to ever do that."

"Yeah. I do," she says quietly. Then she laughs. "You're pretty trusting, you know."

"Actually, I'm not," I reply. "I don't trust many people the way I do you."

She looks up at me. "You mean that?"

"Yes."

I don't perceive my statement as particularly romantic, but I can see it hit that way for Jackie. She starts kissing me fiercely, but I pull back before she gets too carried away.

"We don't have to do this, you know."

"You don't want to?"

"I don't want you to feel like I expect it. You're never under any obligation to do anything with me." Maybe her talk of the law has spooked me more than I care to admit.

"You've never pressured me," she replies. "It's my choice too, right?"

I nod.

"Then this is what I want." Her face forms a trademark Jackie expression – a straightforward, challenging look. I feel a rush of affection for her and kiss her again.

Later, I stretch out across the backseat and she maneuvers herself carefully on top of me, like I'm a beach towel. I haven't had sex in a car this often since I was in high school myself.

"So?" I murmur in her ear. "Still wondering if this is wrong?"

She laces her hands together on my chest and rests her chin on them, holding my gaze.

"Nothing that good could really be wrong."

***

The next two months pass peacefully. Life hums along for all of us with zero drama, exactly the way I like it.

Until a chance encounter with Isabel and Jackie at a shopping center leads to Isabel inviting me and Alicia over for dinner. There's nothing I can do to prevent it, as I explain to Jackie when she asks me if I can somehow get out of it. We've been to Isabel's house half a dozen times, at least, but not since my relationship with Jackie escalated. She hates the idea of containing her guilty conscience while she's sitting across the table from Alicia, and I'm not wild about the prospect myself.

But reason says it will just as hard for Jackie and a lot more suspicious if I don't go, which means the best way through this is to get her to relax a little. So when I see her in the hallway between periods a few hours later and she still looks stressed out, I walk up to her.

"Ever hear the expression 'fake it till you make it'?" She scoffs. "I'm serious, Jackie. You look like you're facing down a firing squad. You're making this a lot harder on yourself than it needs to be."

"Whatever you say, Mr. Harrison." She looks at me coldly, pronouncing my last name with a special variety of strained sarcasm I rarely hear from her. "I better get going."

Chapter Seven

JACKIE | *DAVID*

I start dinner on the late side so that I'll still be working on it when they arrive. The longer I'm out of the picture, the better I figure the evening will go.

I like to cook, and David does too. Over the last year, he's taught me how to make a few things. We never made this dish together but he gave me the recipe and told me to try it sometime. I'm determined to do it justice.

Not that I'll be able to taste much besides the bitter combination of jealousy and guilt that fills my mouth when I'm around Alicia. Standing on the street with her for ten minutes while she and Gran chatted was excruciating. I have no clue how I'm going to get through a whole meal.

I glance down at my clothes for the millionth time. I went with my nicest, most flattering jeans and a layered blouse that Gran's always after me to wear more. I also wound my hair into a careful French braid. None of it matters. Alicia's going to look better than me anyway.

I hear the doorbell ring and wash my hands with exaggerated slowness. I make it to the living room as Gran is answering the door.

"Welcome!" she greets them. I hang back, watching them come

in. David looks the same way he always does, which to me is perfect. Alicia has on a green wraparound dress that somehow makes her look even more striking than usual. I can't help comparing myself to her, with disastrous results.

"Hi, Jackie," she says, looking genuinely pleased to see me. Time to fake it till I make it.

"Hi, Mrs. Harrison," I reply. "I love your dress." Complimenting her feels like biting on tinfoil. It's going to be a long night. I quickly excuse myself to get back to the kitchen while Gran takes them to the patio for drinks. She pours wine for herself and Alicia, but David asks for water.

"Jackie, can you please bring David a glass of water?" Gran calls through the cracked kitchen window. I've already filled a tumbler with ice water, which I bring out to him.

"Thanks," he says. One of his fingers brushes mine as he takes it from me. "Do you need any help with dinner?"

"That's okay. I'm just about finished."

"What are you making?" Alicia asks. "It smells crazy good in there."

"Herb crusted stuffed chicken and artichoke hearts."

"Oh, David makes that sometimes. Did you give her your recipe?" she asks him.

"Yes, I did." He smiles in recognition.

I suddenly wonder if I've made a tactical error in choosing it. "I, um, wanted to make something you'd like. If I don't screw it up, it should be pretty good."

"It will be. Jackie's becoming quite an accomplished chef," Gran informs them confidently.

"I wouldn't go that far," I reply.

"You did great with the food for the barbeque last summer," David says. He sounds so natural it's creeping me out a little bit. The way he's talking to me, you'd never know anything was different. This could be any of a dozen conversations we've had in front of Gran and Alicia before.

"Well, that didn't totally count. Since you helped." My face gets hot when I remember the last time we cooked together. I'm not as good at this as he is. "I better get back inside. I'll be done soon."

Gran and Alicia carry most of the conversation throughout dinner, which might have made things a little bit easier except that Alicia keeps talking to me. I'd almost forgotten how approachable and friendly she can be.

"This is excellent, Jackie," she says as she spears a forkful of chicken. "It's as good as David's. Very impressive. The only thing I could make in high school was toast."

"That's still about all the cooking you can do," he kids her. The tender inflection of his teasing is agonizingly familiar. It feels like a knife twisting between my ribs when he directs it at her.

"Hey, I definitely added macaroni salad to my repertoire at one point," she tosses back. "Anyway, this is great."

"Thank you." I try to think of something else to say. Gran's been teaching me how to make conversation with adults since I was a kid, and I know she expects better from me. But I can't do it right now. I can't do it with Alicia. It's taking all I have just to answer her questions.

"When did you learn to cook?" she asks me.

"I was eleven or twelve. My dad doesn't cook much and I got bored eating the same thing all the time, so I started experimenting one day." By then, I was eating almost every meal alone anyway.

"Remind me how long you've been living here again?"

"Three years this summer." I wonder suddenly how much Alicia has heard from Gran about why I moved here. She probably knows more than I'd like, but there's nothing I can do about that.

I hope David doesn't tell her things about me.

"They've been good years," Gran says, smiling at me. "Jackie's done very well here."

"Yes, she has," Alicia agrees. "I remember how proud David was when she won that contest right after school started."

"He deserved to be, after spending all that extra time with her."

David says nothing, but he looks pleased. He's not one to argue with a compliment.

"Isabel mentioned you were thinking of getting a job, Jackie?" Alicia asks.

"Yeah, this summer." I slice my chicken into a row of identical bites. "I would have gotten one sooner but most places around here won't hire fifteen year olds. Hopefully I'll have a better chance after my birthday."

"When is that?"

"Week after next."

"Sixteen is a big milestone," Alicia remarks. "Are you having a party?"

"I'll probably just have a couple of friends over." Thinking about a birthday party feels childish, and reminds me again that all I want for my birthday – or ever – rightfully belongs to her.

Luckily, David jumps in to rescue me. He's been fairly quiet all through dinner and when he does speak, he directs his questions and comments to Gran the same way Alicia's been focusing on me. I hope it doesn't seem strange that he and I aren't talking to each other.

When everyone seems to be done, I go in the kitchen to get dessert ready. I'm counting down the minutes until this evening is finally over. As I'm cutting up strawberries, Alicia comes in. Her sudden presence startles me and the knife slips, slicing into my palm.

"Ow! Shit." Several drops of blood hit the board.

"Oh, Jackie!" Alicia gasps. "I'm so sorry. Oh no, you're bleeding."

"I'm okay." I go over to the sink and run cold water over my hand. "Ugh. This is disgusting. At least we're already done with dinner." Part of me is relieved to have ruined the dessert. Maybe they'll leave now.

"Let me help you," Alicia says as she comes over to me. "Is it bad?"

"I'll be okay. I should wrap this…" I trail off as Alicia lifts my hand to take a closer look. I breathe in a hint of lilac and the subtle scent takes me back immediately to the last place I smelled it. Which was in their bedroom.

I feel like throwing up.

"Are you okay?" She puts her other hand on my shoulder and I can't stand the way she's looking at me. She's acting – as much as I try to suppress the thought – almost like a mom might, not that I would know. The idea upsets me on too many levels to count.

"Sorry," I say, pulling my hand back. "I think I might be sick. Give me a second." I run to the bathroom, close the door, and grab a dark blue hand towel to press against the cut because it's the first thing I see. At least it won't stain. I slump over the sink trying to breathe through my nose.

"Jackie?" Gran calls. "Are you all right? Alicia said you cut yourself."

"I'll be okay. I just need a minute."

"I'll get you the first aid kit."

"Thanks." I lift the towel, relieved to see that the bleeding is finally slowing down. It stings like crazy but it isn't too deep. Gran passes me a kit and I hastily bandage my hand.

When I emerge from the bathroom, all three of them are waiting for me with concerned looks on their faces.

"Oh. This is awkward," I say. "I'm fine. It's not bad at all. Sorry about dessert."

Alicia waves a hand at me and I try not to stare at her wedding ring. "Don't worry about that. Dinner was plenty."

"You look really pale, Jackie," David says. "Are you sure you're all right?"

"Yes," I say, sounding slightly irritated even to myself. "I have a thing about blood. That's all."

"I never knew that," Gran says. She wouldn't have, since I'm completely making it up. But what am I supposed to tell her?

"Well, we should probably be going," Alicia says after a brief silence. "It's a school night and David gets up early."

"Before you go, Alicia, did you want to take a look at the books?" At first I have no idea what Gran is talking about, but then I remember her mentioning some old books that she wanted to donate to the school during dinner.

"Oh yeah, I forgot. Lead the way."

"They're in the garage." Alicia follows Gran and just like that, I'm alone with David. He comes a little closer to me and takes my hand, turning it over to see my palm.

"Are you sure you're okay?" he asks again.

"Yes. It's only a cut. I don't know why you're making such a big deal." I pull my hand back.

"Because you don't look okay. At all." He looks at me quizzically. "That wasn't so bad. Was it?" I shake my head, looking at the floor.

Maybe not for *him*.

Chapter Eight

JACKIE | **DAVID**

Jackie's performed remarkably well throughout the evening, but I'm worried about her. As soon as we're alone, the tension she's carried all night begins to seep from the edges of the mask she's been wearing. I'm not sure it would be noticeable to someone who doesn't know her as well as I do, but I can see it.

Hoping to distract her, I ask to see her room. I've never been in there.

She turns and leads me down the hall without a word. Her bedroom is very tidy, which doesn't surprise me, but it's awfully generic. She doesn't have posters on the wall or photos of friends tacked up. No lava lamps or tea lights or any of the absurd things teenage girls typically use to decorate their rooms. Despite her long tenure here, this could practically be a hotel room. I wonder if she's subconsciously staying prepared in case she has to leave at a moment's notice. The idea makes me a little sad.

The biggest clue to her personality is a bookshelf on the far wall of the room, which I step over to examine. More than a few of the books on this shelf used to be mine.

I smile as I come across my old worn copy of *The Crucible*. I gave it to her last year when her class was studying the play. The paper she wrote about John Proctor was the one I encouraged her to enter in the contest. It was inexplicably perceptive, considering this was long before our own affair started.

Maybe she had a feeling.

"I know this isn't easy for you," I state quietly. Jackie has all but fallen into her desk chair, rubbing her forehead with the heel of her hand.

"I can't take much more of this, David."

"We'll be leaving soon."

"Oh. Here you are," Isabel says a moment later. Jackie rises instantly and I turn around as Isabel comes into the bedroom and gives me a mildly reproachful look which makes me realize I just screwed up. I'm nowhere near her granddaughter, but propriety is important to Isabel and she doesn't like me being in here at all. I give her what I hope is a chastened expression, counting on her good favor to excuse my blunder. Isabel has always liked me.

We go back into the living room to say our goodbyes, and Jackie suffers through a brief hug from Alicia. She's still holding up, but only just.

"That was a great dinner," Alicia says as we're pulling out of the driveway.

"It was. Jackie must be doing a lot of cooking these days."

"She's a good kid."

"Yes, she is." I navigate carefully down the dark dirt paths that lead back to the main road. They look different at night.

"Remember when we first met her? She was like a skittish horse, all nervous and darty. She seems much more confident now. A lot calmer."

"Yeah. She's doing well. It says a lot about Isabel."

"And you." I shrug. "It's obvious that you've had a big impact on her. You've helped her come out of her shell."

"Well. Like you said. She's a good kid." I would really like to move off the subject of Jackie, but I can't think of a subtle way to do it. Since I was barely listening during dinner, I can't even turn the conversation to anything we discussed.

"She's lucky to have you as her teacher." She pauses for a beat. "And her friend." I glance at Alicia in mild surprise – her comment seems overly generous, considering our history. Granted, it's been a long time since my indiscretion. Years. Long enough, apparently, that Alicia no longer feels reflexively suspicious of my female students even when she should. I'm not sure whether that says more about me or her, but I'm not complaining.

I reach for some kind of rational answer. "That's why we went into teaching, right? So we could be a positive influence for kids who need it." I feel like a politician.

"I miss that sometimes."

"You're still helping your students. You can advocate for them a lot more as an administrator than you could when you were a teacher."

She nods. "You know, Isabel told me Jackie's dad didn't even call over Christmas. Didn't so much as send her a card. Nothing."

"Nice guy." Jackie told me that already, during a brief window we managed to sneak in during winter break. She said it in a fairly convincing impression of indifference which didn't fool me for a minute, but I understood. It's the same façade I maintained at my dad's funeral.

"Isabel thinks that's part of why Jackie's drawn to you. You help fill in that part of her she's missing. And you know what she's going through."

I actually don't think the fact that Jackie and I both had drunks for fathers is anything more than a random biographical footnote we happen to share. It rarely comes up, because she doesn't obsess over her past and neither do I.

But however Alicia wants to explain any closeness she sees between us is fine with me.

"You know, I bet you would have made a pretty good dad."

I laugh. "I doubt that. I'm happy to stick to teaching." Alicia and I never wanted kids of our own. Neither of us are especially fond of babies or young children, and we're both too self-absorbed to be parents anyway. "And you." I squeeze her hand, and watch a flash of streetlight reflect against her teeth as she smiles at me.

***

When Jackie's not in class the following morning, I'm instantly alarmed. Especially when I check the attendance records and see that she attended her first and second period classes. If she ditched my class, she's avoiding me. I'm pretty sure I know why, and I need to get in front of this.

I text her and try to calibrate my expectations correctly. It'll be a while before she can answer, because she's careful not to ever risk getting caught texting on the phone I gave her.

But hours pass and she doesn't answer.

I walk across the campus after school lets out, strategically routing myself where I can see the school bus pickup. And I spot her getting on. She was in school all this time.

This can't continue. I go back to my classroom to finish what I was doing and pack my things. I'm heading out to the faculty parking lot when Alicia intercepts me.

"Hi, babe," she says. She looks a little tense.

"Hey. Everything okay?"

"I'm going to be late tonight. Three seniors got caught doing coke in the gym. They were arrested and their parents are completely losing it. Kathryn and I have to give a report to the police. It's a whole thing. It'll take a while. I'm sorry."

"Don't worry about it," I say, trying to hide my relief. "I didn't have anything special planned for dinner. Maybe I'll go out for a bit. Text me when you're on your way home."

"I will."

"Good luck with the rogues."

"Thanks. They're all on the honor roll too. I am so not in the mood to deal with multiple rounds of, 'my angel child would *never* do anything like this!'"

I laugh. "See, this is why I'm not really interested in your job."

She shakes her head. "I'll see you at home later."

I get into my car, silently blessing the unknown seniors for their marvelous timing.

By the time I reach Jackie's street, the bus has come and gone and she's walking toward her house when I pull up behind her. I feel like a stalker, which makes me equal parts aggravated with myself for letting my emotions get the better of me, and Jackie for childishly trying to dodge me and whatever's going on instead of dealing with it.

I roll down my window. "Jackie, where were you today?" She doesn't answer but she does stop walking, staring at me with her huge brown eyes. "Come for a drive with me."

"I don't feel well."

"Then I'll come in with you. We need to talk." I'm surprised to hear myself say it, and Jackie must be too. I've only been in her house once with no one else there. Isabel works long hours, and it's tempting, but that's the exact reason I haven't given in since we started having sex. It would be too easy to talk myself into doing it again, and again, and grow complacent to the danger.

Jackie lets us in and pulls off her shoes. She flicks on a light near the couch as I take a deep breath and force myself to speak calmly, be the man she knows and trusts. If I'm harsh with her, she's going to shut down completely. "Look. I know last night wasn't the greatest evening we've ever spent together, but I thought it went all right under the circumstances. What's going on with you now?" She sits down and doesn't speak. I try again. "This is about Alicia, right?"

She nods, finally. "Seeing you together like that was too much for me."

"I'm sorry if it hurt you, Jackie. You know that's not what I wanted." I kick off my own shoes to go sit down across from her. Isabel doesn't like shoes on her carpet. "But it's not like you found out anything you didn't already know. Alicia has always been who she is. She —"

"I told you I didn't want to do this!" she finally explodes. "I haven't seen her once since this whole thing with us started. I *knew* it was going to mess with my head. Knowing about her is one thing. Sitting through dinner with her, and watching the way you look at her — and how freaking perfect she is — I couldn't deal with that. I can't do this anymore."

"Jackie, look…"

She bolts to her room and I follow her. Except for the fact that her bed isn't made this time, it looks the same as it did last night. She's curled up on her side, facing the wall. Away from me.

"I'm still not going to tell anyone," she says without turning. "If that puts your mind at ease."

For some reason, this riles me more than anything else she's ever done or said. "Don't ever say that again," I reply tightly. "Don't insult me by implying that's what I'm worried about right now." I sit down on her bed. "I don't want to leave you like this. *That's* what I care about."

I sit still, determined to wait her out. She eventually turns to face me, and I'm really wishing we were still in the living room. This is a highly inconvenient moment for the effect that being in bed with Jackie is having on me. I hold out my arm anyway, inviting her to move in closer. Which she does.

"You don't really want to stop seeing me, do you?" I say.

"Of course I don't. I love you like crazy. But I can't keep going like this. Before, I could sort of block her out. All day today, I just kept seeing her face. I wish it didn't make any difference to me, but it does. I don't want to be this person, David." She looks at me earnestly. "You get that, right?"

"Yes. I get it." I resist the urge to tell her that she already is that person, just like I am. That not being with me anymore can't change what's already happened. I don't want to make her feel worse.

This is for the best. It is. I always hoped she would be the one to break things off. I wasn't expecting it to smart this much, though.

"Are you sorry this happened?" I ask her.

"No. I just wish it could have been different. Like exactly what it was, but without the guilt." She relaxes her body a bit more, fits against me more snugly. "Maybe I should find someone else, someone I don't feel guilty about being with." She looks at me as though testing the waters, and I nod agreement.

"I always figured you'd move on sooner or later, Jackie. I know it's easy to forget sometimes, but I *am* your teacher and you're only fifteen. Even if Alicia wasn't in the picture, we still couldn't be together in a normal way. You deserve someone who can give you more than I can."

"I don't know about that. You set the bar pretty high."

"Good." The idea of her walking around school with some boy hanging all over her doesn't thrill me. "Just promise me you won't rush into anything."

"I won't." Her hand drifts along my arm. "This is so nice. It's been a long time. I'd almost forgotten what it felt like to be out of your car."

"I was just thinking the same thing."

"We should have come here more often." Her fingers are skating lightly over my neck now. It's very distracting.

"Too risky."

"I know." She reaches down and starts playing with the belt loop on my hip. "It feels like we're breaking up. But that's stupid, right? We weren't together in the first place."

"I think we were. We definitely had something. Not everything needs a label."

She leans in and starts kissing me, and she means business. I push her hand away reluctantly.

"You know we don't do this here."

"You're already in my bed," she points out. "What time is it?"

I pull my phone out of my back pocket. "A little after four."

"Gran never gets home before seven."

I stare at the ceiling, assessing my options, but I finally concede.

"Okay. Just this once." I pull her on top of me. "Let's make it count." I try to put everything else from my mind and focus only on giving us both one last really good memory.

A parting gift, of sorts.

***

It's late afternoon when I leave Jackie's house, and I drive around aimlessly for a good hour. The shattered look on her face when I left is all I can see right now.

I'm a lot more upset than I should be, considering this was inevitable. If anything, I should have had an exit plan in place and not left it up to her.

But the truth is, I wouldn't gamble everything again for someone I didn't care about as much as I do Jackie. So it's natural that I don't want to let her go.

It wasn't this hard with Lily, not even close. To this day, I still don't know what I was doing with her. I was a lot younger back then, far more selfish, and I guess it was the challenge that excited me. The danger.

I cared about Lily in my own way but it didn't hold a candle to her love for me, which bordered on worship. I'm not especially proud of that. I know she got hurt. Of course, there's an outer limit on how much remorse I can feel about that now. What she tried to do to me in the end categorically destroyed any lingering fondness I had for her.

When I finally go home, Alicia's already there. She's on the couch with a bowl of leftovers and a glass of wine, Maggie dozing at her feet.

"Where were you?" she asks.

"Just out driving around," I reply truthfully. Maggie comes up to me and I scratch her ears. "How'd it go with the students?"

"Not so bad. It turns out they got the drugs from a kid who graduated from South Point a few years ago, so the parents have a convenient scapegoat."

"Good," I say as I sit down next to her. Maggie jumps up between us and circles once before getting comfortable again. I stroke her head.

"Something wrong?"

"No, not at all. Want a refill?" I ask, nodding to her glass.

"No thanks. I'm going to head upstairs."

"Okay. I'll be there in a few minutes." I go to the kitchen and warm up some leftovers for myself. I'm not at all hungry, but I'm not quite ready to go up to bed with Alicia either.

What I should do is take this as an opportunity to refocus my energy on my marriage. Move forward with my life, and put Jackie firmly in the past.

Of course, that's not going to be so easy considering I'll see her every single day.

Chapter Nine

JACKIE | *DAVID*

For the last two hours, I've been wrapped around the pillow that David shared with me, pretending he's still here. Wondering how long it will take for his familiar scent to fade from my sheets. From me. Trying to accept that this blown-apart sensation is now my full-time reality.

What the hell have I done?

I hear a soft knock at the door and sit up in a panic. I didn't realize it was so late.

"Yeah?"

Gran opens the door, wearing her work clothes. She must have gotten home a few minutes ago, but I didn't hear her car.

"Hey. I didn't know you were home already."

"Are you feeling all right? What are you doing in bed?" She narrows her eyes.

"Oh. Nothing. I..." Shit. I meant to change back into normal clothes before she got home. After David and I were done, I pulled on a pair of shorts and skimpy tank top to walk him to the door. Then I got right back into my bed. "Actually, I guess I'm not feeling very well," I revise hastily. "I didn't sleep great last night so I thought I'd go to bed a little early."

"Without any dinner?"

"Yeah. I'm not that hungry. I think I might be coming down with something."

When she steps inside, I scramble to my feet immediately. I can still feel David's presence so acutely, it seems impossible that Gran won't sense it too. Even if she can't, I don't want her in my room right now. It feels too private in here, after what happened earlier.

"Maybe some toast would be good." I head toward the door and she follows me to the kitchen. She rests her hand on my forehead.

"You don't seem to have a fever."

"I'm sure it's nothing major. I just need to catch up on some sleep."

"Is something bothering you?"

"No, why?" I grab two slices of bread and put them in the toaster.

"Because you were acting a bit peculiar last night as well. As though you were distracted by something. And because I know you don't sleep well when you're under stress."

"I have midterms coming up. And I'm kind of behind." I silently will her to accept the excuse, which is partially true.

"Dear, you always do well in school. There's no sense in pushing yourself so hard you get sick."

"I won't. I promise."

"Have you given any more thought to your birthday?" Gran asks.

"Oh. Right. I think I'll have Nicki spend the night."

"Is that all?" Gran sounds disappointed. "You can invite more than one person. Or if you like, you can take a few friends to a restaurant. I'd be happy to treat."

"Thanks, but that's okay. I'd rather have Nicki over." If I could, I'd skip the birthday thing completely. I'm in no mood to be sixteen. Not if that's the age I have to deal with losing David.

"Well, it's up to you." Gran starts boiling water for her own dinner. I make myself sit at the table while I chew on toast that tastes like shoe leather and try to make halfway normal conversation with her so she won't get any more suspicious than she already is. Mercifully, she gets a call from one of her friends a few minutes later and I take advantage of the interruption, motioning to her that I'm going to take a shower.

I breathe a sigh of relief once I'm alone in the bathroom. I turn the water on as hot as it will go and pull my clothes off for the second time this afternoon, watching my body disappear beneath swirls of steam in the mirror. It reminds me of the first time David saw me completely naked, in his room. Even though it was nothing he hadn't seen before, I'd felt a little embarrassed at first.

It didn't take long for that to change, though.

Everything did that day.

***

I agree to let Gran take me and Nicki out for Mexican food before we head back to the house for my birthday sleepover. Gran offered to let it be the two of us, but like everyone else, Nicki really likes Gran and she was happy to have her join us. The two of them trade stories all throughout dinner while I listen. Nicki fills Gran in on the latest PG rated school gossip and Gran tells stories of her own high school exploits. Not for the first time, I suspect that teenage Gran had a lot more in common with my best friend than with me.

After dinner, Gran goes out with one of her friends while Nicki and I seal ourselves up in my room with a bottle of peppermint schnapps. We haunt Instagram, watching one stupid video after another and passing the bottle back and forth until it's half gone.

"Oh, shit," I say as I stand up to get some water and wobble. "What are you doing to me, Nicki? I haven't been this drunk in months."

"Me either," Nicki replies, and we both giggle. I go to the bathroom and grab a box of crackers on the way back. Even though my head is spinning, I'm feeling better than I have since the breakup. Possibly because I can no longer feel anything.

"Here." I hand the crackers to Nicki. "Eat something. I don't want taco puke all over my bed."

"Yup, that would be gross." She sits up and closes the laptop. "Hey, happy birthday by the way." She gave me my present earlier, a gift certificate to Sephora.

"Thanks. I'm glad you came over." I sit on the bed. "I know you wanted me to have a party but I felt like something more low key."

"Totally fine. I'm just glad you're having fun. You've been acting weird lately but you seem better tonight."

"Well, that's because I'm wasted." We both burst out laughing and I decide it's a good time to take a drink of water. "Hey, Nicks."

"Hey, Jackie."

"Can you keep a secret?" Oh God, this is such a terrible idea. My brain rapidly starts skipping ahead, trying to plan out the conversation like a chess match. The problem is that I'm not clearheaded enough for this, and I can't afford to say too much. Nicki's way smarter than a lot of people give her credit for and if I let the wrong detail slip, she'll figure out the whole thing.

But seeing David in class this week has been unbearable, and now I have no outlet. He's been my only confidante for months. Maybe I can weave enough truth into an improvised story to get some of this weight off my chest.

Nicki sits up straighter. "Hell yes. Especially if you're going to tell me *why* you've been acting weird lately. I knew there had to be something going on."

I take a drink. "Okay. So the truth is… I've been seeing someone."

Nicki actually squeals, that's how much she's been looking

forward to hearing this from me. "Yes! Wait, who?"

"You don't know him," I say quickly, trying to invent a plausible way I would come to hook up with someone she didn't even know. "He's in college."

"An *older* guy. Nice. How come you never introduced us?"

"Because, well, it was kind of a secret."

Nicki's eyes light up and she waits to hear my explanation. She loves drama.

"He already had a girlfriend."

Her mouth drops open. "No way!" She looks stunned and gleeful at the same time. "You total homewrecker! How could you not tell me about this?"

"I didn't tell anyone." This is almost fun. I never get to shock Nicki.

"Well, so what happened?"

I grab a couple of crackers. "I broke up with him last weekend."

"Oh, shit. Why?"

"I couldn't take it anymore. I was tired of being the side piece. You know?"

"He wouldn't break up with his girlfriend?"

"I never really asked him to." I poke the edge of Nicki's laptop. "They're… serious."

"But he was with you!"

"Yeah. I know."

"Whoa. *Whoa.* This is huge. I can't even believe I'm hearing this from you. Wait, does this mean you finally popped your cherry?"

I groan. "God, I hate that expression. But yeah."

"What the *fuck,*" she exclaims in mock anger. "I can't believe you've been doing some guy all this time and not even telling me about it!" She shoves me and I almost fall off the bed.

"Well, now you know."

"Damn. Okay, let me just deal with this for a second." After a minute, she seems to grasp the other part of what I said. "Wait, so… wow. Okay. No wonder you've been so depressed. That sucks."

I nod, feeling the humor of the moment dissipate. I don't trust myself to speak because the alcohol is pushing me dangerously close to tears. She moves closer.

"Hey. It'll be okay," she says, wrapping an arm around my shoulder. "You know what they say, the best way to get over someone is to get under someone. We just need to get you laid again. I'll help." To her credit, this makes me laugh again. Not much, but enough.

"Does that actually work? Seriously, I'm asking."

"What makes you think *I* would know?"

That makes me laugh for real. Nicki's been having sex since she was thirteen. She was the first in our group of friends to do anything with a guy. In fact, my first kiss was a ludicrous attempt to keep up with her, an idea I had to let go of real quick in the end. Nicki tried a bunch of things that year that I had no intention of doing, and I've been behind her ever since. Like I said, it's fun to be the one with a juicy story for a change. It almost makes me wish I could tell her the truth.

"I don't know," she continues. "I guess. But then, I never have to get over anyone. I leave first." It's true. She does. "But you broke up with this guy too, right?"

"Pretty much, yeah."

"So? Maybe it'll be easier than you think."

"I doubt it." I pick up the bottle of schnapps again. "I really love him, Nicks."

"Well, I should hope so. Wow. A girlfriend. I never would have guessed." She shakes her head and repositions herself on her stomach. "But we'll get back to that later. How was the sex?"

I roll my eyes, but this is the one thing I can talk about safely enough when it comes to David. There's no way she could ever identify him from these particular details.

So we spend the next two hours trading stories. I'm surprised myself at how many I've accumulated with him. I don't tell Nicki, but I can't help feeling that despite her major head start, I finally have her beat at something.

***

The following Monday is my actual birthday. When I come home from school, I find a small package outside the door with my name on it. David's handwriting.

I wonder when he had time to bring this over.

I take it inside and open it to find a jewelry box containing a thin chain with a delicate gold maple leaf on the end. There's a note folded beneath the box, and I pull it out. It's two typed lines, no signature.

"For love / The leaning grasses and two lights above the sea"
Happy birthday. I miss you.

I recognized the reference to one of our favorite poems even before I read the note.

I lift the necklace and pinch the clasp to put it around my neck. I also save the note, zipping it into my pillowcase. It's the first one I've ever gotten from him, not counting our texts or the dozens of comments he's made on my papers in the last year and a half.

When I go into his class the next day, he immediately glances at my neck and smiles at me when he sees it there. I touch the leaf and feel a rush of adoration so forceful it almost knocks me over, followed by an equally strong wave of pain.

He comes over to my desk as I slide into it. "Happy birthday."

"Thank you." I can't say more because there's other kids coming into the room already. He turns and goes back to his desk, and I return to my usual practice of not looking at him.

Chapter Ten

Shit. What is she doing here?

I pulled a few strings to make sure Jackie was in my class again this year but under the current circumstances, seeing her so often is starting to feel like a penance for every impure thought I've ever had about her. She never looks at me anymore, but I don't have that luxury with her.

Now it's lunchtime and she's in Matt's classroom. Sitting alone at a desk while Matt's working at his. I feel my breath catch at the sight of her hair in the familiar messy bun. I just saw her this morning, it shouldn't jar me like this, but for some reason the unfortunate coincidence is unnerving me a little.

"Oh, hey, David," Matt says from his desk. Jackie jerks her head at the sound of my name, then quickly returns to whatever she's doing.

"How's it going?" I walk over to him. "Sorry to interrupt."

"No problem. Jackie's just making up a bio test."

I lower my voice so I don't disturb her. There's some district paperwork we need to fill out, and I came by to ask how he's done part of it. Of course, being Matt, he completely forgot he needed to do it at all, and panics slightly.

"I better go get it now," he says, standing. "Can you stay here with Jackie for a few minutes?"

"Oh. Sure." When Matt leaves, I sit on the desk next to her. She closes her iPad and rubs her eyes. We're not quite as alone as it feels, which I'd do well to remember, but it's closer than we've been in weeks.

"How have you been?" I ask her, hoping for a real answer. She touches the necklace I furtively gave her for her birthday. She's been wearing it ever since.

"I've been okay." For the first time in a solid month, she looks me directly in the eye. "I miss you." She might as well have plugged me into a wall socket as she stands up and steps toward me.

The air around us seems to convert to a liquid, splashing us against each other. The fact that this is probably the worst idea I've ever had in my life somehow doesn't register.

Then she's kissing me, barely gliding her lips over mine. I've completely forgotten where we are until the door clicks again and she instinctively springs backwards into her chair.

It's tough to separate my emotions in that moment. I can't believe I almost let myself get caught in such a compromising position. Matt doesn't say or do anything so I'm pretty sure he saw nothing, but it's a little hard to think clearly right now.

He asks Jackie if she finished the test, and she tells him she did. Hopefully her voice only sounds shaky to me. I quickly make my excuses and steal into the hallway, trying not to look at either of them.

***

Jackie comes to my classroom after school, caution completely scattered. I haven't left school with her since the day I took her to coffee because… well. Because it's crazy and irresponsible. Not to mention against school policy.

But I do today because if I don't, I'll do something even stupider. Like finish what we started in my own classroom.

"What was that about, Jackie? Are you trying to get me arrested?" I ask her when we're in the car. "I thought you wanted out."

"Yeah. I did too." Her hand slides automatically into mine. "But that's not really working for me." Before I can respond, she places one of my fingers in her mouth and plays her tongue over it while I concentrate on not crashing the car.

I fully recognize most people would consider me deviant. Sick. Evil. But nothing and no one will ever convince me that this relationship isn't consensual. Today especially.

I don't know exactly how many times Jackie and I have had sex but we're well into the double digits at this point. It's always good – remarkably good, really, considering her previous inexperience – and I've almost forgotten how insatiable she can be. If one of us is being assaulted right now, it sure isn't her. What comes next is a lot rougher than usual, but in all the best ways. At the very end, she grabs hold of me tightly enough to bruise and bursts into tears.

"What the hell?" she asks me, and I try not to laugh at her expression of startled confusion. I take a few seconds to sort myself out, then reach over her for a packet of Kleenex from my glove compartment. I hand it to her and she wipes her eyes.

"Are you okay?"

"Yeah, I'm fine. What is this? I never cry."

"Don't worry about it. It's a physiological reaction, not an emotional one."

"Oh. So this is an actual thing?"

"Yes, absolutely. Not a common thing but definitely a thing."

Now she's laughing. "That's a relief. I thought I was losing my mind. Damn, you're good."

"I'm not *that* good. You just haven't seen me for a while."

"We should break up more often." She cuddles closer to me, her body still shuddering.

I touch her lower lip, which is starting to swell slightly. "I think

I bit you. I'm sorry."

"Don't be. That was incredible." She brings me in for another kiss. "I can't believe I'm here with you again. It feels like it's been forever." It does indeed. There's a rush that comes with reconciliation, and it's making me happier than I can remember being in a long time.

Of course, it can't possibly last. While I'm resting up for a second round, she starts talking about things I wish she wouldn't.

"Do you think he saw anything?" I know she's talking about Matt. All afternoon, I was worried about that very thing but at this moment, I don't really care. Whatever the bill is for the last twenty minutes with Jackie, I'll pay it.

"I doubt it. He wasn't looking in our direction. Plus which, he's my friend. I think he would have said something to me if he thought he saw you kissing me."

She says nothing for a few minutes, looking contemplative. "I guess after this I'll have to start letting you go. Again. This must be what it's like to quit smoking."

"Very flattering metaphor." I smile at her. "Remember, pulling back was your decision, not mine. I'm happy to go back to the way things were before."

"But nothing's changed. You're still married, and you always will be. Right?"

"Maybe not always. I mean, you never know. But yes, you can expect things to stay that way for the foreseeable future." I can see that my words sting, but I can't afford for her to start getting any ideas about this being more than it is someday. I can't even let her in on the small part of me that wants that too. "I'm sorry. But I respect you too much to give you false hope."

"So we're right back where we started."

"Pretty much. Yeah." I start playing with her hair. "Was that such a bad place to be?"

"I don't get how it can be okay with you, if you love her. And

I know you do, I can see it."

"Of course I do. But I love you too, or I wouldn't be here. Trust me on that."

"How can you love both of us? I don't understand."

"This isn't class, Jackie. You don't need to understand everything."

She slides her legs over mine. "Would you love me as much as her if you'd met me first?"

"I can't really answer that, because I didn't. And you're only going to torture yourself going down this road. Don't compare yourself to Alicia. And especially don't start trying to compare your relationship with me to hers."

"Why?"

"Because she's my wife. It's just different."

"I know, but different how?"

"I don't know how to explain it. And honestly, I'm not going to try. I don't want you to take this the wrong way, but my relationship with Alicia isn't really your business."

She swings her legs down and sits up straight, looking wounded. "Wow. Whatever. Sorry I asked."

Now I feel like an asshole. "I'm not trying to hurt your feelings. I'm just not going to discuss personal details about my marriage with you."

"Fine." She tries to look indifferent and misses badly.

"Look at it from my perspective. I'm sure you wouldn't like it if I was talking to her about you." The English teacher side of me notes the irony in that statement. "All I'm going to say is that being married is hard in some ways. Not specifically for me and Alicia. It's hard for everyone."

"But?"

"But there's good parts of marriage too. It's complicated. I'm sure you'll see for yourself one of these days."

"Uh huh." After a few minutes, she lets me pull her back over.

"Has she ever done this?"

"Done what?"

"Cheated on you."

"I think that would come under the heading of personal details," I reply, then decide to throw her a bone. "But no, not that I know of. Why?"

She shrugs. "I don't know. I kind of wish she had. Maybe I wouldn't feel so bad then."

"I know what you mean. Of course, if she were to do something like that, it wouldn't be with a student. It takes a special kind of jerk to take advantage of a student."

"You're not taking advantage of me." She sounds annoyed. "I'm not a child."

"I didn't say you were, but that's how most people would see this."

"Well, I'm not most people and I say it's fine." I smile at her indignant expression. She always ends up defending me, even when she's pissed at me.

"And your opinion is the only one I care about, Jackie."

She nods, and her hand starts exploring my body. I've won, and I intend to be a gracious winner. I get ready to make her happy again.

Chapter Eleven

JACKIE | *DAVID*

When David drops me off at home, I sink to my bed in a lightheaded daze. Ever since that moment in Mr. Mintz's room, I've been on some kind of sensory overload. It's been a long time since I've felt so utterly at David's mercy, so overwhelmed by what he can do to me.

It takes me back.

By the time I spent the night at his house, David and I had done a lot together. But not everything. I couldn't bring myself to have sex for the first time in a car.

"I wish we could go somewhere else," I'd told him one afternoon, feeling frustrated.

"Like where?" He was kissing my neck and shoulders.

"Somewhere with, I don't know. A bed."

He stopped what he was doing and smiled. "That could be arranged."

"Really?"

"I do have a house, you know."

"That you live in with your wife." I looked away.

"She's going to be out of town next week," he said. "She'll be in Seattle for a conference. I was trying to decide whether to tell you about it. Guess you settled that debate."

I considered his words, not wanting to jump to conclusions. "Are you saying you want me to come over to your place?"

"If you can and you want to, absolutely."

"Of course I want to."

It was almost too easy. Gran never questioned it when I told her I was sleeping at Nicki's. David only lives about a mile away from the school, so I walked to his split-level townhouse. I'd been there once before, when Alicia invited me and Gran over for a Christmas party they threw my freshman year.

My heart hammered as I lifted the latch and made my way to the sliding glass door on the back patio, as he'd instructed. I suddenly felt panicked that Alicia would be there, that she'd come home early or something. How would I ever explain what I was doing?

But he walked up right away when I tapped on the glass. The first thing I saw when I got inside was a huge black and white wedding photo over the fireplace that I'd somehow managed to forget about since last time. I didn't have a ton of time to dwell on this, though, because he wrapped his arms around me and kissed me.

"You came," he said. "I'm glad. Are you nervous?"

"A little." I couldn't lie to him.

"Don't be. You don't ever need to be nervous with me. Nothing is going to happen here that you don't want."

"I know." I hadn't been worried about that. I always felt safe with David. It was the enormity of what I was getting into that scared me.

I wondered if he was nervous too.

Maggie came up to me and gave me an overexcited doggie greeting – she loves visitors. She followed us as David showed me the parts of his house I hadn't seen the night of the party, which mainly consisted of the two upstairs bedrooms.

Alicia likes pictures. By the time we got to the master, I'd seen way too many of her with David. The last one was sitting on their dresser, propped in a silver frame.

It gave me more of a jolt than the others because they both looked impossibly young, barely older than me. Alicia's hair was longer than I'd ever seen it in person. David was holding her from behind and they were standing on a bridge.

They looked so happy.

I lifted the picture to study it more closely while David watched me. "That was in San Francisco. We took a trip there when we were dating." I nodded and put it back. "What are you thinking?"

"I don't know," I said, reaching down to pet Maggie. I wondered if she knew I didn't belong there. If she was trying to look out for Alicia in her absence.

I hoped she didn't think badly of me.

"I feel a little guilty, I guess." I glanced at the bed, wondering which side Alicia slept on. This was not in any way helpful.

"I do too," he replied. "But it's not like this happens every day. You're the only person I've been with since Alicia."

"I am?"

"Yes." He looked a little offended. "Do you really think I go around doing this all the time?"

It actually hadn't occurred to me one way or the other, but for some reason I was relieved. "No, of course I didn't think that."

"Things happen sometimes," he continued. "We can't always control how we feel about other people. I can't help the way I feel about you."

"Neither can I." As if he didn't know.

He touched my cheek. "Would you rather go somewhere else?"

I shook my head. "No. I like seeing where you live. I'm surprised you don't mind, that's all."

"It doesn't matter to me where we are. It doesn't change what's real for us."

"That's true."

He kissed me. It hadn't taken me long to figure out that the slow, almost polite way David starts out is designed to build in a way that turns me inside out, every single time.

I know how to do the same thing to him, now.

"Hang on a second," he whispered. "Let me get rid of our third wheel over here." For a confused second, I thought he meant the picture of Alicia. But then he guided Maggie from the bedroom and closed the door.

I was glad. I didn't want her to see this.

***

It took ages for my heart to stop racing when we were done. He wrapped a blanket around us and pulled me in close. Almost as close as we'd been a few minutes earlier.

"You can relax, you know." I did my best but my heart was working overtime to accommodate the sensation of his body pressed against mine. My hand traveled across his skin as though I'd been charged to create a map of it from memory.

"I don't even know what to say."

"That's all right."

"Is it... always like that?"

He ran his fingers through my hair. I love it when he does that. "No. That was unusually good, especially for a first time." I sighed in relief.

"I thought it was going to hurt. Everyone says it hurts at first."

"Only if the guy doesn't know what he's doing." He took a sip from a glass of water on the bedside table, then held it out to me. I took a drink. "Are you hungry?"

I nodded.

"I'll go make us something."

"Can I help you?"

"I'd love that." He smiled at me as I watched him pull his clothes back on. "I'll be in the kitchen. Take your time, okay?"

Cooking dinner with him made me almost as blissful as the sex had, because it allowed me to fantasize that we lived together, that this was my life.

And he wasn't done with me yet, not by a long shot. I was almost dizzy from the continual building and release of pressure inside me, from the new cravings that coursed through me as David expertly manipulated my body. It was clear that he'd been holding back with me up until then, because I learned more from him that night than I ever realized there was to know. And even that pales in comparison to what he's taught me since.

I got better at keeping my eyes away from the photos.

The only bad moment came sometime in the early hours of the morning. I cried out in my sleep and sat up, unsure where I was at first.

"Jackie, it's me." I felt his hand on my shoulder. "You okay?"

"I had a nightmare."

"I'm sorry. Come here." He pulled me down. The steady rhythm of his heart against my back was reassuring, but it still took me a while to stop shaking.

***

In the morning, he got up and took a shower. I laughed as I heard him singing to himself, and pulled on the shirt he'd been wearing the night before to use the downstairs bathroom.

When I got back into his bed, I could see him in the shower from across the room. I was tempted to go and join him like he'd done with me the previous night, but I wasn't that daring yet. A few minutes later, he got out and wrapped a towel around his waist. He saw me watching and came over to kiss me. He smelled fresh and soapy.

"Good morning."

"You were singing," I noted with amusement.

"Yeah, I do that." He walked over to the sink and I heard

the whir of an electric razor. I got up and followed him, hoisting myself up on the counter to watch him shave. I couldn't get over the fact that I was allowed to see him do something so ordinary, and yet so intimate.

"How are you feeling?" he asked, reaching down to stroke my leg. "Still good?"

"Yes." I was actually a little sore, but David didn't need to know everything.

"What was your nightmare about?"

"Oh." I'd been hoping he might have forgotten that. "I was driving, and I ran a red light and crashed into a group of people. And then…" I paused, not sure whether I should tell him about the next part. "Alicia got in the car next to me."

"Oh yeah?"

"I asked if I'd hit her, and she said, 'Not yet.' But she had blood on her face. It freaked me out." Her face was half blown off, in fact, but I figured that was TMI for sure.

He laughed. "I think it's better for both of us if you don't read into that too much."

"Definitely."

He changed the subject. "Are you in a hurry? Do you have time for breakfast before you go?"

"Sure," I said, grinning. "Want me to make something?"

"I can do it."

"You made dinner last night. It's only fair," I said. I slid down from the counter and before I knew it, I was voicing a thought that had been bothering me since I woke up. "David. I'm not going to get pregnant or anything, am I?"

He smiled at me as he splashed water on his face. "I love how innocent you are. Hand me that towel?" I passed it to him. "No, you're not. That's why we used protection."

"It's not a hundred percent though."

"Nothing is. But I was very careful." He closed his arms around me. His skin was still warm from his shower, and I turned my head to look at our reflection in the mirror.

"So," he said flippantly. "Now that I've officially molested you, do you hate me?"

"What? No." I knew he was joking, but I didn't like it. "I could never hate you. Last night was amazing. I wish I didn't have to go home."

"You said yourself, you don't have to go yet." He began gliding his hands down my rib cage until they reached the bottom of the shirt I was wearing. "Is this mine?" I nodded, and he laughed again.

"I felt like wearing it for a while. I'll give it back."

"Don't," he said. "Keep it." His fingers floated along my spine. "It's going to be hard for me to see you in class after this, Jackie."

"Same here," I said, overwhelmed all over again by his nearness. I reached down and pulled the towel from his waist.

I didn't end up leaving his house for several more hours.

Chapter Twelve

JACKIE | **DAVID**

I'm feeling pretty good as I walk toward my classroom. I woke up thinking about Jackie. I couldn't help it. Right or wrong, I'm happy to be seeing her again, happy to know that in less than three hours she'll be here with me, able to look me in the eye for a change.

Almost the moment I walk into my classroom, the silence is shattered by my class phone. I go over to answer it, but I don't even get a chance to say hello.

"David?" It's Kathryn, Alicia's boss. And mine. "I need to see you in my office. Can you come right away?"

"Uh. Sure." My heart rate skyrockets.

"Good." She hangs up without the formality of a goodbye.

Fuck. So much for wondering whether Matt saw anything yesterday.

***

"What should I do if someone ever finds out, David? What do I say?"

"The main thing to remember is that innocent people don't panic. How would you react to someone asking you if we'd slept together if it had never happened?"

"I guess I'd be confused. I'd want to know why they were asking."

"Exactly. But you wouldn't act guilty or defensive, because you'd know it wasn't true. If someone's asking you about this, then they either suspect or they actually know something. If it's only suspicion, they'll go by your reaction to know if they should keep digging."

"And if it's not just suspicion?"

I grinned at her. "Then I'm screwed. Why do you think I'm so careful?"

"But you never forced me into anything, doesn't that make a difference?"

"Nope. Unfortunately, our relationship is illegal no matter what you think of it."

"Why?" She sounded outraged.

"You're too young to officially consent. It doesn't matter that I always ask your permission. I could still go to jail for touching you, especially since I'm your teacher." I put my arm around her. "But really, try not to worry too much. You're in control here. I'm literally putting my life in your hands."

***

Jackie brought that up, not me. Call it hubris or whatever, but I've never worried about this too much with her. It's so against what parents want to believe in the first place and beyond that, their protective instincts work in my favor.

I discovered that with Lily. When her parents found out, I don't think I slept that entire week. But nothing happened except that they took her away.

It's hard to imagine Isabel turning me in either. Above everything else I know about her, she is completely devoted to her granddaughter. She'd never want Jackie to be humiliated in court, nor would she want something like this getting out to all of her friends. If there was a way for her to go on believing nothing bad happened to Jackie, that's probably what she'd do.

And at the end of the day, nothing bad *did* happen to Jackie. I feel no guilt over anything that's ever happened between us. I know in my heart I've never hurt her. Certain kids grow up fast, no matter what anyone thinks of it, and Jackie's one of them. She's no child, hasn't been for a long time.

I straighten my spine as I walk toward Kathryn's office. If I've singled Jackie out at times and I know her better than my average student, it's because she's talented and I see a lot of potential in her. I like her, but I've certainly never been inappropriate with her. That's what I tell Kathryn. A year ago it was the truth and if I put myself back in that place, it'll still ring true. It's like a form of method acting.

Over the years, I've been called in here a handful of times to help Kathryn deal with some serious situation involving one of my students. I once had a kid turn in a paper that was quite obviously a desperate cry for help, and I reported it to her immediately. It turned out he had stolen his dad's pistol and hidden it in a corner of the garage, planning to kill himself.

That's the only time I've ever seen Kathryn's face look the way it does now, wiped completely clean of expression. She told me once that the worse a situation is, the more she retreats into a lack of emotion.

"Sit down, David." I do, closing the door behind me.

"What's wrong?" I ask, trying to sound curious rather than concerned.

"I'm going to get right to the point. I need you to tell me if you are having a sexual relationship with one of your female students. Jackie Culver."

"Jackie?"

"Yes. Jackie."

"Wow." I sit back in my chair, determined to react with dignity. "Don't you know me better than that, Kathryn?"

"I thought I did." She pauses. "You know I should be contacting the police, right? I'm not even supposed to be talking to you about this. But I care about Alicia, and out of respect for her I decided to give you a chance to come clean with me first to see if this is something we can possibly contain. You've been alone with Jackie outside school. Want to tell me about that?"

I shake my head. "I wish I could straighten this out, but I have no idea what you mean. Unless – is this about the fact that I gave her a ride yesterday?"

Kathryn doesn't reply.

"Okay. I did do that, and I know the district has a policy against giving rides to students. But to be honest, I didn't think much of it. Jackie's grandmother is friends with Alicia, so we all know each other. When she missed the bus, she asked if I would mind driving her home."

"And you did. Which, as you said, is very much against policy unless the student is a member of your own family. You know that."

I nod. "Yes. I'm sorry. I really didn't think it would be a big deal but you're right, that was a lapse in judgment. It won't happen again."

"What about kissing her? Is that going to happen again?"

"What are you talking about? Who told you I kissed her?"

"That's hardly the point. You need to tell me the truth here. If you don't, it'll be even worse for you." For the first time, a hint of rage comes through her icy tone.

"Look, Kathryn, I've known Jackie a long time. She hasn't had a lot of positive male influence in her life, so I try to fill that role for her. That's all it is. I would never hurt her, and I've certainly never kissed her." Kathryn's disbelief breaks through her expression – she's all but rolling her eyes. "What are you going to do now?"

"I'm going to call Jackie in from class and ask her about this. In the meantime, you're going to tell Alicia that you're sick and you need to go home."

"What? Why?"

"Because I can't have you trying to contact Jackie."

"That makes no sense," I say tightly. "She's not even in my first period class, and if you're going to call her down here anyway, why can't I stay and teach while this gets straightened out?"

"This is not up for debate," she says. "Go home and stay there. Wait for me to call you." She looks me in the eye. "If you've been sleeping with a student, David, you're finished. I will personally make sure of it. That's a promise."

"Fine. Do what you have to do." I leave her office and immediately spot Alicia in hers. She sees me too.

"David? What are you doing down here?"

"I came to tell Kathryn I need to head home. I'm not feeling well. It hit me really suddenly."

"Oh," she says. She looks bemused, no doubt thinking that I seemed fine an hour ago.

"I'll call you in a while," I say, heading for the door.

I feel so stupid now for what I was thinking yesterday, that I'd be willing to pay any price necessary for what happened between me and Jackie.

That was a lot easier to think when I didn't actually have to fork anything over yet.

Chapter Thirteen

JACKIE | *DAVID*

I'm not the least bit surprised when a student aide shows up a few minutes into my second class holding a note I'm positive is for me. I've been terrified that Mr. Mintz saw something yesterday, even though I've spent the past fifteen hours trying to convince myself otherwise. He's normally one of my friendliest teachers and he barely looked at me as I left the room.

I know David doesn't worry about these things as much as I do but I had a sick feeling that this time, he should.

Yesterday in his car, I was ready to completely concede defeat and spend the rest of my high school career collecting as many stolen afternoons with him as I could. In spite of Alicia, in spite of everything. I was even starting to think I could handle it. It was hard to hear a lot of the things he said about her, but it also felt like a more adult conversation than any we'd had before. David always treats me well but it's not often I feel like his equal.

Anyway, it was enough of a distraction at the time. But the reprieve is over.

My history teacher barely glances at the note before setting it aside and ignoring it. We're in the middle of team presentations and she's the strictest teacher I've ever had when it comes to interruptions. But as much as I appreciate her putting off this moment on my behalf, I don't think it's going to work. Sure enough, a moment later her desk phone rings. She answers, sounding disgruntled.

"Yes?" A pause. "We're in the middle of presentations right now. I'll send her when they're done." The students up front look on uncertainly. "All right." She hangs up and motions to me.

"Mrs. Connell wants to see you right away in the main office. Take your things," she adds. "If you're done before the end of the period, go and wait in the library. I don't want the presentations interrupted again."

We're supposed to be taking notes that we'll be turning in so this is going to affect my own grade, but that's the least of my worries.

Halfway to the office, I dash for the nearest bathroom and reach instinctively for the cell phone David gave me, but then I remember I didn't bring it with me since I assumed I'd see him this afternoon. Not that it matters. He'll be in class right now anyway. Plus, we've talked about this before. If I don't admit to anything, he can't get in trouble.

I make my way to the main administrative building and into the principal's office. I'm momentarily frantic that Alicia might be in this meeting, but she doesn't seem to be here. Her office door is open and no one is inside.

Instead, I see a no-nonsense middle-aged woman waiting for me near the front desk. Her hair is dark brown and streaked with gray, and she looks at me over the top of narrow glasses.

I've never personally met the principal of South Point, but David has a lot of respect for her. He told me once that Mrs. Connell was primarily responsible for Alicia getting appointed as the vice-principal.

"Are you Jackie?" she asks me.

"Yeah."

"I was beginning to get worried about you. Come on back."

I follow her into the largest of the individual offices and receive a shock. Gran is sitting at the small conference table.

Oh fuck.

"Gran? What are you doing here?"

"Mrs. Connell called me. Have a seat, Jackie," Gran replies. She looks grave.

"Am I in trouble?" I know full well I am, but I have to act like this could be about anything.

"Not at all," Mrs. Connell says. "But we do need to talk to you." She closes the door and sits across from me. "Do you want some water?"

My mouth is bone-dry, but I don't want anything from her. "That's okay."

She nods. "Thank you for coming down, Jackie. Let me say again, you're not in trouble. You can relax about that. But I do need you to listen carefully to my questions and tell me the truth, okay?"

"Uh. Sure. Okay."

"I need to ask you about David Harrison."

Stay calm. That's what he always told me to do. "What about him?" I glance at Gran anxiously, but she's looking at the table.

"I'm sorry to have to ask this, Jackie, but I need to know if he's having a romantic or sexual relationship with you."

"Huh?" I attempt a confused expression but it probably just comes out as stupid, and I can hear my voice go up an octave. "What are you talking about? Mr. Harrison is my teacher."

"I understand that. But I have reason to believe he is, or has been, more than your teacher."

"I don't know what you mean," I say, clasping my hands under the table. I'm feeling woozy but determined not to let David down. "He's a great teacher. Actually, I guess he's more like a mentor to me. But we're not having any relationship like… that."

"Has he ever kissed you?"

"What? No." I try to look disgusted.

"That gives me a problem, Jackie. Because I heard from a very good source that you two were kissing yesterday. Here, at the school."

I try desperately to shut off my thoughts so they won't show up on my face. I can be pissed at myself later.

"That's not true. I have no idea why anyone would say that. Gran, you don't believe this, do you?" She doesn't reply. "Was it a student who said it? Kids make up really crazy rumors."

"No," Mrs. Connell says. "It wasn't a student." She shifts her chair along the table so she's sitting closer to me. "Listen. Jackie. I understand that this is hard to talk about, but —"

"It's not hard at all. It's just not true."

"Listen, please." I shut up. "You're only sixteen. What Mr. Harrison is doing with you is illegal, and I'm obligated to report it. I don't have a choice. It's the law."

I shake my head again. "Maybe the person who told you this made a mistake or something, but he's just my teacher. I was in his class last year too."

"I know. I was there earlier this year, when you won that award." Mrs. Connell pauses. "You spend a lot of time with Mr. Harrison outside class, right? He helped you with your essay and so forth?"

"Yeah. I told you, he's a really good teacher. He's the best teacher I've ever had. That doesn't mean he's some kind of pervert. Besides, he's married." Now my voice is shaking. Perfect. "He and Mrs. Harrison came over to our house last month. Gran, tell her."

"I did," Gran says, sounding pained. "I told her that when he came over, I left you two alone for a minute and before I knew it you had disappeared to your bedroom."

"Come on. You can't seriously think we were doing anything." My voice is climbing higher. "Mrs. Harrison was right there! *You* were right there!"

"So you've been alone with him on multiple occasions," Mrs. Connell says.

"Yeah, at *school,*" I say. "In the classroom, when I went there at lunch or something." I fight to keep my rising panic from showing. "You don't believe me, do you?"

"You acted strangely that night they were at our house, Jackie." Gran's voice is so low I can hardly hear her. "You barely looked at David or talked to him all through dinner. I thought it was odd at the time, but I didn't understand it. Now it makes sense." She puts her hand on my arm. "Darling. Tell the truth."

"I am!" I resist the urge to pound on the table. "You don't understand."

"Explain it to us, then," says Mrs. Connell.

"There's nothing to explain! You have this completely wrong! David isn't like that at all." The moment the words are out, I realize my fatal slip. Which of course, Gran catches.

"David?" Gran says, her eyes widening.

"M-Mr. Harrison, I mean," I stutter, but it's way too late. *"You* call him David. It just came out that way. Gran, you have to believe me!"

The silence that echoes throughout the room is the loudest I've ever heard.

"What happens now?" Gran asks at last.

"As I said, the law requires me to report all allegations of abuse. Even suspicions of it." Mrs. Connell places a hand over her eyes briefly.

"But I just told you, whatever you heard wasn't right." I know I'm losing my cool but I have to stop this train before it runs us both over. "Please, please don't report this. You're going to get him in trouble and ruin his reputation. Once something like this gets around, it never goes away. Please!" My voice is getting louder involuntarily, like an invisible hand is turning up the volume on my words.

"Isabel," Mrs. Connell says. "I think you'd better take Jackie home."

"All right," Gran says.

"Call me when you get there," Mrs. Connell says. "We'll talk about where to go from here."

Gran rises slowly, looking shaken. I bury my face in my hands as she puts a hand on my shoulder and leads me out to the parking lot. I know I handled that horribly but I can't think how to fix it.

"How could you think he would do something like this?" I ask Gran, barely coherent. "How could you think *I* would?" She doesn't reply. "Gran, why don't you believe me?"

She gets in the car and starts it without looking at me.

"What about Mrs. Harrison?" I gnaw the inside of my cheek until I taste blood. "She's your friend. Are you really going to let her think her husband was cheating on her, even though he wasn't?"

"What happens next is out of my hands." My grandmother's voice sounds harsh. "How long has this been going on, Jackie?"

"I don't know what I can say," I answer. "I don't know how to make you believe me. I know I haven't always told you the truth, but I swear I am now!" I curse my younger self for all the stupid lies I told Gran when I was mad at her, or just bored. My record isn't great.

"That night, when he was in your bedroom…"

"Will you let that go already? Even if he *was* doing whatever you think he did with me, do you really think he would be stupid enough to do it there?"

"It's not normal for a grown man to be alone with a young girl in her bedroom, much less his own student," she says. "And the way you wouldn't look at him all evening… I can add two and two, Jackie."

"This is insane." I stare out the window. "Who did Mrs. Connell hear this from, anyway?"

"From what I understand, one of your other teachers witnessed

David kissing you in a classroom yesterday. And then you left with him after school?"

"He was giving me a ride home!" I ignore the first part. "What's the big deal?"

"And when you got home? Did David come in?"

"No, why would he come in? He dropped me off and left." At least that much is true.

"Jackie." Gran stops for a red light and shifts to look at me, finally. "I will do whatever I can to help you through this. But you have to stop lying."

"I'm not lying." I wind my backpack strap around my hand, barely aware I'm doing it. "I don't care if you believe me anymore. I would never have sex with a teacher." I twist the strap harder until it cuts off the blood flow and try to switch my tone from guilty to angry, because I definitely think it's coming off the former. "I'll never forgive you for thinking I could do that, Gran. Never."

When we get home, I go straight to my room and fling myself on my bed. After a few minutes I can hear Gran's voice in the kitchen and go to my door to listen.

"… very upset, of course… I agree. I certainly don't think she should hear it from the police." Gran's voice is pinched and high. "She gave me a strong tell. This is a nightmare… yes. Thank you. I'm sorry you have such a difficult conversation ahead of you."

I fight a sudden, irrational urge to pull the covers over my head like a little kid.

Chapter Fourteen

JACKIE | **DAVID**

I get home and start pacing the living room frantically. It's freaking Maggie out, she's watching me with a look of concern.

"It's bad, girl," I admit. "Real bad." Maggie should know, she was the sole witness to the one time I brought Jackie here. I felt her disapproval when I booted her out of the bedroom. Right before. But like all good dogs, she accepted my decision and kept on loving me anyway.

If Matt told Kathryn we were kissing, it's going to take some kind of cover story to get me out of this. I go back to that moment in the classroom with Jackie, try to picture what Matt might have seen. It must have been quick, a split second glance through the glass. I was sitting on a desk when Jackie came over to me.

We were barely touching, truth be told. But I wasn't exactly pushing her away, either. How can I possibly explain that?

I'm going to have to say it was some kind of lapse in judgment on her part. As much as I hate the idea of throwing Jackie under the bus like that, she's not the one who could go to prison over this. A teenager kissing a teacher isn't great but it's understandable.

Forgivable.

I spend the next three hours working out a script for when Alicia inevitably hears about this. Not knowing what Jackie might say under the pressure of Kathryn's thousand-yard stare, it's tough to develop the specifics. But I've got the general concept in place when, sure enough, Alicia turns up long before school lets out.

"What the fuck is going on?" she asks me without preamble. Maggie runs up to her, thrilled to see us both in the middle of the day, but for the first time in my memory Alicia ignores her. "Kathryn said Matt saw you kissing *Jackie?* You have something you want to tell me, David?"

I nod. "Sit down." She throws her purse on the table and sits across from me. Alicia has a fierce temper, and I'm a little surprised she's not yelling. I'm sure that's coming.

"Look, I'm not going to lie to you. Something did happen yesterday. I didn't tell you last night because I didn't want to embarrass Jackie or hurt your relationship with Isabel. I had no idea that Matt saw it."

"I can't believe you're making me go through this again." Her arms are crossed over her chest. "Go on."

I take a deep breath. "Jackie told me that she has feelings for me. She thinks she's in love with me. And while I was trying to figure out how to respond to that, she kissed me. Really briefly. I was already pulling away when Matt came back and she panicked."

"She did this in his *classroom?*"

I shrug. "I doubt it was something she planned to do."

"And I suppose she's never tried anything like that with you before." Alicia's tone is deadpan.

"No. She hasn't."

"You were just an innocent victim of circumstance. Like with Lily."

"This was nothing like Lily, Alicia –"

"Kathryn said you left with her after school."

"That was stupid. I admit. She came to my classroom and I told her that I couldn't have that kind of relationship with her. But I was trying not to be a jerk about it, because I could tell this was something she'd been holding onto for a while and I didn't want to completely crush her. She started getting emotional and I felt bad."

"So you decided to take her for a little ride." She sneers.

"Look, I know how it sounds. But I couldn't just tell her to leave when she was so upset. I told her I would give her a ride home and we could talk."

"You have a history with one of your students already. And now you're telling me that when another sixteen year old girl tried to *kiss* you, you decided to deal with that by taking her off campus, alone. In your car."

"You've known Jackie since she was thirteen, Alicia. You know she's not a bad kid. She didn't do this to hurt us. She's lonely and she's mixed up and she depends on me – you said it yourself. She doesn't have all that many people in her life she can talk to, or trust. I wanted to help her."

She buries her face in her hands. "How could you have been so stupid?"

"I don't know."

"You could lose your license over this, David."

"I realize that."

"So yesterday afternoon, you were out driving around with her. *Talking.*"

"Yes."

"And what did she say?"

"She was very apologetic. She said that she hoped I didn't hate her. Things like that."

"You didn't touch her."

"No. Absolutely not. We talked, I drove her home, and that was it."

Alicia's pretty face is clouded with rage. "I think you'd better go. Spend the night at a hotel or something. I can't stand to be in the same house with you right now."

"Alicia. You know I wouldn't do this."

"How can I possibly know that, after Lily?" she snaps. "Besides, even if you're telling the truth, it almost doesn't matter. Unlike before, this one isn't just between you and me. Kathryn suspended you and no matter how this shakes out, you've probably ruined your career. Not to mention what you've done to mine. Assuming you're not lying now, what you did do was fucking idiotic. How did you expect me to react?"

I take a deep breath and close my eyes. "You're right. I'm sorry."

"That's not good enough," she says.

I go upstairs to pack a change of clothes and my toothbrush. When I return, Alicia is sitting in exactly the same spot. The only difference is that Maggie is trying to sit on her lap. She's a big dog, so this might be funny under other circumstances. I start walking toward the door.

"Wait."

I turn around. "What?"

"You say you never had any kind of relationship with her, right?"

"Beyond the one you already knew about, no."

"Then unlock your phone and leave it here with me, David. I want to go through it."

"Fine. If that's what you need to convince yourself I'm telling the truth." I thank myself profusely for having the foresight to get another phone. I've never contacted Jackie on my regular one.

I pull out my phone and place my thumb on the sensor to unlock it. Then I put it on the table.

"Knock yourself out." She takes it without looking at me, starts scrolling through my emails. "I'll talk to you tomorrow."

Maggie whines slightly as I head for the door without her.

***

I check into a hotel in the center of town, then use the business center console to access my email and send a short note to Alicia telling her where I am before taking the elevator to my floor.

The room is airless and dark, and I turn on the noisy air conditioning before flopping onto the bed. My brain feels jammed.

It's weird not having my normal phone. I pride myself on not being as addicted to the thing as most of my colleagues and students, but it still feels a bit like I'm missing a finger. Instead, I pull my little flip phone from my pocket and start scrolling through my messages with Jackie, stopping to read random snippets.

Most of them are harmless. Flirtatious but not dangerous.

I keep going until I find the texts I *really* should have deleted a long time ago. The ones I had to verify for myself that Jackie deleted off her own phone.

what are you doing? It was nighttime when I'd texted her, which I usually don't do, but by then I had formed the impression that she kept her secret phone with her at all times. Just in case. So I wasn't surprised when she answered.

Lying in bed. You?

Same here.

Alone?

She knew I wouldn't be texting her if I wasn't, but I let it go.

Yep.

Me too. Want to come over? I could take a walk and meet you away from the house.

I would love that but I don't have my car right now. It's in the shop.

The next text took longer to come in, like she was gathering her courage.

Maybe we could do something else instead ;)

I'd smiled. Hadn't that been, indeed, what I was hoping would happen? But I was glad she suggested it instead of me.

Let's talk ground rules first, I texted back.

I bet I can guess.

Oh yeah?

No pictures, no names, and delete the texts after.

I'd laughed.

I like that you pay attention.

I texted her again, a fairly unoriginal start to get things going but between Jackie's imagination and mine, things got out of hand within seconds. I almost wish I could use this as evidence in my favor.

We should act out the real thing tomorrow :)
That was her last text of the evening.

Before I took her home the next day, I made her hand over her phone so I could see for myself that the messages were gone. Even though we had stuck to the ground rules, I couldn't deal with the prospect of someone finding her phone and becoming very interested in tracking down the guy who'd been sexting her.

Not that it was any worse than anything we'd done together in real life, both before and after that night. But somehow it seems more damning on the screen.

It's funny. Jackie never asked if I deleted them from my own phone.

Chapter Fifteen

JACKIE | *DAVID*

Sometime around midafternoon, David texts me asking if I can talk. I call him immediately and he picks up on the first ring, all business.

"Are you alone?"

"Yeah. Gran went down the street. What about you?"

"I'm in a hotel. Alicia doesn't want me at home right now."

"Why?" I whisper, horrified. "What did you tell her?"

"I didn't tell her anything. She's angry about the situation. How'd it go with Kathryn?"

"Not good. I told her and Gran that nothing happened between us, but they didn't believe me. I can't believe I got you into such a big mess. I'm so sorry." I sigh. "Do you hate me?" I'm afraid to hear the answer but I have to ask.

"No, of course not." I breathe for what feels like the first time all day. "I know you didn't mean for this to happen."

"So what now?"

"I'm suspended, which means there's going to be an investigation. The police will want to talk to you."

"Oh God. What do I say?"

"We can talk about that, but the first thing is to stay calm. What did Isabel say?"

"She's not exactly your biggest fan anymore. I think I blew it by letting you go in my room that night. She said she thought it was strange." I'm honestly surprised at how much she's making of that.

"Terrific."

I hesitate. "What did you tell Alicia? You must have said something."

"That it was a misunderstanding."

"And that was enough for her?"

He laughs. "Not really. I'm in a hotel for the night."

"Well, tell me exactly what you said and I'll say the same thing."

"I didn't say much, Jackie. Just that Matt didn't understand what he was seeing. But I'm not sure what to do now. Even if you were to say that you initiated the kiss–"

"I will. I'll say that." I don't care what happens to me. And maybe if I take the blame, he can slide out of this.

"I love you for being willing to do that," he says after a long pause. "But it all depends on what Matt saw."

"Even if he thought you were kissing me back, that's not illegal. Is it?"

"I'm not really sure," he replies. "I imagine it's enough to get my teaching license revoked."

"Fuck."

"It's not just that, anyway. According to Alicia, Matt also saw us leaving together. That's going to take some explaining."

Gran told me that, I suddenly realize, but it didn't click until now. "How the hell did he see *that?* His room is on the other side of the school."

"I don't know." After a moment, David speaks up again. "Maybe you could say that after you tried to kiss me, I offered to drive you home so we could talk about it."

"Oh. Yeah. That's good. That's the kind of thing you would do. Think anyone will buy it?"

"I have no idea. But it's probably my only chance."

"I'll do my best."

"I know you will." I've never appreciated David's ability to stay composed more than I do right now. "Listen. I won't pretend I'm not counting on you. But I know you can do this."

I'm quiet for a long time.

"Jackie? You still there?"

"I'm here." I wish he was. Stupid thing to wish, but I do.

"Remember, if you don't tell them that we've been seeing each other, they might *suspect* – but they're not going to be able to prove it."

"I won't tell them anything," I say, trying to sound tough. "I'm going to say that I came on to you, and you turned me down like you were supposed to. I'll fix this, David."

"I'm not worried." I doubt that, but it helps to hear that he believes in me. "And thank you. If you can, let me know how it goes tomorrow. I love you."

"I love you too." I hold down the red button and watch the tiny screen power off, wondering how everything could have fallen apart so quickly.

When Gran comes back home a half hour later, I'm hiding in my room again. I can't help resenting her for not believing me, which I know isn't fair. It's not her fault that she can tell when I'm lying. I gave her a lot of practice.

"Alexa!" I say sharply, and the small circle on my desk lights up. "Play Cobra Starship mix."

I was hoping for a distraction but the first song Alexa picks out is "Dirty Little Secret" by All-American Rejects. When I hear it, I start to laugh so hard it spooks me. Even Alexa is judging my life choices.

Before I know it, I'm crying for the first time since this whole thing started.

Unless yesterday counts.

That thought makes me cry even harder and before I know it I'm curled into a tight ball beneath my covers, laughing hysterically and crying at the same time.

I don't know how long this goes on before Gran comes in. But my pillow is wet.

"Alexa, volume at five percent," Gran says, and the music becomes barely audible.

I don't bother to pretend I'm not crying, and Gran doesn't pretend not to notice. Instead, she sits down on the bed with me and puts a hand on my shoulder.

"It's going to be okay, dear." Her voice is quiet.

"No it isn't." I can't give her the story David and I came up with, not now. To my relief, Gran doesn't try to say anything else. She just sits there with me.

Finally she gets up and leans over to kiss me on the cheek.

"I love you," she says softly. Hearing the last words David said to me from her makes me cry all over again. Only two people in the world really matter to me, and I could lose them both over this.

***

The following morning, I wake up with my eyes still swollen. I look terrible. I must have cried myself to sleep. I haven't done that since I was a little kid.

Gran is making tea in the kitchen when I come in, and she looks mildly surprised to see me.

"I think you need to stay home from school today," she says, carrying a steaming mug to the table.

"No way." I am resolute on this. I can't erase what happened but I can save David from it, and that's the only thing I can live with doing. "I'm going to school. I need to fix this."

"Darling, you look awful. Why don't you go back to bed and I'll call Mrs. Connell and tell her –"

"Gran, please, let me deal with this in my own way. I want to set the record straight so Mr. Harrison can come back to school."

She pauses. "Jackie, I think we need to be realistic about the chances of that." I trace the pattern of the tablecloth. "Sit down. What do you mean by setting the record straight?"

I sit and take a deep breath. Here goes nothing.

"This is all my fault, Gran. I'm not going to let his career get ruined over something that I did."

"Tell me."

I feel my stomach flip over. "I didn't tell you the whole truth yesterday about what happened at school."

"No offense, dear, but that was pretty obvious. So what did happen?"

"The truth is that I do have feelings for him. For Mr. Harrison," I say. "And I… tried to kiss him. That's what Mr. Mintz saw. It was really stupid and I totally regret it."

"I see." Gran's face is unreadable. There's a reason she always beats me at poker.

"But it – he turned me down. He said that he couldn't do anything like that with me. And *nothing else happened,* Gran. He only drove me home afterward so that he could talk to me. He said he was worried about me."

Gran stares at me without responding.

"I panicked. I didn't want to get him in trouble."

"So you're telling me that this is as far as it went. You tried to kiss him, he turned you down. And that's the only time he ever touched you."

"If you can even call that touching." I twist my hands in my lap. "I'm sorry, Gran. I'm sorry I lied and I'm sorry I did it in the first place."

"Why do you think you did it?" she asks.

"I don't know. I've had these feelings for Mr. Harrison for a long time now. He's really different from every other guy I know. But it was a mistake. I get that now. He said it wasn't wrong for me to feel what I did for him, but it would be wrong of him to act on it." I can't stop twining my fingers together beneath the tablecloth. "He was nice about it. I should have told you the truth yesterday, but… I was embarrassed. And scared."

"But you want to tell the truth now?"

"I can't stand the thought of Mr. Harrison getting in trouble over this, because it wasn't his fault."

Gran doesn't speak for a long time, and I hold my breath while I'm waiting for her response. I feel like a defendant waiting for a verdict. If I can get her to believe me, everyone else will be easy.

"Jackie. Do you know how much I love you?"

That was *so* not what I expected her to say.

"Of course I do. You're the only one who wants me around." My voice catches a little because I really don't like to think about that. This is part of why it's hard to deal with other kids my age. No matter what crazy shit they get up to, their parents still want them. Even Nicki's.

Gran's told me a bunch of times that my parents would have bailed on any kid, that what they did isn't on me. And I know she believes that, because Gran has never lied to me. But that doesn't make it true.

"I don't care what you do with your life, your career, or anything like that," Gran continues. "The only thing that matters to me is that you grow up to be a person of integrity. I want you to be a person *you* feel proud to be."

"I know, Gran." She tells me this all the time.

"That's not to say I don't expect you to make mistakes. Everyone does. But there are the kind of mistakes you can recover from, which is most of them, and there are the kind you can't."

"Okay." I'm not sure where she's going with this. "Which one do you think it is, what I did?"

"Only you can decide that. But I will say this. If you're telling me the truth about what happened, then I agree with you that the best way forward is to tell Mrs. Connell, and the investigators, and anyone else who needs to know. Make this right."

"That's what I want to do."

"But Jackie, I have to tell you that I think you're lying to protect David, and–"

"I'm not, I swear!"

She continues like I haven't spoken. "– this is probably your only chance to come clean. If you change your story later, it's going to be very difficult for everyone to believe you."

"That's why I'm going to tell the *truth*," I say, standing. "I better get going. I'll be late."

Chapter Sixteen

JACKIE | DAVID

After a fitful, endless night, I go downstairs to check my email again. There's a short note from Alicia, and another from Kathryn. I open the one from Kathryn first.

David,

The police have opened an investigation. Please make yourself available today to speak with them.

I sigh and open the one from Alicia, sent far earlier in the morning than she's usually awake. I imagine she had a rough night also. All it says is that she dropped off my phone at the front desk. I go to pick it up, then get a terrible cup of coffee from the lobby before returning to my room.

It's not quite nine o'clock yet, the earliest I could get in touch with Alex Cruz, my union representative. The guy teachers call when they're stuck in jams like this. I call anyway and leave a message, and he returns my call barely ten minutes later.

"Good morning, David."

"Hi. Thanks for calling me back so quickly."

"No worries. What's going on?"

"There's a little problem with one of my students," I say.

"Something one of my colleagues thinks he witnessed. It was a misunderstanding."

"What kind of misunderstanding?"

"He thought he saw us kissing, and unfortunately I made the mistake of driving the student home after that. So as you can imagine, it didn't look good."

Alex is silent for a full ten seconds.

"Hello?" I say at last.

"I'm here. That's really unfortunate. Today's climate, I can't say I like your odds on this."

"What's going to happen?"

"Well, first of all, don't say anything to me right now. Actually, don't say anything to anyone that you don't want repeated. You're in a very tricky spot. I'm inclined to say you should talk to a lawyer, instead of the police."

"Won't that just make me look guilty? Look, it's a bizarre situation but I didn't do anything wrong. You see, my student –"

"Hold on, David." His voice is firm. "I know this isn't what you want to hear but if you put your hands on a student, or if the administration thinks that you did, your termination is pretty much a done deal. And if I was you, I'd be more concerned about keeping myself out of jail."

"Are you serious?"

"I can only advise you on your position with the district. And all they can do is take away your job. I have to be honest – that outcome is almost a certainty if you were driving around alone with a student that someone saw you kissing."

"I *wasn't* kissing her though."

"Why does he think you were?"

I gnaw on one of my fingernails. Time to play this card and hope for the best. "Because she was trying to kiss me."

Dead silence again.

"I can see how it might have looked, but there's nothing going on between us."

"Right after that happened, you were seen driving around with her?"

"Just leaving with her, I think."

"Ah, yeah. That isn't good."

"So what do I do now?"

"As I said, in your shoes I wouldn't speak to the police at all. But I'm not really allowed to give legal advice. For that, you need a lawyer."

"Am I going to get arrested?"

"Well, it all depends. Mostly on what this girl says. You put yourself in an incredibly vulnerable position. The district has a policy against giving rides to students for a reason and when you add in this kiss, or whatever it was, it's not looking good for you." He clears his throat. "I'm sorry."

I feel sick. "My wife is the vice-principal. I don't know if that makes any difference."

"It could. Or it might make things even worse because the principal will be under more pressure not to give you special treatment. Who's your principal?"

"Kathryn Connell."

"I know Kathryn. She won't hesitate to cut you loose if she thinks that you've done anything to jeopardize your position, no matter who your wife is. My best advice is to get yourself a lawyer, right now. And make sure you're covered legally."

***

I luck out — one of the attorneys Alex recommended has a clear morning and invites me to come down right away. His office is less than a mile away, so I head over.

"How's it going?" Marshall Adler says as I walk in. He's a genial, avuncular-looking guy in an expensive suit. At least it's expensive for this town.

"Hi. David Harrison." We shake hands.

"Good to meet you. Have a seat. Do you want some coffee or anything?"

"Please."

He pours me a cup from a French press on his desk. "All right. Let's get down to it. My fee is two hundred an hour, so you don't want to waste any time. Explain to me what's going on, and it'll help if you tell me the truth. Save us time later. Whatever you tell me is completely confidential, even if you confess to a crime."

I nod, and open my mouth to speak. I'm about to tell him the same thing I told Alex, but at the last minute I decide to take his advice. I might as well lay out exactly what I'm facing.

"I'm a teacher at South Point High School. And I've been having a… personal relationship with one of my students," I say, forcing myself to look him in the eye.

"How old is she?"

"She's sixteen."

"Sophomore, junior?" He's scribbling notes.

"Sophomore. She was also in my freshman class, last year."

"And when you say personal relationship, we're talking sexual."

I only hesitate for a few seconds. "Yes."

"Her age when that started?" Marshall's voice is detached. He could almost pass for an accountant quizzing me about a questionable deduction.

"Fifteen, but it was just a few months ago. She had a birthday recently."

"Okay. And what's the current situation?"

I describe as briefly as possible what happened the other day, and what Matt saw. As I finish, Marshall puts down the pen and looks over the table at me, rubbing his chin.

"I know how this must sound, but –"

"It's David, right?"

"Yes."

"David, let's be really clear on something. My personal beliefs aren't relevant here. You're a client, I defend you, it's that simple. We don't need to get into a discussion about the morality of your actions and frankly it's not in your fiscal best interest. My job is to keep you out of prison. Let's focus on that, shall we?"

"All right."

"First question – what's Jackie going to say when the police question her this morning?"

I go over the version of events we came up with last night. Marshall sits back in his chair.

"Well, here's the thing. She's probably going to end up telling them everything."

"I don't think she –"

He holds up a hand. "I understand you two worked out this little story but the fact of the matter is, it's not very believable. Even if it was, she's a young girl who's about to have tremendous pressure put on her by highly trained individuals whose job it is to get people to tell the truth whether they're planning to or not. If she doesn't end up doing that, great. But it's the most likely outcome and we need to start preparing ourselves for it now."

"What does that mean?"

"It means that you don't talk to the police. Not now, not ever."

"Won't that make me look guilty?"

"You *are* guilty. You're guilty of a felony offense here, probably more than one depending on the nature of how they charge you and the extent to which you're telling me the truth now."

"Everything I've told you is the truth."

"Better hope. Statutory rape carries a sentence of a few years at the most. Forcible rape, you could get ten. Or more."

I recoil. "I never forced Jackie into anything. I'm not like that."

"Good for you but it doesn't really matter. You've been sleeping with her so no matter what she feels for you, that makes you a criminal. You could be in for a rough ride here. And that's why it's so important that you say nothing."

"But if I don't give the police some kind of statement, I'm going to lose my job."

Marshall nods. "Look, I'm not so much in the business of telling people what they want to hear. My only concern, as I said, is keeping you out of prison. Any other priorities you might have are all secondary to the very real possibility that you could do prison time for this. You need to let that sink in."

I sigh and lean back. In some ways, it's almost a relief to hear the worst case scenario laid out.

"So when they call, what do I say?"

"Tell them that you've engaged a lawyer and you cannot answer any questions without him being present. Give them my number and I'll tell them that out of caution, I'm advising you to give no statements. In the meantime, I'll find out what the girl has told them and see where we are."

"So what do I do now?"

"First thing is to go home and think of a way to come up with five thousand dollars. If you're arrested, you'll want to be ready."

"Five grand? Are you serious?"

"That's my standard retainer. Hopefully this doesn't go to trial but if it does, you'll run through it pretty quickly."

I stand, slowly. "Okay. I'll get the money but it might take me a couple of days."

"You can pay by the hour until then. I accept credit cards."

"All right."

"We say nothing to the police, right?"

"Yeah, I got it." I make my way toward the door, trying to figure out what the hell I'm going to tell Alicia. "Look. I know it doesn't make any difference to you, I get that, but…"

"Yes?"

I shake my head. "Never mind."

Chapter Seventeen

JACKIE | *DAVID*

As soon as I walk into school, it feels like heads are turning my way. That has to be paranoia though, right? How could anyone know what's going on other than me, David, Gran, and Mrs. Connell?

And Alicia, of course.

Nicki and I usually meet in the quad before school. Today she's already here, and races over as soon as she sees me.

"Jackie! What the hell is going on?"

"What do you mean?"

"I heard this insane rumor that Mr. Harrison got suspended because of you."

"*What?*"

Before she can respond, two girls I know from gym walk past us.

"What's up, slut?" one of them asks me cheerfully.

"*Excuse* me?" Nicki retorts aggressively. They ignore her.

"We heard you got caught doing Mr. Harrison," her friend says to me. "Lucky you." They walk on, snickering.

"What the fuck," I mutter. "This cannot be happening."

"What's going on?" Nicki grabs my elbow. "That's not true, is it?"

"Of course not." I pull my arm back. "This is so stupid. One of the teachers thought he saw something and it got blown completely out of proportion."

"So you haven't been…?"

"No! Come on."

"Well, that guy you were telling me about…" Nicki pauses. "You never told me his name. And you said he had a girlfriend, so…"

"That wasn't Mr. Harrison! Are you nuts?"

"Sorry, I just –" Nicki cuts herself off and starts over. "It's just that he wasn't in school yesterday." Nicki's in his sixth period class.

"People get sick, Nicks."

"And you weren't here either." I start digging through my backpack for aspirin and pop two in my mouth. "You were here before school but Maddie said you got called down during first period and then no one saw you after that."

"Why can't people mind their own business? Some teacher saw him giving me a hug and freaked out, that's all."

"So why do you look like you've been crying?"

"Because the whole thing was bullshit and they're trying to use me to get Mr. Harrison in trouble. I care about him, not in a creepy way, you know, but –"

"No, I get it. He's a good guy."

"He is. And he doesn't deserve this. How did you even hear about it?"

"I think one of the aides said something. Everyone's talking about it."

"That's just great." I feel like stabbing myself. No matter what I do now, the damage to David's reputation is done and it's probably permanent. "I have to go."

"Where are you going?"

"I'll talk to you later, okay?" I don't wait for Nicki's response. I just head straight to the main office, trying not to look at anyone on the way there.

As I push the front door open, I almost crash into Alicia.

I wonder if I'll ever be able to smell lilac again without wanting to puke.

"Oh, God." I gasp. "Sorry, Mrs. Harrison." Alicia doesn't respond, just fixes me with this icy glare. How many times have I wondered what she'd think of me if she knew? It's even scarier than I imagined. She looks like she could easily kill me without thinking twice about it.

I struggle to come up with more words. "I'm… I'm really sorry. About all of this." She *still* says nothing. "I'm on my way to see Mrs. Connell now. I'm going to tell her what happened. It was totally my fault, not his. He didn't do anything wrong, and I'm so sorry."

"You'd better get going, then." Alicia puts a hand on my shoulder, which makes me want to scream in terror, and leans over to whisper into my ear.

"This is *absolutely* your fault," she hisses.

Trembling, I wrench away from her and scramble for the door to Mrs. Connell's office.

"Jackie." Mrs. Connell's voice sounds so normal. "Are you all right?"

That's got to be the stupidest question I've ever heard. "Sure. I'm fine."

"I'm glad you're here. Come in, please." I sit down in the same chair I did yesterday, and she closes the door. "I should tell you that a police officer is on her way. I made the official report yesterday. Mr. Harrison has been placed on leave for the time being. He'll be questioned as well, but the detective wants to talk to you first."

"Good, because you're making a mistake," I say. "Please let me explain. I should have told you this before."

Mrs. Connell holds up her hand. "It's all right, Jackie. Your grandmother told me what you said. You'll need to tell the officer when she arrives but there's no need to make you keep repeating it."

"Oh." I sit up a little straighter. "So, okay, you know what happened. It was my fault. Can Mr. Harrison come back to school now?"

"Well, I'm afraid it's not quite that simple." Before she can continue, there's a knock at the door and Mrs. Connell stands. As I expected, it's a cop.

"That was fast," Mrs. Connell remarks. "Come in."

"Hello, Jackie," says the officer as Mrs. Connell closes the door. "My name is Amy Keller. I'm a detective." She hands me a business card and sits down. "I wrote your case number on the back of my card. I'm here to talk to you about this business with your teacher, David Harrison."

"I know," I say, feeling my face burn. "Look, this is all a mistake. It's a misunderstanding."

Keller ignores that. "Do you need anything before we get started?"

"No. That's okay." I take a deep breath. I know I have to do this, but I'm scared. If it comes out later that what I'm telling her isn't true, am I going to get in trouble? I've been afraid to Google the answer.

Mrs. Connell sits across from us with her arms folded.

The detective speaks again. "Okay, Jackie, before you tell me what happened, I want you to know a little bit about what we're dealing with, okay?"

"Fine." Anything to keep putting off the moment where I have to start lying.

"Are you familiar with the concept of statutory rape, Jackie?" I don't like the way she keeps saying my name. I know what this is, I've seen cop shows. She's trying to bond with me so I'll talk.

"Yes, of course. But —"

"Well, there's actually a few different laws related to this kind of thing," she says, pulling a notebook from a pocket on her vest. I glance down at the gun and mace on her hip, and look away again. It freaks me out to think that I'm dealing with a person who uses those things on a regular basis.

She continues. "It gets a little confusing, and different states handle this differently. But here in Oregon, for example, there's a felony called rape in the third degree. And that's any kind of sex between a minor who is fourteen or fifteen and a person who's at least three years older than them. There's another one called second degree sexual abuse, and that's sex between a minor and someone who's at least twenty-one and their teacher or coach."

I close my eyes, reminding myself sternly that these are just archaic rules written in a book somewhere. I've always known David is technically breaking the law by being with me, and I guess that's reasonable since most kids can't handle this kind of thing. But I'm not a kid. Whoever wrote that law didn't know David or me because if they did, they'd never call it any kind of rape. What we do is as far from that horrible word as a thing can be.

The cop watches me carefully as she keeps talking. "There's a few more but I think you get the idea. The point here is these are very serious crimes. And it doesn't matter if the younger person, you in this case, consented to the sex or not." Outside the office, I hear the bell for first period. Finally, she waits for my response.

"Okay," I say finally. "But I don't know why you're telling me all this, because we never had sex. Or anything like that." Quickly, I launch into the same story I gave Gran this morning. The officer listens, scrawling notes in her pad. I wonder what she's writing about me.

"So, you see? It was all my fault." The officer exchanges a glance with Mrs. Connell and puts down her pad.

"This happened in Mr. Mintz's classroom, right?"

"Yeah. The day before yesterday."

"How did you happen to choose that moment?" she asks.

I hesitate. "What do you mean?"

"Well, it was lunchtime and there must have been a few people in the halls." She points to the door with her pen. "I've seen how your classrooms are set up. There's usually several windows. It seems like a strange place to proposition someone."

Can't argue with that. "I told you, it was stupid. I don't know what I was thinking."

"From the way you describe it, Jackie, you kissed Mr. Harrison and he pulled away. Right?"

"Pretty much. Yeah."

"But that's not exactly what Mr. Mintz says he saw." She flips to another page in her pad. "He said that when he walked up to the door, he saw Mr. Harrison sitting on one of the desks. He said that you were standing in front of him. Does that sound right to you?"

"I don't know." I can barely remember that moment.

"Because as I'm picturing that in my head, I feel like Mr. Harrison had a lot of chances to ask you to move away before you leaned in to kiss him. Actually, he didn't really stop you at all from the sound of it. *You* pulled away, when you heard Mr. Mintz come in. Isn't that right?"

"I'm not sure. It all happened really fast."

"And you said that he told you he couldn't have that kind of contact with you. But if Mr. Mintz walked back in and you both left the room, when did you have this conversation?"

"After school, when I went to Mr. Harrison's classroom. He only drove me home after that because he wanted to talk to me about why I'd done it in the first place."

"Doesn't that seem odd to you?" she asks. "Put yourself in Mr. Harrison's place. A student tries to kiss you. You tell her no… and then get into a car with her, open yourself up to any kind of claim she might make after that? Wasn't that a little unwise?"

"I don't know. Maybe." I try to keep from sounding defensive. "Or maybe he knew I would never say anything bad about him."

Keller settles back in her seat. "He drove you straight home?"

"Yeah, that's right."

"Okay. Did you know that your grandmother had a tracking app installed on your phone?"

"A what?" I feel another surge of adrenaline, and wonder how many of these my heart can take before it gives out.

She pulls a piece of paper from her pocket and unfolds it in front of me. It looks like a map of town with a route outlined in red.

Fuck. If she can tell where my phone was that day, I'm screwed. I have no idea how to begin to explain that.

"Your phone tracker shows that you left school, then drove down the highway for almost ten miles. Pretty much in the opposite direction from where your house is." She follows the route with the tip of her pen. "*Then* it shows you driving back to your house." She slides the map across the table to me. "Why did you say you went straight home, Jackie?"

Shit. "I told you, we were talking. Driving and talking."

"After he rejected your advance, he drove you all the way outside of town and back. To have a conversation."

"That's what I said." But I can see that she knows I'm full of shit.

"See, Jackie, that's a little bit hard for me to accept," Keller says mildly. She puts her pen down on the table. "I've been doing this for a while. I understand that Mr. Harrison is someone you care about, that you want to protect him."

I wish I was a better actress. "I am *not* trying to protect him. Or if I am, it's because I don't think he deserves to lose his job because of something stupid that I did." I take a deep breath. "My grandma was telling me this morning, you can't recover from certain mistakes. I don't want this to be something that haunts me forever. I want to fix it. Mr. Harrison has done a lot for me and I don't want to hurt him."

There's a long pause and eventually Keller closes her notepad and says, "You can go back to class now, Jackie. I think I have all I need for now."

She doesn't have to tell me twice. I take my things and leave the office, not even bothering to get a pass for my first class. Instead, I go straight to the bathroom. And that's where I remain for the rest of the period, reviewing each of my failed answers to the only test in my life that's ever mattered.

Chapter Eighteen

JACKIE | **DAVID**

When I pull up to my house, Alicia's still at school. Which is good, because I still haven't worked out how to explain the fact that I just took out nearly the entire balance of our savings account to cover my possible retainer. I have no idea what I'm going to do if it ends up costing more than that.

She comes home about an hour later, around lunchtime. She walks in without looking me in the eye, and tosses her purse on the table. I have an instant sense of déjà vu.

"Is it okay that I'm here?" I ask.

She shrugs. "You had to come back sometime."

"Alicia, look, I —"

"David, I thought about this all night." She walks over to me. "Before this goes any further, I need you to look me in the eye and tell me that nothing happened between you and Jackie."

I put my hands on her shoulders. "Nothing happened. Except what I already told you. I did a stupid thing driving her home after, but that's the extent of this. As far as I'm concerned, nothing and no one could ever come between us. I wouldn't risk that again, not after last time."

She's silent for a long moment, sizing me up. Alicia's no fool. The biggest point in my favor is that she *wants* to believe me.

At last, she nods.

"Fine." She shrugs my hands off her shoulders and goes over to the couch. Maggie leaps up and lays her head in Alicia's lap, and I go to sit down across from them.

"I ran into Jackie earlier," she informs me.

"Oh," I say. "What did she say?"

Alicia's eyes fill with contempt. "She said she was *sorry*. Told me that this was all her fault and she was on her way to tell Kathryn what really happened."

That explains a lot. It's probably what pushed Alicia over the line into blaming Jackie instead of me. I nod, trying to keep my face neutral. "She really does feel bad about this."

"She should. I told her I agree with her. It is her goddamn fault."

"You said that?"

"Pretty much."

"Alicia. She's just a kid. She made a mistake…" I shut up. Defending Jackie is not a good idea, even though she deserves it.

"Well, that *mistake* is probably going to cost you your job. She must have known this could get you in trouble. And she sure as hell knows you're married."

"True."

"Have the police gotten in touch yet?"

I shake my head. "I called my rep and he suggested I call a lawyer. So I did."

"You went to see a lawyer?"

"This morning. And he doesn't think I should talk to the police at all."

"Why not?"

"Basically, he thinks that losing my job is pretty much a foregone conclusion and I should be more concerned about keeping myself out of prison."

"He's not wrong about your job, but why should you go to

prison? Even if you kissed her, that's not illegal. Unless you're lying about everything and it was a lot more than that." Her eyes narrow.

"I'm not and it wasn't. But I'm not in a great position to defend myself. I was alone with her a lot if you count all the time I spent with her at school, I know where she lives… the optics just aren't good."

"So he thinks you could go to jail, even though nothing happened."

"Right. That." I take my glasses off and rub my eyes. At that moment, Marshall's number flashes on my phone. Speak of the devil. I answer and walk into the kitchen.

"Hello?"

"David, Marshall Adler here. Got a minute to talk?"

"Sure. I'm at home with my wife." I glance at Alicia, who's watching me closely.

"I assume she doesn't know the whole story here?"

"That's correct. What's going on?"

"Well, Jackie apparently said exactly what you told me she would to the police."

I crumple onto one of the breakfast bar stools, my phone pressed to my ear. "Thank God."

"Not so fast. This isn't over."

"Okay. What now?"

"They still want to talk to you, and my advice is still that you not do that. Scuttlebutt is that the principal – Kathryn, I think her name is?"

"Yeah."

"She's very serious about firing you if nothing else. I looked over the policy you sent me, and I doubt she's going to have any trouble with that. So I see nothing to be gained by you giving a statement to the police they could use against you."

"Use against me how?" Alicia is staring at me from the living room, her body completely still. "From what you just told me,

Jackie made it clear I'm not guilty of any crime."

"But we both know that's not true, and it's not like the police are going anywhere. She could change her mind at any time. Maybe a counselor gets it out of her, or whatever. And if that happens, this all comes alive again. In my opinion, that's not an unlikely scenario."

"Okay. I understand."

"It's your choice, of course. But my recommendation, my *strong* recommendation, is to refuse any police interviews, accept your termination, and move on as best you can. Oh, and one more thing. You cannot have *any* contact with this girl, do you understand me?"

"I wasn't planning to." That's a lie. I actually haven't given any thought at all to what would happen with me and Jackie, but he's right. Breaking off our relationship, permanently this time, is the obvious thing to do.

Maybe I didn't want to let myself think about that.

"Good. If she should contact you, make sure she understands. It has to be completely over between you because everyone's going to be on high alert now. Any benefit of the doubt you might have enjoyed before is gone forever."

"I hear you." I sigh. "Okay, I better call my rep and see what the situation with my job is."

"Remember, don't get into a debate with your boss over this. You don't want to slip and say something that could backfire on you later."

"Okay."

"Last thing. Since you're not being charged right now, I don't need that retainer after all. I'll send you an invoice for today. If you do end up getting arrested, ask for a phone so you can contact your attorney and then call me right away. Don't say *anything* else to anyone."

"All right."

"Okay, David. Good luck."

"Thanks for calling." I put my phone down on the counter and lean forward, hanging my head.

"What did he say?" Alicia asks.

"Good news and bad."

"Tell me."

"I'm not being charged with anything, but it looks like Kathryn is determined to fire me."

Alicia nodded. "I know, she's mad as hell. She came by here last night."

"Well, to Jackie's credit, she told the police what really happened but I guess Kathryn doesn't believe her. And because I did violate the policy, she can fire me if she wants. It's discretionary, right?"

"Yeah, but typically we wouldn't terminate a teacher for a first offense." Alicia comes over to me. "I'll see what I can do. No promises."

"I'm so sorry about this." I'm not apologizing to look good. I really do feel badly. I never wanted this thing with Jackie to affect Alicia.

She sighs. "I'm still not sure I believe you, just so we're clear. And I'm still pissed."

"I don't blame you on either count. But at least Jackie told the truth. At least she's not making things worse."

"I still can't believe she did this. I mean, I could tell she had a little crush on you but we both know that's nothing unusual." Her voice hardens. "She didn't seem like the type to act on it."

"I know." I'm grateful Alicia can't read my mind, because my focus on this conversation is being inopportunely interrupted by a flood of Jackie memories right now.

One occasion in particular keeps playing in my mind, the only other time I visited her at Isabel's house. It happened last year, not too long after we started seeing each other. I texted her after she missed my class.

Everything okay? How come you're not in school?
I'm home sick.
Sorry to hear that. How bad?
Just a stomach bug. I'll be okay.

I made chicken soup for dinner that evening. While I was letting the broth simmer, I texted Jackie again. She'd already told me she still felt awful and would likely be out the next day as well.

What time does Isabel go to work?
Usually around noon. Why?
I was thinking maybe I would come over after school tomorrow.
Really? :)
If you want me to.
Of course I do.

When the soup was ready, Alicia and I ate it together. There was plenty left over. The following morning, I took the portion I allotted for myself and stashed it in the lounge fridge. As soon as school was over, I drove over to Jackie's house with it.

Isabel's car was gone. I went to the door and rapped it lightly.

"Come in," I heard Jackie say, and I did. She was laying on the couch wrapped up in a blanket.

She looked fairly miserable. Her skin was pale and her nose and eyes were red-rimmed. She was surrounded by a pile of books and a garbage can near her feet that was half-filled with tissues. Her hair was damp, like she'd just gotten out of the shower.

But she lit up to at least half her full wattage when she saw me.

"Hey. I can't believe you came."

"I told you I would." I went over to the couch and sat down beside her. "How are you feeling?"

"Pretty crappy. But better now that you're here."

I held up the container in my hand. "I brought you some soup."

"You did not."

"It's a rule. You get sick, you get soup."

She smiled. "That's so sweet. Thank you."

"Are you hungry?"

"Yeah, I am actually. I've been living on saltines and ginger ale."

"I'll heat some of this up for you if you want."

"That would be great."

I went into the kitchen and found a bowl, spooning some soup into it, and heated it up for a couple of minutes. While it was in the microwave, I poured her a fresh ginger ale and brought that over to her as well.

"Thanks, David." She blushed a little. At the time, she was still getting used to calling me that.

"You're welcome," I said as I settled down next to her. She started to eat.

"This is really good. Did you make it?"

"I did."

"I can't believe you did that for me." She grinned at me again and I reached out to tuck her hair behind her ear. "None of my other teachers came to visit," she added jokingly.

"They better not have."

When she was finished with her soup, she curled up next to me. I reached over for one of her pillows, inhaling the faint coconut-lime scent from the shampoo she uses. I placed it on my lap so she could lay her head down and shook out the blanket a little to cover her with it more evenly.

"I'm glad you came," she said. "I missed you."

"Same here." I slid my hand into hers and started stroking her hair. "Isabel's still at work?"

She closed her eyes. "That feels so good. Yeah, she won't be home until at least eight or nine."

"Good." I didn't like to think of Isabel's reaction if she were to walk in and find me cuddling with Jackie on her couch. But I have to say, it didn't feel weird to be there. It felt natural. Innocent, even.

"How long can you stay?"

"How about I stay until you fall asleep?" I started tracing small circles over her forehead. She looked like she was halfway there already.

"Wish we could really take advantage of the house being empty," she murmured.

"You're feeling too lousy for that," I said. "Besides, I'm not going to do anything with you in your grandmother's house. It wouldn't be right."

"Yeah," she said. We sat there in silence for a few minutes, and I thought she had drifted off when I heard her say something else.

"Sorry, Jackie? I didn't catch that."

"I said, no one ever took care of me like this before. Except Gran."

I kissed her forehead. "Everyone needs taking care of sometimes."

***

Jackie told me once that this was one of her favorite memories with me. I couldn't understand why at first, and she couldn't really explain it. But it made sense eventually.

Cooking her dinner and even going out of my way to bring it to her didn't feel like a big deal to me. What I didn't realize then, even though I should have, was how much that simple gesture would mean to a person with Jackie's history. How large even small acts of caring loomed in her emotional landscape. Feeling like she matters to someone has a way of taking her over.

The funny thing was that I thought almost nothing of it at the time. It certainly wasn't calculated to make her think or feel any particular way.

I'd just wanted to see her.

Chapter Nineteen

JACKIE | *DAVID*

A horrible, endless day passes. No one seems to know what to say to me, including Gran, but everyone at school has a lot to say behind my back.

I go to my usual meeting place with Nicki before school on the quad, but she's a no-show and dodges me at lunch too. By Friday, I'm about to conclude that she doesn't want to be seen with me when she finally turns up about two minutes before first bell.

"My mom's at work," she announces. "Want to ditch?" Somehow this feels like the first nice thing anyone other than David has said to me all week.

"Let's go." I grab my stuff and we walk back to her empty house in silence.

"The school is going to call Gran when I miss first period," I say idly. It doesn't seem to matter that much right now. School has never seemed less important, and I can't concentrate anyway. Still, ditching never sits well with Gran.

"Aren't you already in trouble?" she asks, digging around in her drawer.

"Yeah." That doesn't quite feel right. Gran doesn't seem angry, she seems lost. Like she has no idea how to handle things for the first time in my life, which is worse than her being mad at me in some ways. But I don't know how to explain that.

"So, more trouble won't hurt anything." She finds what she's looking for, a multicolored vape pen, and holds it out to me.

I'm about to refuse but before I can overthink it, I put it to my lips and take a little hit. The recklessness of it feels kind of good.

I hand it back to Nicki and she inhales on it as well, then returns it to her drawer. She comes to sit next to me on the bed.

"I'm sorry about yesterday." She doesn't have to explain what she's talking about. "I shouldn't have avoided you like that. I was really thrown off, that's all."

"It doesn't matter," I say, even though it does.

"It matters to me. I'm not going to bail on you when you need me. And don't tell me you don't, with the whole school calling you a slut."

"It's all good." I stare out her window. "That's what I am."

"No you're not," she says stubbornly. "I've known you forever. If you did do what everyone is saying you did, there had to be a reason."

I look down at my hands. I don't normally bite my nails but this week has kind of turned me into someone else. Even my cuticles are a bloody mess. I moved on to them after I ran out of fingernail.

"What have you heard?" I ask her finally. I don't particularly want to hear the answer, but I do want to make sure the right gossip is going around.

"Basically that you tried to come on to Mr. Harrison and he got suspended for it." She moves a little closer to me. "Is that what happened?"

"Yeah. Pretty much."

She shakes her head and laughs dryly. "I have got to stop underestimating you."

"It was the stupidest thing I've ever done in my life."

"Why did you do it?"

"I have no idea."

"Was it about that guy? The one you told me about?"

I'm about five seconds from admitting to her that there was no other guy, that it was him all along. But I can't do it. I can't tell Nicki or anyone. The only way we'll survive this is to stick with the story. "Maybe a little."

"Because when I told you to get under someone else, I didn't mean a teacher." She grins and I shake my head.

"Now you tell me."

"I mean, don't get me wrong. As teachers go, he's not bad. I totally would."

I laugh a little. I know it's fucked up but hearing that from Nicki makes me feel kind of validated. She usually likes her guys big and brawny, which is so not David.

Without warning, I go from laughing to crying. I hate crying. It makes me feel like I'm falling apart. That's probably why I never do it.

Nicki reaches over and puts an arm around me. "Don't cry. You know how it is," she says. "They'll get bored with this and move on to something else eventually."

"I don't think they're going to move on from this one anytime soon." The pot is starting to do its work, and I'm feeling faintly disconnected from the world. It doesn't suck. Maybe this is the answer. Maybe I should start experimenting with random substances and random boys. It seems to work for Nicki.

I let myself imagine going with her to one of the house parties her older brother is always throwing. Wearing something that makes me look like the slut I am, for one night. Spending that night with someone else.

But as soon as I start picturing some guy touching me in all the same ways David did, my brain refuses to go any further. Because he wouldn't be David, and I don't think I can deal with that. I'd probably have to be completely wasted to even consider it. So what would be the point?

Having worked through this scenario in my mind, I no longer feel any need or desire to see it play out in real life.

When the pot wears off, I go back to school. Much to my surprise, Gran never even texts me about the classes I missed. That's so far from her normal pattern that it's disturbing. Almost scary.

***

I've been checking my phone whenever I can, but I haven't heard anything from David. I'm desperate for news, but I know I have to wait and be patient. When he finally does call, it's after school and he sounds distant.

"Hey, Jackie. Sorry it took me so long to call you."

"What's happening? I've been going crazy."

"I had to wait until I got a moment alone. I've been dealing with the school and my lawyer all week."

"You had to get a lawyer?"

"Afraid so."

"So… what's going to happen?"

"Well, you did your part, that's for sure. Because of you, there's no legal case against me. That's the good news." My fingers find the edge of a dish towel and I start obsessively kneading it. "The bad news is, I've more or less been fired. Kathryn's letting me teach until the end of the year, but then I'm gone. She's transferring you to another English class." My heart sinks.

"If you were fired, how can you keep teaching?"

"I wasn't officially fired. It's complicated. It has to do with Kathryn's relationship with Alicia and the school's reputation. Basically, she wants me gone but she's also trying to avoid publicity and drama. So the deal is that if I make it through graduation with no further 'incidents,' she'll let me resign."

For the millionth time, I curse myself for what I now can't change. It's impossible to picture South Point without David. He's the best teacher there, never mind what he is to me.

"Jackie, there's something else."

I already know what it is by his tone. "You can't see me ever again."

"Right."

I'm happy to go back to the way things were before.

That can't happen now. A future for us in any form no longer exists.

"This is basically like a restraining order. Kathryn and my lawyer both made it crystal clear. If I'm seen with you ever, for any reason, I'm dead. I *have* to get through the year with no issues, or I'll never get a job again." He pauses. "You understand, right?"

"Yeah."

"I don't blame you for any of this but it's the end of the road for us."

"I know."

"And I'm sorry to ask this, but I need you to delete all of our messages from this phone."

"I already did." I didn't, but I promise myself I will as soon as we hang up.

"Good. Thank you."

I really need him to say something else. Something I can wrap my broken heart around like a hot water bottle on a cold night. He's done it so many times before, made me so happy with nothing more than his words.

But this time, there's nothing but a silence so final I could die in it.

"I should go," he says eventually.

"Okay. I…" I can't say anything either. My throat feels like it's closing up. "Bye, David." I hang up quickly before I can humiliate myself.

I think back to Alicia's face when she stared me down outside her office. And I find myself resenting her more than ever before, almost hating her. It's not fair that David has someone to sleep with during all this and I don't.

Not that she's likely to be doing anything with him right now. Or who knows, maybe she is. I don't exactly want to imagine it. The point is, she's there with him and I'm not.

I go into my bedroom and stare at my books. I pull out *The Odyssey* and flip through the pages randomly.

The epic poem was way too slow-paced and old-fashioned for most of the kids in my class and we only covered about a third of it, but I fell in love with the story and the verses. I read the whole thing.

I put the book back on the shelf and sit down hard on my bed. Wondering what it will feel like when David's been lost to me for twenty years.

Chapter Twenty

JACKIE | **DAVID**

I tried to pretend it didn't, but the conversation with Jackie gutted me as much as it did her. I could hear the pain permeating her voice like tiny vines inside a tomato and I had no idea how to comfort her. At least the first time we ended things, I got to kiss her goodbye.

Before my resolve can melt away, I take my little phone out to the garage and snap it in half. I put the two pieces beneath my back tires and pull my car out, running over them. When I go back in to inspect them, the screen and keyboard are fractured beyond repair.

So that's it then. My last line to Jackie is officially destroyed.

I put the pieces in my pocket, then take Maggie for a long walk around the neighborhood. When we reach the park, I dump the fragments into a trash can. All evidence gone.

Come tomorrow, it'll be like none of this ever happened.

When I get home, Alicia's pouring a glass of wine. She's been drinking a lot since all this happened. I don't love that, but I don't exactly have a lot of moral high ground with her at the moment.

"Hi," I say cautiously, unhooking Maggie's leash and hanging it on the wall. "How was school?"

"It was fine. Nothing unusual."

"I'm still going back on Monday, right?"

"Haven't heard otherwise. Kathryn moved Jackie to a new English class yesterday." Alicia's mouth tightens as she says Jackie's name.

"Good." I go and sit at one of the counter stools across from her. "Have you heard from Isabel at all?"

"Isabel? No, why would I?"

"I just wondered if she reached out."

She takes a drink. "What's she going to say? 'Sorry my kid tried to ruin your marriage'?"

"Yeah. Good point."

We sit in painful silence for another few minutes, and then Alicia pours herself another glass of wine and heads upstairs to the spare bedroom. It's ostensibly an office too, but we rarely use it except when we have guests. Or during times like these, when she's too pissed off to sleep with me.

I go upstairs to our room and pull my shirt off to check my back in the mirror. Jackie left several deep scratches across my lower back in alternating angry shades of pink and bright red that day in my car and I've been waiting anxiously for the worst one to heal. It's starting to fade now.

I lean against the wall and sigh. It's been months since she was here, but it feels like yesterday.

***

"You're making me feel self-conscious," she said.

"How do you mean?"

She rolled over in bed to look at me. "You're so much better than me. Compared to you, I feel like I'm awful."

I smiled and shook my head. "You're not in any way awful. You're new at this, which is not the same thing. I have, what, a seventeen or eighteen year head start on you? It'd be pathetic if I wasn't at least a little bit better."

"I guess."

I kissed her. "Innocence is sexy in a different way, Jackie. Trust me." She looked skeptical, so I took a different tack. "Besides, I can teach you anything you want to know."

"Yeah?" She moved closer still. "Anything?"

I laughed.

"Sure. What'd you have in mind?"

She told me.

***

I don't know why being in my bathroom so often brings that moment to mind since it didn't even happen in here, but it does. And it arouses me every time.

The thing is, I know remembering that moment has the same effect on her.

I would hate for anyone to make Jackie feel bad about what happened between us. If people knew, they might make her believe that her experience was something sinister when it wasn't, twist her memories of everything we said and did into something that was wrong instead of how it actually made her feel at the time.

I was there. I saw the way she looked at me that night. The way I conduct my personal life is problematic at times, I admit that. I've manipulated countless girls and women, using them to boost my ego when I wasn't really interested in them. I've cheated, and I've slept with other people who were cheating – including Alicia. I never said I was a saint.

But I always treated Jackie with respect. Even now, I can't think of anything I could have done to make my behavior more ethical, short of not being with her at all. And would that have been for the best? Should I have ignored what she felt for me, left her hanging and wondering forever?

I know I changed her. But it wasn't for the worse.

None of that matters, though, because the world writes me off as a creep.

A rapist.

The word would make me laugh if the situation weren't so dire. Rape, sure. That seems like a reasonable term to describe what happened to a girl who jumped me every chance she got and continually asked for more.

Also, I'm pretty sure *rapists* don't bring their victims soup.

***

I get to school so early on Monday that it's still dark outside. I'm not eager to find out my colleagues' reactions to everything that's happened, so I want a bit of time alone to compose myself and catch up before dealing with that.

But on the way to my classroom, I pass by Jackie's locker which has a brand new graffiti addition. Someone must have spray painted it over the weekend.

TEACHER'S PET SLUT, it says. In big red letters high enough to fill half the wall.

I stare at it for a minute, consumed with fury for whoever did this to her. I momentarily consider texting Kathryn about it, before I remember that I'm supposed to be staying out of anything having to do with Jackie.

And so, hating myself for my cowardice, I continue to my classroom instead.

Chapter Twenty-One

JACKIE | *DAVID*

I can see the graffiti covering my locker from fifty feet away, even though I can't read what it says until I get closer. When the words become clear, I hear jeering around me as the other kids watch my reaction eagerly.

I try to reach inside me for some of Gran's inner strength, to make my face as blank as possible. As though I can't even be bothered to care.

But I can't believe this is happening. Who spray paints lockers anymore, anyway?

While I'm trying to decide what to do, Mr. Mintz comes down the hall. He looks at my locker, which is hard to miss, then at me.

Until a couple of weeks ago, Mr. Mintz was my second favorite teacher and I know he's always liked me. If this had happened before, he absolutely would have dropped whatever he was doing to help me deal with it.

But now, he looks away and keeps walking as if this has nothing to do with him at all, even though he's literally the reason it's happening.

Bastard.

Not knowing what else to do, I go up to my locker and get my books. I'm a little afraid to open it, but fortunately the inside looks normal.

I'm not even going to try to clean this shit off, why should I? I didn't do it. Everyone's going to see it, which I'm sure was the goal anyway, but I'm going to pretend it's not even there.

***

When I get home from school, Gran is waiting for me.

"How come you're not at work?" I ask. Gran manages a restaurant downtown, which is why she's usually gone in the afternoon.

"I'm going in later than usual. What's this about someone spray painting an insult on your locker today?"

"You know about that?"

"I hear things. Why didn't you tell Kathryn?"

I shrug. "I thought it would be better if I ignored it. Kind of thought that's what you'd want me to do."

"You could have told me."

"I didn't want to make it a huge thing. I'm just trying to get past this." I sigh and sit down. "Everyone knows what I did and they hate me for it. There's nothing I can do to change that, right?"

"Probably not." Gran is always honest with me, no matter what.

"So what do you want me to do exactly?"

"Well, what I would *like* you to do is tell me the truth about what happened. If I know the whole picture, perhaps I can help."

"There's nothing to tell that you don't already know." She's never going to believe that, and I'm never going to tell her the truth. It feels like Gran has me in checkmate. I can't move in any direction without going down, so I'm just staying put. As long as I do that, I haven't officially lost. But we also can't move forward.

"Can I go start my homework?" I ask her. She nods, her hands clasped in front of her face.

I want to tell her that if there's anyone in the world I would trust with the truth, it's her. Except that isn't true anymore. That one person is David now and has been for a long time. We're the only people who know our secret and it has to stay that way at all costs.

No matter what.

****

The sense of relief I feel when school lets out for spring break is so intoxicating it reminds me of actual happiness. Someone cleaned off my locker, but it doesn't matter. *Slut* is starting to feel like my new name.

The only time I feel okay is when I'm asleep. I lose whole hours in emptiness and it's wonderful. So I fully intend to basically spend this entire week in bed, shutting the world out and trying to forget everything I possibly can, as often as I can.

Except it doesn't work out that way, because Gran wakes me up at a gruesome hour on the very first day of my vacation and announces that we're going for a hike.

I groan. "Gran, I don't want to do that. I'm too tired."

"I am not giving you a choice," she says, sounding sympathetic but firm. I make an aggravated noise and bury my face in the pillow.

"Not right now."

"Darling, I can't let you languish in your room all week long."

"Why not?"

"Because you're going to get sick." I snort. "I know you want to hide, Jackie, but that's not the answer. You're starting to get depressed."

No shit.

"Gran, please, can't you leave me alone?"

"No. I can't." She pats my shoulder through the blanket. "Be ready to go in fifteen minutes."

I sigh, but I know damn well that Gran is immovable when

she's convinced of something and arguing with her is a waste of time. I throw back the covers and pull on a pair of jeans and a sweatshirt. They're looser than normal, and I realize I've lost weight in the past two weeks without even trying, something that most girls in my class would kill to do. I should tell them that being too stressed out to eat works wonders.

I yank my hair into a sloppy ponytail and go into the kitchen.

"Why do we have to do this again?" I ask as I pour myself a glass of orange juice.

"Because we do," Gran says simply. "I can't let you keep wasting away like you've been doing. As your grandmother and your guardian, I feel that it's time for me to step in here."

"Whatever." I pull on my oldest pair of shoes and Gran drives us to one of our old favorite hiking spots near a waterfall. She won't even let me listen to music on the way. She tries for the first few minutes to make conversation but eventually gives up.

I feel guilty for being so distant, but what does she want from me? If she would just leave me alone, this would be so much easier.

Once we arrive, it's not so bad. I can hear the water thundering even though we can't see it from here, and I can't deny that it's a gorgeous day. Almost involuntarily, I find myself sucking in the fresh clean air.

Of course, Gran has to *notice*. "Better?" she asks me with a small smile.

"I guess."

We start walking, and even though we're still quiet, it's a lot less painful than when we were sitting in the car. I feel kind of weak, though.

Annoyingly, Gran sees that too. She hands me a small backpack containing a bottle of water and a few of my favorite snacks.

"Thanks," I say grudgingly. I pull out a little baggie of cheese popcorn and start munching on it as we walk. "You know, I'm not anorexic or anything. You don't need to worry about that."

"I know," Gran says. "But all the same, you're not eating enough. Are you?"

I shrug, scuffing at the dirt with the toe of my sneaker.

"Jackie, I have to tell you that I'm completely at a loss right now. I have no idea how to help you. You've gone somewhere deep inside yourself where I can't reach, and I'm worried about what you might find there."

I cram more popcorn into my mouth and nod, but don't look at her.

"I can't help but feel that I'm failing you," Gran continues.

"You aren't failing me," I manage. "This isn't about you, Gran." The statement comes out a lot meaner than it sounded in my head and I rush to soften it. "What I mean is, this isn't your fault."

"I wish you would talk to me."

"I keep telling you, there's nothing to talk about. I made a mistake and believe me, I'm paying for it. Can we just leave it at that?"

"You know, I used to think of David as sort of a surrogate father to you."

"Well, he wasn't." Gross.

"Let me finish, please. I understand now that he was important to you in other ways. But can you make room for the possibility that perhaps you were looking for an older man to make you feel loved because you don't get that from your own father?"

Gran has too many shrink friends. "I don't care about Dad," I reply. That's not entirely true but I want it to be, which feels close enough. "He doesn't give a damn about me, so why should I give a damn about him?"

"I don't blame you for feeling that way," Gran says.

I scoff. "Now you're going to tell me he really does love me, he just doesn't know how to show it. My mom too, I guess, wherever she is." I kick at a pebble, trying to ignore the tightening in my chest that comes every time I think about my mother. I haven't heard from her in so many years it feels like she belongs to a different lifetime. A different kid.

And maybe by now, she does.

"I'm not going to tell you anything like that." I lift a low tree branch and duck under it but Gran is so short she barely has to lower her head. "Whether or not your parents love you is hardly the point, is it, if it's not the kind of love you need?"

I can't think of anything to say in response to that and we reach the waterfall in decent time. I walk straight to the edge and sit down next to the wooden posts marking the safe space. This is one of the only things I can do better than Gran. She doesn't do heights.

I can really hear the water roaring now and it almost drowns out the sounds of other people chatting nearby. Taking selfies. Laughing. I try to shut them out completely and let myself get lost in the stunning sight. I hate that Gran is always right, but this is making me feel a *tiny* bit better.

I sit there indulging in a fantasy that David is next to me, and run my fingers along my palm like he did so many times, trying to imagine what he'd say to me if he were here now.

Promise me you won't rush into anything.

I look around, startled. It's almost like I could hear his voice for real.

"I couldn't if I wanted to," I whisper back. Let's face it, no one will ever love me the way I love David, and anything less wouldn't be worth it. I know David loves me, but I'm not and never will be his only love. That's part of what's divided us from the beginning – he had lots of relationships before me. An entire marriage, even.

But for me, it's always been him.

I've wondered so many times what it was like for him to go home to Alicia after being with me. Whether he kissed her when he came through the door. If he had sex with her. He must have, at least some of the time.

I hope he showered first.

When we got together, I used to torture myself thinking about whether she was better than me. It's not that David ever gave me any indication he was comparing us. That was all me. I couldn't help it.

Speaking of unfortunate comparisons, I feel bad for whoever I do end up with next. Whatever he's like, I'll never be able to stop measuring him against David.

I feel a hand on my shoulder and jump.

"How are you doing?" Gran asks me, deliberately looking away from the edge of the cliff.

"I'm good," I say, standing up and brushing off my pants. "Sorry. I was in some kind of trance."

"That was the whole idea," she replies, sounding pleased. "Nature is very good for that."

"Uh. Yeah." If Gran only knew what I've been thinking. "I'm ready to head back now."

So okay, the hike wasn't quite as bad as I expected. Good thing too, because Gran takes me on three more that week. Each time I'm a little less resistant.

But in between, I sleep.

Chapter Twenty-Two

JACKIE | **DAVID**

Spring break was deadly, much too long. I tried to occupy myself with grading more than a hundred papers, but I'm a fast grader and it only took me a couple of days.

Alicia and I are still tiptoeing around each other. She's not visibly angry anymore but things aren't back to normal either. Normally we go on a little trip for spring break, at least three or four days of it. That didn't even occur to me this year until the week was half gone.

It's hard for her to avoid me in our small house, but not impossible. Especially since I've been trying to stay out of her way, let her process this in her own time.

At any rate, it's a relief to be back in school even though my colleagues' reactions to my return have been a mixed bag. A few are trying to act like everything is normal, which clearly takes a concerted effort, but most are avoiding me. No one has the guts to bring it up to me directly.

No one except Matt, that is. He's been solidly in the avoidance camp but he finally approaches me in the lounge when I'm making coffee our first day back from break. It's my usual duty since I'm almost always the first to arrive.

"Hey, David." He comes up to me, looking nervous. I raise my eyebrows but say nothing. "I, uh, saw your car in the lot. Can we talk for a minute?"

"About what?" I stare at the coffeepot, waiting for it to do its work.

"About the whole thing with Jackie." He sighs. "I want to explain what –"

"There's nothing to explain." I keep my voice cool. "You were just doing your job, right?"

"Look, if I'd had any idea of what was really going on…"

"You could have known that, if you'd asked me." I've had more important things to deal with than how Kathryn came to know what happened that day. I know Matt told her, but I haven't been dwelling on it.

Still, what I told Jackie was true. Because of Alicia's position, there tends to be a little distance between me and most of the other teachers at South Point but there are a few that I've come to consider friends over the years, and Matt is one of them. He's even been to our house for Thanksgiving with his husband.

So maybe I haven't wanted to think about the fact that Matt set all this in motion.

"David. I'm sorry."

"Why didn't you come to me first?" I'm in a tricky position here because objectively, Matt was completely in the right. Our flat-out lies about it notwithstanding, what happened between me and Jackie that day was my fault as much as hers and the truth is, Matt had an obligation to report what he saw.

But maintaining the delicate house of cards we've built around whatever he witnessed depends utterly on my ability to pretend I've been falsely accused because of him.

For this to work, I have to help Matt believe that *he's* the lousy friend. Not me.

"I tried." His voice is earnest. "I was literally on my way over to ask you about it after school when I saw Jackie heading to your car. With you."

Ah, so that's how he happened to see us leaving. When the science wing is clear on the other side of campus.

"You could have talked to me the next day, or called me that night even. You didn't have to go straight to Kathryn."

"I panicked." He holds his hands wide. "I don't have any better explanation than that. You have to understand, I came back from the office and I couldn't be sure, but it looked almost like the two of you were kissing. Then I saw you leaving with her. So yeah, I jumped to conclusions." He runs a hand through his hair. "I've been killing myself over it ever since Alicia went off on me."

"She did what?" This is news to me.

"She cornered me the day after you were suspended and kind of laid into me. Said that Jackie came onto you that day and it happened so fast, you didn't have a chance to react."

"She shouldn't have done that." Getting involved in this, especially to scream at Matt for doing what he was supposed to do, is not a good look for her. If Kathryn finds out, it's going to cause Alicia real problems of her own.

On the other hand, I'm kind of heartened that she was defending me. At her own expense, even.

"Well, you know how Alicia gets about you," he says with an attempt at a smile. "She's protective of her man."

"I didn't know she confronted you." I sigh. "Look, Matt, I understand it looked really bad. I do. I just wish you could have waited to ask me about it before you blew up my whole life. If you'd heard my explanation and still felt like you needed to talk to Kathryn, I would have understood. At least then you would have had the full context."

"I should have. No question. I owed you that much. I know it probably doesn't mean anything now, but I went to Kathryn before break and asked her to reconsider her decision."

"What'd she say?"

He scoffs. "Well, let's just say she wasn't in the mood to hear me out."

"Of course she wasn't. She only wants to hear from people who think I'm a child molester." I roll my eyes. "Sorry, do I sound bitter?"

"Yeah, I don't get that," Matt says, sounding eager to criticize Kathryn from my side of the fence. "She's known you even longer than I have. This is not the kind of thing you would do."

I stare at him. *"You* thought I would."

"No, I didn't. That's why I was so relieved to hear there was an explanation." He looks uncomfortable again. "Look, are we okay? Or… *could* we be okay, someday?"

I take a swallow of coffee, feeling it burn my throat as I consider things. For whatever reason, I was starting to take stupid risks with Jackie, doing things I'd told her were off limits from the start. For God's sake, I let her kiss me at school and then left with her, not to mention making love to her in Isabel's house before that. Who knows what I might have done next?

If I look at this a certain way, Matt almost did me a favor.

"I don't hate you," I say finally. "Can we leave it at that for now?"

"Yeah. Yeah, sure."

I clap him on the shoulder. "We should get going." At that moment, both of our phones chime with a text message from Kathryn reminding us of the early-morning staff meeting she set for the first day back.

***

"I'll make this quick," Kathryn says once we're all in the library. "I know we all have a lot of work to do, but this is important and it needs to be said before school resumes." Alicia is standing next to her in a distant approximation of something like unity.

"I want to address what happened here last week," Kathryn

continues sternly. "I know you are all aware of what I'm talking about, and I'm telling everyone together so this is very clear and there's no confusion. I expect all of you to pay attention to the bullying policy *always,* and not turn a blind eye when you don't care for the student being bullied. Alicia and I are fully committed to ensuring that this stays a safe environment for every student here. I'm putting all of you on notice right now that we expect the same commitment from each of you."

A couple of the other teachers are sneaking curious glances at me, which I ignore.

"When a student's locker is spray painted with a sexual slur, and I don't hear about it until *five hours* after the fact – from another student, no less – that tells me that we have a problem. When you don't immediately report that kind of thing to me or Alicia, you become complicit in it. You contribute to making South Point an unsafe place to be, and that's offensive to me. I don't care what the provocation for the graffiti might have been, it's unacceptable." Matt is turning red next to me. He must have seen it too. "Going forward, if you see something like that, you need to assume no one has told us yet and do it yourself."

"We're all striving toward the same goal," Alicia says, her voice noticeably less vehement than Kathryn's. "No matter how we feel about any one student personally, it's important to uphold the values that we stand by as a school."

There's a long silence.

"That's all," Kathryn says finally. "Have a good first week back, everyone." The bell is due to go off in about five minutes, and everyone disperses abruptly. I walk over to Alicia.

"What brought that on?" I ask her quietly. Kathryn is already marching back to her office.

"Apparently, she got a call from Isabel over break," Alicia explains. "She's not happy about the way the whole graffiti thing was handled. Kathryn wanted to make sure it didn't happen again."

I roll my eyes, trying to pretend I think that's stupid, but I'm privately grateful Kathryn is looking out for Jackie since I no longer can.

"I should go," she says.

"Matt talked to me this morning," I inform her. She stops and turns back toward me.

"What'd he say?"

I give her a faint smile. "He says you stuck up for me."

"I guess you could say that." She looks at me dispassionately. "So what, you think you're off the hook now just because I defended you?"

"Am I?"

She moves a little closer to me, even though no one is close enough to hear us.

"I still say you were fucking stupid."

"I still don't disagree."

"All right then." She turns again and starts to walk away. I head to my classroom to start getting ready for first period.

About two minutes later, my phone vibrates with a text from Alicia.

Come by for lunch today.

I smile to myself as I power down my phone. It might take a while but we're going to get past this. She's going to get past this.

Just like she did the first time.

Chapter Twenty-Three

JACKIE | *DAVID*

"Jackie?"

I look up at my new English teacher, hoping she didn't ask me a question.

"Yeah?"

"You're wanted in the principal's office." I was zoning out so hard I didn't even notice anyone come in here. I stand up and throw my book in my backpack, then take the pass from her and leave.

What does Mrs. Connell want now?

On the way over, I decide that this is probably another attempt to get me to talk. I'm starting to see for myself that she's every bit as tenacious as David described her to me once, and I prepare to be a surly teenage stereotype in response.

"Hello, Jackie." Mrs. Connell motions to the familiar table where someone is already sitting. Someone who looks up at me expectantly as I walk in.

I've never seen this person before in my life so this makes no sense at all, but I feel like I know her. Maybe because she looks a little like me – or how I might look in a few years, anyway. She has a similar build and her hair is almost the same shade as mine, but a lot longer and wilder.

144

"I want you to meet someone," Mrs. Connell says. "This is Lily. She used to go to South Point."

"Hi." Even that one word feels like an escaping prisoner. I have no idea who this girl is but she's not here to bring anything good to my life, I can tell that much by her face.

"I didn't graduate from here," Lily adds. "My family and I moved away in the middle of my sophomore year. That was about eight years ago."

"Okay…?"

Mrs. Connell breaks in. "Lily would like to talk to you about Mr. Harrison, Jackie."

"What? Why?"

Lily gestures to a chair. "Do you want to sit down?"

"Why?" I ask again.

"I'll explain, if you let me," Lily says. "All I want you to do is hear me out."

I don't want to hear her out. I want to get away from her. But instead, I find myself sitting down as though I have no control of myself. Like that's anything new.

"I'm going to give you some privacy," Mrs. Connell says. "Lily, you two can use my office as long as you need it, okay?"

"Sure. Thanks, Mrs. Connell."

Suddenly I'm alone with this older girl who waits for me to look at her. And when I do, I recognize something in her eyes. Something that scares me.

I stare at her, and finally she clears her throat and speaks. "Sorry. I know this is weird. Meeting you is messing with me more than I thought it would."

"I don't understand why you're here."

"When my parents moved us to Portland, I didn't really stay in touch with anyone," Lily says, which doesn't sound like an answer. "But later on, I reconnected with an old friend who teaches here now. It took me awhile to get up the courage, but eventually I asked her to keep an eye on David for me. Let me know if she heard anything about him. Last week, I finally got that call." She sighs. "I know what happened between you two, Jackie. At least, I have a pretty good idea."

"Everyone *thinks* they know what happened," I say defensively. This can only be a trap, and I'm not falling for it. "But they don't. You don't even know *me.*"

"I know David," she replies solemnly. "I know him the same way you do. I was involved with him."

"Bullshit. I don't believe you." My body says otherwise though, judging by the ice water that surges through my veins.

"I didn't expect you would." Lily gives me a sad smile. "I wouldn't have either. But see if this sounds familiar, okay? David probably told you that you were different from all his other students, because you were mature enough to handle yourself with him."

"No," I say defiantly. "He did not say that to me."

He said it. More than once.

"How about this then – he felt *somewhat* guilty for cheating on Alicia with you but people can't always control how they feel about each other."

"No." This time my voice is a lot quieter.

"No?" Lily says gently. "I guess he doesn't have a birthmark under his left hipbone either? Right here?" I look up in horror as Lily taps the same spot on herself. "It's a perfect circle, almost the exact same size as a dime."

"I don't…"

"Did he say you were the only girl he had touched since Alicia?"

"Stop," I cry out. "Please stop."

Do you really think I go around doing this all the time?

"Jackie, you have no idea how much I wish it wasn't true." I want to cover my ears, hide under the desk, anything to stop the flow of words from Lily. But I hear them anyway, along with something I know she can't fake – a level of pain that at least equals my own. "If I had done things differently, he might not have been around to hurt you like this. I'd give anything to change it."

My head feels too heavy for my neck suddenly. "You're telling me that he… that David…"

"We got together right after I turned sixteen," Lily says. "He'd usually drive us somewhere way out in the woods. I told him I wasn't ready to have sex, and he said that was okay. He just had me go down on him instead. And vice versa."

Saliva floods my mouth.

"Alicia was still teaching at the time," she continues. "History. I had them both, back to back. She was actually a great teacher but I almost failed her class because I couldn't think about anything around her except what a traitor I was."

"I can't deal with this," I say, rising from the table. I get as far as the door, then stop.

I can't seem to leave, either.

"I get it, Jackie. When my friend called last week and told me your version of events, I kind of spun out too," Lily says softly. "But then I knew I had to come back."

"*Why?*"

"Because you need to know who David really is. And if you're anything like I was, what other people tell you about him is pretty meaningless. I figured you would never believe it, unless you heard from someone else who's been there."

I turn back toward her.

"I don't believe you anyway."

"No?"

"So what if you know about his birthmark? That doesn't prove anything."

"Tell me how you know I got it right, then."

I have no answer to that, obviously.

Why does she look like me? It's not that we could be twins or anything but I definitely look way more like her than Alicia.

Did I *remind* him of her?

"I really loved him," Lily says. "In my mind, I was responsible for the whole thing, not him."

"Maybe you were."

"No. I wasn't, Jackie, and neither were you. David's almost twenty years older than you. And he was already twenty-six when he was with me. Do you really think either one of us could have manipulated him into doing something he didn't already want to do?" She pauses. "How long has it been going on?"

I don't have to answer. This could still be a trap Mrs. Connell set up somehow. Although even for her that seems a little extreme.

"October," I hear myself reply.

What am I *doing?*

"And he's been having sex with you." It's more of a statement than a question.

"Why are you here?" I ask her. "What do you want me to do?"

"I can't answer that for you. I can only tell you what I wish I would have done."

"I guess that means you think I should tell everyone what happened." My teeth are clenched so hard I sound like my jaw has been wired shut.

"If he's done this to both of us, it's a safe bet there have been others."

Oh hell no. That's not even a remote possibility. There has be an explanation for Lily, and there is *no way* that David's done this with other girls. That's not him.

"It's okay if you're not ready to think about that," she adds hastily, seeing my face. "I've had a lot longer to process this than you have. But Jackie, please, consider this. You've been so quick to take this whole thing on yourself. When did he show any kind of willingness to protect *you?*"

I think about that. From what I hear, David is okay. Nicki says he looks fine, at least. Whereas I'm still getting shit on a daily basis, like the paper shoved in my locker this morning. When I opened it, I found a disgustingly graphic cartoon of a girl on her knees in front of a boy.

And scrawled across the bottom: ***YOU'RE A SKANK WHORE.***

It wasn't a threat or anything, but I still felt a sickening fear cut into my gut like broken glass when I read that.

"How would he have protected me?"

"Well. He could have told the truth. Taken responsibility for his actions the way a partner who truly loved you and a real man would have done."

"But he would have gone to prison," I whisper.

"And that has always been a risk for him. Look, let's say he stood up for you and admitted what he did. He'd probably serve a sentence for rape, but by the time he got out you'd be over eighteen. No one could stop you from being together if you wanted."

I can't respond but my expression is apparently all Lily needs to see.

"But he didn't do that, let alone wait until you were eighteen in the first place. Instead, he let you take *all* the blame. I'm guessing he hasn't even been talking to you?"

I hesitate. "He can't. He's not allowed."

Lily nods. "So, my parents found out about us. That's part of why we moved. When we left, I told David that nothing was ever going to change for me, that I'd do anything to be with him. I promised him we'd make it work. And he said that even though he loved me, I needed to move on because things were getting too complicated for *me.*"

"What happened?" I ask in spite of myself.

"Oh, I tried to keep it going anyway. After a few *really* neutral emails, he basically ghosted me." Lily's laugh carries a bitter note. "I won't even try to describe how pleasant that was. I'm sure you can imagine. The point is, he cut me loose when being with me was too risky for him. Just like he's abandoned you now."

But it's not like he *wanted* to abandon me.

I need to move, but this room isn't exactly built for pacing. The best I can do is stumble over to Mrs. Connell's window as I gather my courage to ask something else.

"Did Alicia know?"

"I didn't think so, at the time," Lily replies. "I wouldn't swear to that now. I wrote her an email a couple of years ago, confessing. I told her what happened and fell all over myself apologizing."

"What did she say?"

"Not a lot." Lily sounds grim. "She thanked me for 'taking responsibility for myself,' and I haven't heard from her since. My guess is, whether she found out from me or some other way, she's known the truth for a long time now. She stays with David anyway. Still lets him work with students. You can interpret that however you want."

"Look, what do you want from me?" I whirl around, angry. "If you think what he did with you was so wrong, *you* tell the police what happened and *you* press charges."

"I can't," Lily says heavily. "In Oregon, crimes like this can't be prosecuted after six years. I'm about two years too late."

"Well, why did you wait so long?"

"Because it took me years to accept that David was even *as* guilty as I was. Forget about more than that." Lily runs a hand through her hair and I can't help thinking again how much it looks like mine. That one thing is still bothering me more than almost anything she's said. "When my parents found out, they mostly wanted to pretend it never happened. They definitely wanted me away from David, hence the move. But they weren't interested in holding him accountable."

"They thought it was your fault too?"

"Pretty much. But I try not to judge them too harshly for

that. They also thought they were protecting me. When I was in high school, most people didn't understand the dynamics of sexual abuse, or how damaging it is to keep quiet."

It *wasn't* abuse.

At least not with me.

After a moment, Lily stands up and walks over to the window beside me. I stiffen automatically.

"I'm not saying coming forward wouldn't have been a nightmare for me. It's okay if you can't bring yourself to go that route. I could never ask you to do something I wasn't able to do myself. That's not why I came here." Lily tentatively places her hand on my shoulder and every instinct in me wants to jerk away. But for some reason, I don't. "I came for you. To be here for you, if you want me to be."

"Why?"

"Because in spite of what I just told you, and the fact that I know full well David alone is responsible for this clusterfuck, I can't completely get past my own guilt. I don't think I ever will."

I stare at her in confusion.

"I feel like by staying quiet, I let him do this to you," she explains. "So if I can do anything now to help you get through it, and I mean *anything,* that's what I'm going to do."

I clutch the edge of the table, feeling like I'm about to black out. I won't let this be true. I can't let anyone change the way I feel about David, because his love made me who I am.

Unfortunately, my brain seems to be believing her without my permission.

And she can tell.

"Oh, Jackie. I'm so sorry." Before I know it, she's hugging me and I'm not fighting it. Something deep inside me has decided all on its own that Lily's not the enemy.

Seconds later, I pull away.

"Did… did you say you live in Portland?" I barely know what

I'm asking. Anything to change the subject.

"Yeah. I do."

"How long are you here for?"

"As long as I need to be. I'm a grad student and I work part-time, but I cleared my schedule for the week."

"You don't even know me and you did that for me?"

Lily squeezes my shoulder. "I also did it for me. Which I realize might not make much sense to you." It doesn't.

"So what happens now?"

"Whatever you want. You tell me how you want to do this, and that's exactly what we'll do."

"I don't know. I need some time to think."

"Perfectly understandable."

"But if you wanted to stick around… that would be okay."

Lily gives me a real smile then, the first one I've seen since meeting her. "Sure. Do you want me to come back and pick you up after school? Talk some more?"

Before I can answer, we hear a soft knock on the door.

"It's me," Mrs. Connell says.

"Come in," Lily answers, and the door swings open.

"I came to check on you. I hope I'm not interrupting."

"You're not. I think we're done for now."

Mrs. Connell turns to me. "Do you want to go back to class, Jackie?"

"Sure."

"I'll write your teacher a note."

As she's doing that, Lily takes a Post-It note from the desk and writes down her cell phone number and email. She hands the little sheet to me and I pocket it.

"I'll pick you up in front of the school after last period, okay?"

"Okay." I walk out of the office without saying anything else.

I don't go back to class. I doubt Mrs. Connell expected me to, since I didn't even take the note she wrote for me. Instead, I wander out to the soccer field and sit on the bleachers for the rest of the morning.

Trying to figure out how I can possibly learn to live in a world where there's such a thing as Lily.

Chapter Twenty-Four

JACKIE | **DAVID**

It's early afternoon, barely four o'clock, and Alicia and I are both home together. That's pretty rare, but during lunch I convinced her to come home with me right after school let out rather than staying a couple hours later like she usually does.

"Why?"

"Because I want to do something with you. Something fun. Take our minds off everything."

She acquiesced without a ton of enthusiasm but I had my window. That's all I ever need.

I went to the grocery store and picked up all the ingredients to make her favorite dessert, then brought them home to her. She laughed in spite of herself when she saw what I had in mind. Alicia does *not* cook.

I've been trying to show her how to use a piping bag for the past twenty minutes and it hasn't been pretty, to say the least. But to my relief, the plan itself is working. She's starting to relax around me, resemble her usual self.

"I have never seen anyone have so much trouble with this." I look around at the spectacular chaos in my kitchen and try very unsuccessfully to suppress my laughter.

"So you're saying I'm not going to make it to MasterChef this year?"

"Are you kidding? Gordon Ramsey would kick your ass for the mess in here alone."

"Oh well. I'm not sure that was ever a dream of mine anyway." She threads her arm through mine so automatically and naturally I could almost forget how long it's been since she touched me.

"You have other talents." I wipe a smudge of flour off her cheek and kiss her where my finger was.

"What about you? I thought you could teach anyone anything."

"Apparently I was wrong about that." I grin at her and she smacks me on the arm.

"Asshole. You have flour in your hair, by the way." She brushes the top of my head.

"So do you."

"Maybe we should go get cleaned up." She raises her eyebrows, and I know I've won. I draw her closer and kiss her properly for the first time in weeks. Her response is as welcome as it is predictable.

***

Usually I'm out seconds after my head hits the pillow but for some reason, I can't sleep tonight and I'm awake long after Alicia. When I'm sure she's asleep, I carefully untangle myself from her and go downstairs to clean up the kitchen, then open the back door so I can watch the spring rain that started sometime in the past two hours.

Maggie wanders in to join me, her eyes sleepy. She's my buddy. Day or night, she likes to follow me around. I sit down next to the open door and she flops across my lap.

"What's up, girl? You can't sleep either?" I scratch her ears. "Not sure why I can't. But hey, at least me and Mommy made up, right?"

Maggie makes a happy little noise. I lower my head to whisper a confession in her ear, not the first I've made to her.

"I miss her, Mags." She gives me a major side-eye, and I shake my head. I swear she understands what I'm saying somehow. "I know, I know. Not supposed to."

I do, though.

Trying to cook with Alicia reminded me of when I showed Jackie the same thing last summer, only with considerably more success. Isabel was hosting a Fourth of July barbeque fundraiser for the local women's shelter, and Alicia volunteered us to help.

We arrived early and when we got there, Jackie was in the kitchen prepping about a million pieces of chicken for the grill. Alicia stayed outside with Isabel to set up tables and chairs.

"I forgot you like to cook," I said to Jackie in greeting and she jumped. "Sorry, did I scare you?"

"I startle easy." She looked over at the platters I was carrying. "Let me wash my hands and I'll help you unload all that."

"No need. Keep doing what you're doing." I laid everything out on the kitchen table and then went back to her. She was wearing yellow shorts and a blue tank top, and her hair was pulled into two French braids with a bandana over them. I could see swimsuit tan lines on her back where the tank top dipped a little.

She looked very pretty and a hell of a lot more grown up than I remembered from the end of her freshman year. I'm still not sure how she pulled that off in a mere seven weeks.

"How can I help?" I asked her.

"Um. Do you want to make the salad?"

"Sure." I started pulling out ingredients from the fridge. "How's your summer so far?"

"Not bad."

"You been reading anything good lately?"

"I finally finished *The Great Gatsby.*"

"And?"

"It sucked. It was so boring. I kept waiting for it to get as good as you promised it would be, and it never did." She shook her head in exaggerated displeasure. "You let me down big time on that one."

"Seriously? It's one of my favorites."

"I just don't share your love of F. Scott Fitzgerald. He takes, like, a year to get to the point."

"So does Dickens and you don't have any issue with him."

"Must be a style thing." She washed her hands and got an enormous bowl for me to use.

"Thanks. That chicken looks like it's going to be good."

"Hope so. I'm trying this new thing with lemon pepper and cayenne." She holds out the marinade so I can smell it.

"Very nice. I can't wait to try it."

"Hopefully someone coming tonight knows how to work the grill because Gran and I both suck at that."

"I can handle the grill," I promised her. When she finished getting the chicken ready, I helped her decorate a pie and a cake for dessert, hence the piping bag tutorial.

I think about forty people came to the fundraiser, which is way too many for Isabel's place in cold weather but no big deal when it's nice out. She has a sizable piece of property, but a pretty small house. Go figure.

Everyone raved about the food, and I was quick to share the credit with Jackie. Her eyes lit up every time she heard me do that.

Alicia and Isabel were busy mingling with everyone all throughout the evening and I didn't see anyone Jackie's age there. She held her own nicely with the adults for a while — it's always been very important to Isabel that Jackie have that skill — but by the time the fireworks started she was looking pretty bored.

I came up behind her and gave one of her braids a friendly tug. She turned to look at me.

"Hey, Mr. Harrison." It was starting to get chilly, so she'd pulled on a sweatshirt and jeans at some point.

"You sound so formal," I teased her. "I don't really mind if you want to call me David when we're not in school."

"That's okay. I think it would be kind of weird calling you by your first name." A firework exploded and turned her face an interesting combination of green and orange. "Everyone thinks I'm a total suck-up as it is."

"Does that bother you?"

"No. I don't care. They'd think I was weird anyway. I always have been."

"Well, then I say weird suits you. Not that it matters what I think."

"Yes it does." She suddenly got very busy pulling the sleeves of her sweatshirt down until they almost covered her hands. I smiled and changed the subject.

"Great job on the food tonight. It's all anyone can talk about."

She shrugged. "I didn't do that much. You did most of it."

"You've got to learn how to take a compliment, Jackie."

"Okay." She looked back at me. "Thank you."

"You're welcome." I pulled her closer, in a side hug. She seemed a little surprised at first, but then I felt her hand move cautiously around my waist.

"I'm glad you gave *Gatsby* a try," I said. "That makes me happy, even if you didn't like it."

She rolled her eyes. "It was *so* bad."

"I'll try to make you a better recommendation next time."

"Yeah, do that." She nodded vigorously. The porch lights went on right about then, and we let go almost at the same time.

***

Things were so natural between us even back then. We had a long history of easy, innocuous touches way before I ever thought about kissing her. I'd put a hand on her elbow to guide her out of the way when we collided in the kitchen, or she would touch my arm to get my attention. Now and then I would hug her, like I did that night.

Of course, I wasn't unaware of how she felt about me, or the effect that my touch had on her. It was no different from the way Lily reacted to me in the beginning, or any of the numerous girls between them with whom I never went one step further.

The difference with Jackie was that I liked being with her for other reasons besides the way she looked at me. That's how I knew I was in trouble.

The next time I asked her to call me David, she never called me anything else again. Except when other people were around to hear it.

Chapter Twenty-Five

JACKIE | *DAVID*

I honestly try to attend my afternoon classes, but it's pointless. My concentration is shot. When Lily promptly pulls up after the final bell, I've already been waiting outside for twenty minutes.

"Want to get some coffee?" she asks me as I get in her car. I nod, and she drives off without another word. On the way, I try to gather more clues about her. Her car is on the older side, but it's clean – normal clean, not obsessively spotless like David's. She's got a piano cover of a Chainsmokers song playing, and there's a little wooden hummingbird hanging from her rearview mirror.

We pull into a Starbucks near the school and she orders something with matcha in it. I think that's a kind of tea. She asks me what I want and I request a white hot chocolate, feeling shy when she pays. We take our drinks to a lone table in the corner.

"What do your folks say about all this?" she asks me as we sit down. It's as if our last conversation was paused until this moment and all we have to do is push play again.

"I live with my grandma. And she hasn't said much lately. She doesn't exactly know what to do with this." I take a sip of my drink. The warm milk feels good in my stomach, since I couldn't even think about food in the post-Lily hours of my day.

"Parents never really do. Is she supportive of you?"

"Um. She's trying to be," I admit. "But she wants me to tell her what happened and, well. You know. I can't really do that." Lily nods. "I haven't been able to tell anyone."

"Do you want to tell me?" Lily asks, almost casually. "I'm not a mandatory reporter. And I've been exactly where you are. So I have no intention of repeating anything you tell me to anyone else, including your grandmother."

I consider this. Lily says things so matter-of-factly that it's easy to believe her. "You promise?"

"Yes. I promise."

Before I know it, I'm pouring out the whole thing. The award, the night at his house, the breakup. As I talk, I can feel the heat of our secret burning a hole in my chest but somehow telling Lily doesn't feel like I'm betraying David.

It hurts in a different way. Telling her this, and watching her listen, reminds me of the time I took a bad fall in a driveway when I was eight, and the doctor had to dig tiny pieces of gravel out of my arm for almost an hour. I cried so hard that Gran's shirt was soaked.

But when I finally stop talking, I feel lighter. Almost like I could float.

Silence falls over the table.

"Wow," Lily says at last. "He's getting bolder, that's for sure."

"Was that how it happened with you?"

"Pretty much. Only with you, he went much further. And hearing about it firsthand is kind of... ridiculously creepy." Lily stirs her tea thing. "It feels almost like he was practicing on me. For you."

I don't like that thought, and push it away immediately. "Can I ask you something?"

"Anything you want."

I pick up my neglected cup, which is starting to get cold. "When you were with him..." Lily waits. "When you were doing all of the stuff you did with him, did you like it?"

"Yes, I did," she says simply. "I liked it all, and it's okay if you did too. That's normal."

"I did," I assure her. "It all felt good. He never forced me into anything."

"He didn't force me either, Jackie. That's not how David does this. He wants you to think that everything you did was consensual. And he's very skilled, so of course he made you feel good."

"It *was* consensual." Even now, I feel a need to protect him. Or at least make sure I'm being clear about this. "I'm not a little kid. All of my friends are having sex. I know he's older, but I wanted him. So that's not… rape." I can barely get the word out. It was wrong when Detective Keller said it, and it's wrong now.

"We're not talking about a couple of years here. You were fifteen. He's thirty-four, and he's your teacher. That's illegal for a reason. Plus which, he's married."

"Yeah. And it's not like I didn't know about her, the whole time." Maybe Lily can understand this too. "I kind of hate myself for that. You know?"

"Do I ever." She nods. "And I have to be honest with you, Jackie. That one takes time. The thing is, even if you threw yourself at him like the way you described it to the police, it was still his responsibility to say no. An ethical teacher would have actually responded to that by distancing himself from you. And if he had? It might have embarrassed you a little, but in time you would have remembered David as a decent person who cared about you in the right way."

My throat catches. "I love him."

"I know you do," Lily says. "Hell, I still feel like I love him sometimes, even after all these years and knowing what I do about him now. That's the whole point. David understands that a person's first love is powerful, and he gets off on being that person for impressionable young girls."

"I don't think I can do this." My head hurts.

"You don't have to do anything right now." Lily rests her hand over mine. "Look, Jackie, I would never have come here to crush you like this if I thought there was a chance you would remember your time with David in a good way. I came here, in part, because I know it's already killing you."

I can't speak.

"Isn't it?"

I nod.

"Does it help to talk about it?"

"I don't know." My voice sounds so weak. "You're telling me that he's not who I thought he was and I'm not sure I can take that." I sigh. "I already felt so guilty about Alicia. That's why I tried to break it off. But then I did it all over again, because I love him, and this time I ruined his life."

"You didn't ruin anything," Lily says patiently, with a slight emphasis on the first word. "But one thing at a time. Remember, Alicia's not off the hook here. She allowed David to be around you in the first place, even after I told her what happened."

"I don't get that." I sit back in my seat. "I always thought if she found out, she would never forgive him."

"I can't answer that one for you," she says. "I can tell you what I think, but it's just a guess."

"That's more than I have."

"The way I see it, she can't let herself believe that she's married to a rapist who targets their students. So assuming she believed me at all, I think she must have found a way to revise what I told her into a story she could live with. And I have no idea how you and I fit into that story. Though I think it's safe to say we probably don't come off too well in it."

I pull the plastic lid off my cup and start bending it.

"If I told people… and David went to prison…"

"That might not happen," Lily reminds me. "Our justice system is a long way from perfect, when it comes to this stuff. You'd want to prepare yourself for either outcome, as best you could."

"But if he does, and it's because of me, how would I ever get over that?"

"I know this is hard to accept, but if he did go to jail it wouldn't be because of you." I don't have the heart to argue with her, and it must show on my face because she nods. "Okay. We'll put a pin in that one for now."

***

I don't have people over much so I fully expect Gran to be surprised when I call her to ask if I can bring a random girl to our house, but the only question she asks is what I want her to pick up from the store for dinner. There are times when I'm grateful she's so light on her feet.

Lily and Gran hit it off right away, and Lily can't stop raving about the meal I made even though I don't think sliders and sweet potato fries are anything special.

"I can't believe you can cook like this," she says to me. "I never cook."

"Well, I imagine you're a busy woman, being in grad school. And you work too?" Gran asks.

"Yes, at Powell's."

"The giant bookstore."

"That's the one. I help organize author's events, that kind of thing. I love it."

"What are you studying?" I ask her.

"I'm getting a master's in social work."

"How did you get interested in that field?" Gran asks.

"I'm lucky that way. I've known what I wanted to do since high school."

"And you went to high school here too, Jackie says?"

"I did." Lily looks at me and somehow that simple question

changes the entire atmosphere of the room. Everyone goes quiet.

"Gran?"

"Yes, Jackie?"

I cross my wrists on the table and rest my chin on them. "I think I should tell you what Lily's doing here," I say slowly, even though telling her that represents a gigantic step on the road to telling her everything.

"There's no need, darling. Mrs. Connell called me this morning. She explained about Lily."

Oh. No wonder she didn't question it when I asked her if I could invite Lily over. I wonder how much Mrs. Connell actually knows. What she told Gran.

"It's all right," Gran says. "I'm glad she's here."

"You are?" I glance at Lily, who's listening to our exchange with interest.

"Of course I am." Gran's thin arms sweep across the table, clearing dishes. "I'll clean up the kitchen. Lily, dear, do you have somewhere to stay tonight?"

"I'll get a room downtown," she says.

"You'll do no such thing," Gran replies, waving a hand at her. "We have a perfectly comfortable sofa bed, and fresh sheets in the linen closet. You'll stay here."

"Are you sure?"

"Yes," she says firmly. "It's the least we can do."

Lily looks at me.

"Is that okay?" she asks.

"Yeah," I say. "It's good." Amazingly, I really mean that. I want her to stay.

***

After Gran helps us make up the sofa bed, she claims to be tired and heads to her room. Gran never turns in this early, so I know she's just trying to give us some privacy to talk more.

And we do. Before I know it, three hours have passed. I've never connected with anyone as easily as I do Lily and I guess that's logical, since I've already told her my darkest secret and it's the same as hers.

When I realize how late it's getting, I go take a shower and come back to find Lily in a long-sleeved T-shirt and running shorts with a book in her lap. She's wearing reading glasses, like David does sometimes. The association makes me a little uncomfortable.

"What are you reading?" I ask her.

"Something for school." Lily tilts the book so I can see the title. It looks boring. I sit down on the sofa bed gingerly, and she puts the book aside. "How are you feeling?"

I rub my arms. "Pretty fucked up, to tell you the truth."

"I'm sorry I dropped this on you. I didn't make that decision lightly, trust me."

"I know," I say. "And I think… you did the right thing. It just feels like my brain is exploding. I want to do the right thing too, but I don't even know what that is. He doesn't *really* belong in prison, does he?"

Lily pats the space next to her. "Come here." I do, and she puts her arm around me. I can't even explain how weird it is that I'm okay with this. I'm not big on physical contact with anyone besides David and Gran, let alone strangers. But Lily doesn't feel like a stranger anymore. "It's totally okay if you're not ready to make any major decisions. Honestly, I'm not worried. You'll figure out the right way forward for yourself in the end."

"How do you know?" I murmur, my eyes half closed. It's late and I'm tired. The long, emotionally exhausting day is taking a toll on me.

If she answered, I don't remember. The next thing I'm aware of is coming back into consciousness slowly, and hearing Lily's voice in the kitchen. I reach for my phone and discover that it's nearly two in the morning.

"… don't be sorry. It's nothing to be sorry for — well, unless you're David."

My heart freezes. Was I completely wrong to trust Lily? Is she telling Gran everything I told her earlier?

"Well said."

"But for everyone else, for *me,* it's just what it was. And I'm fine now, I promise. I have a good life."

"Still… I understand you can't tell me anything Jackie may have shared with you about her and David." I let my breath out in a rush when I hear that and realize that Lily kept her word. "But I presume whatever happened is not too different from what he did to you. And I hate the thought of Jackie having to survive something like that after everything she's already been through. I'm worried about her."

"How could you not be?" Lily's voice is gentle. "You love her. I love her too, and I barely know her. But you don't have to worry, Isabel. Jackie's going to be okay. Better than okay, would be my guess."

"She's strong. That's for certain."

I don't feel strong. At all.

"And she has you, and you want to help her with this. I can't tell you how much that matters."

A long pause. I hear one of them set a glass on the table.

"Tell me, what do you wish your parents would have done after they found out?"

I strain to hear Lily's answer. I know I don't want Gran storming in like the cavalry, but I have no idea what I do want from her.

"I wish they could have helped me understand what happened," Lily says. "After we moved, we never really talked about David again. It was like this embarrassing skeleton that no one would acknowledge. I felt really shut out of my own family, and I missed him so much."

I swallow hard. She really does get it.

"I thought David was the only one who loved me, and I kept telling myself that if I held out long enough he would come back for me." One of the chairs creaks. "What I needed was someone to dig me out of the mess he left me in. And help me understand that he was the one who buried me in the first place."

"I can do that." Gran's voice is so low I can barely hear her. "I'll do that for her."

"I know you will," Lily says. "And more importantly... *Jackie* knows you will."

Chapter Twenty-Six

JACKIE | **DAVID**

"We've got a big problem," Alicia says as she comes through the door the following afternoon.

I look up from the *Romeo & Juliet* essay exam I'm drafting, and the spoonful of chili I was about to eat sort of freezes in midair when I see her face. I was hoping to be done with big problems for a while.

"Tell me."

"Lily's been talking to Kathryn."

"What?" I spring to my feet like Alicia's pulled a gun on me. "How could that possibly be?"

"I don't know. She must have heard about Jackie through the grapevine and decided to give Kathryn even more ammunition against you, as if she needed it." Alicia pauses. "Lily forwarded her the message she sent me two years ago."

"You have got to be kidding me." I don't recall the exact contents of the message off the top of my head, but I definitely remember the overall gist. "What is she, campaigning now?" Even as I say this, a horrible idea occurs to me and before I can even think it through all the way, I know I'm right.

Telling Alicia didn't have the intended effect so Lily's plan must be to find Jackie, tell *her* the whole story, and get her angry enough to betray me. That's her endgame. Twisted and yet so perfectly in line with Lily's misguided sense of justice.

I almost fall back into my chair as the picture becomes clear.

"So… so Kathryn confronted you about this?" I ask Alicia, trying to keep my voice stable.

"Yeah." Alicia throws herself onto the couch. The shrieking alarm in my head nearly drowns out her words. "She's apparently decided that I'm no better than you because I didn't 'do something' about it when Lily told me." She scowls. "Maybe I should have. Except it never occurred to me that you'd be moronic enough to put yourself in this position again. And I sure as hell never thought that *I'd* end up paying the price for it."

"What do you mean? You didn't do anything. She can't fire you, can she?"

"Not exactly. She's leaning on me pretty hard to resign, though. She doesn't trust *me* anymore, after reading Lily's message. Which unfortunately I answered. So I can't really claim I never saw it."

Not for the first time, I feel a surge of murderous rage toward Lily. What the hell is wrong with this girl?

Her coming back into the picture is one of the few ways this could get worse. I have no idea how Jackie will react. If we could talk, that would be one thing. Face to face, I can convince her of almost anything. But I have no way to contact her now.

"I so appreciate the mess you've made here, David." Alicia storms upstairs.

I know I brought this on myself, but it still doesn't seem fair for a bullet I dodged eight years ago to find me now.

Goddamn Lily.

***

Things were already rocky between us when everything imploded. It had been a little over two months, and the whole thing was a catastrophe from the word go. Lily came from an ultraconservative, exceedingly religious background. Our relationship placed an untenable level of guilt on her conscience which was just barely outweighed by her extreme devotion to me. But the cognitive dissonance was too much for her, and by then she was starting to act a little crazy.

I was trying to figure out how to exit gracefully before things got even worse, but whenever I hinted at ending things she began to fall apart. I was worried she would snap if I pushed her too far. So we just kept going.

We'd meet when Alicia went out with her friends, which she did much more frequently back then. I hate watching people get drunk, especially in bars, so I'd offer to be the designated driver. In between dropping them off and picking them up, I'd be with Lily.

It was after one such night that she came into class looking like a train wreck. Her hair was all over the place, and she'd obviously been crying. She lingered in her seat after everyone else had left, and I took her in the hallway.

She told me her parents had found out by reading her journal, and my mind instantly went into fight-or-flight mode. I'd been banking heavily on the fact that as long as she kept loving me like she did, she'd never tell anyone. I hadn't accounted for anyone finding out another way.

I tried to calm Lily, but it was all I could do to restrain my own panic. Eating and sleeping were impossible. I began disappearing for hours, driving or running until the middle of the night sometimes. Alicia was understandably confused at my erratic behavior, but I couldn't tell her about Lily. Not unless I had to, not unless she was about to find out from someone else, in which case my marriage would be the least of my problems.

And yet.

Not only did nothing bad happen, things worked out in the best way possible. Somehow, Lily's parents blamed her for what happened instead of me. According to Lily, they were deeply ashamed of her and loath to ruin my life over a "mistake" that she made. Actually, their reaction explained a lot about her own vacillation with me.

I got the impression that the move to Portland was already in the works, or at least a possibility, but it was one of those things that could have gone either way. When Lily told me that they weren't telling *and* that she was moving, I felt like I'd walked away from a gas station holdup clutching a winning lottery ticket.

Lily, I knew, would forever blame her parents for keeping us apart. Not me. It was perfect. I encouraged her to look at the move as a fresh start. I also said a lot of things to assure her that I still loved her and always would, et cetera. Words I calculated to keep her from sensing how grateful I was to her parents for taking care of the situation.

I should have felt guilty, and I do now, but at the time I only thought of myself. I'd like to think it occurred to me that this whole disaster wasn't exactly fair to Lily, but following that thought to its natural conclusion wouldn't have led anywhere I wanted to go.

The day before she left, I reminded her that she'd always have our memories.

"We had something special, Lily," I said when I kissed her goodbye. "You'll always have that to hold onto, and no one can take it away." The frustration and distress she'd caused me was water under the bridge now, and I could afford to be generous.

I answered her emails at first, but I never said much. I crafted careful sentences that didn't imply anything, and wrote one email for every two or three she sent me. When her missives began to get more emotional, I started to let even more time elapse between her emails and mine until I stopped responding altogether. I hoped that would nudge her into moving on and sure enough, she eventually went silent.

It wasn't until about five years later, only six months or so before Jackie came into my life, that Lily reached out again. But not to me.

I came home from work that day to find Alicia on the couch with a drink in her hand and a look on her face which let me know I was in for a long night.

"What are you doing?" I asked, trying to sound like it was normal to find her drinking on the couch in the afternoon, which it wasn't.

"I got an interesting message today," she said, and I could tell it wasn't her first drink. I don't mind when Alicia drinks, to a point, but I definitely mind when she tries to have a serious discussion with alcohol in her system. It always ends with her screaming, and reminds me way too much of my mother. It's the only thing she does that really pisses me off. "From one of our former students. Little trip down memory lane."

"Can we talk about it tomorrow?" I asked, hanging my coat up. "When your buzz has worn off?"

"No, I don't think we can, David." She got off the couch and handed me her phone. "Would you care to explain this to me?"

I saw Lily's name along the top of the screen and immediately felt a stab of horror.

"What is this, Alicia?"

"Read it."

Like I said, I don't remember the whole message because it was really long but it was mostly about how she had felt about me in high school, and how badly she'd screwed up with me. How she wouldn't be "at peace" until she told Alicia the truth. She went into way too much detail about the guilt that she'd been feeling since it happened, and ended with an equally excessive apology.

I read the message twice, my teeth clenched. The second time, I looked carefully for any indication that our relationship had been ongoing. She never said it happened more than once. Finally, I looked at Alicia.

"Well?" She raised her eyebrows.

"Well, what? You actually *believe* this, Alicia?"

"I remember almost every student I've ever had, same as you. And the thing I remember best about Lily was that *she loved you.*" Her voice went up an octave. "We never talked about it, you and me, but I *distinctly* remember that." She took another drink.

"So, she had feelings for me. Like you said, it was obvious. That doesn't mean I acted on them."

"Did you?" she yelled. I sighed. "Never mind! I could tell it was true before you even finished reading that goddamn note."

"Alicia, please. Let's discuss this tomorrow, when you've had a chance to –"

"We're going to discuss this *right now.*"

"I don't want to talk to you now," I said, holding onto my own composure for dear life. "We'll talk and I will explain, but not tonight. You're not in the right frame of mind to have a calm discussion."

"You screwed a student and you expect me to be *calm?*"

I handed her phone back to her, and she yanked it from my fingers. "I don't blame you for being upset, but I want to wait until you're sober before I tell you what she's talking about." I made my way back toward the door, picking up my coat on the way.

"Are you seriously leaving?"

"I'm just going for a walk. I'll be back in a little while. We can talk about this in the morning."

She turned and strode from the room, her glass clutched in her hand. I heard the bedroom door slam a few seconds later, and let myself out.

My head was spinning. I hadn't seen Lily since her last day in school, and so much time had passed since our last correspondence that my original feelings of affection for her had returned. I thought about her more often than I would have expected. I'd even nursed a small, silly fantasy that she'd come back to town one day when she was older and less uptight about sex, and we could finally consummate the thing properly.

I would have liked that.

But now, I felt blindsided. *Six years,* for God's sake. Who does this after more than half a decade? As I walked and my head began to clear slightly, I felt a new emotion bubble up inside me.

Rage.

Growing up the way I did, anything that indicates a lack of control has a tendency to disgust me. That's part of why I hate alcohol. But at that moment I understood better than I ever had before how someone could lose it, with the right provocation. I can't say what I would have done to Lily if she'd turned up on the street in front of me.

I walked fast for almost eight miles. That's how long it took the fury building inside me to settle into a more manageable state of severe agitation. When I got home, I found a blanket and two pillows in a heap at the bottom of the stairs, as though she'd thrown them.

The following morning, she came downstairs looking severely hungover. She rarely drank to excess anymore once we were in our thirties.

I'd heard her stirring before she made her way down, and started some coffee. I handed her a steaming mug as soon as she came in the room, which she accepted.

"All right, I've calmed down," she said, running her hand over her still-mussed hair. "Talk." She crossed her legs and her arms, managing to look vulnerable and livid at the same time.

I laced my fingers together in front of me. "Part of what Lily said is true, but she made it sound like a lot more than it was."

"You cheated on me."

I nodded grimly. "Yes. I won't deny that."

"With a *student*. I'm less interested in the details of how or why, you know?" She sipped her coffee. "Though the fact that she was sixteen certainly makes it more sickening. Is that really who you are?"

"Alicia, it happened once and it was a huge mistake. I regretted it right away and I thought about telling you, but there was nothing to be gained from hurting you like that."

"Yeah, I'm not so sure Lily did me any favor," she said.

"That's how I feel."

"But for Christ's sake, David, she was a teenager! You could have gone to jail."

"I didn't have sex with her." A meager technicality, but Alicia didn't know that.

"That doesn't necessarily matter. With today's laws, you'd have been crucified even if you only kissed her. And obviously, it was much more than that."

"Look, Lily was really religious. It actually *wasn't* a whole lot more than a kiss, but in her mind that was the same as if we'd had some kind of torrid affair." I shook my head. "I'm not saying it wasn't stupid, but I don't think it warranted a guilty conscience on the level she described. I didn't think so then, either. But trust me, she's been carrying this around with her like she killed someone ever since it happened."

"Her *parents* found out?" I nodded. "And they never told anyone? Not Kathryn, not the police?"

"No. They didn't seem to think it was worth ruining my life over. They just moved away, which was a relief."

"They didn't even confront you?" I shook my head. "Wow. If she'd been my kid, you would have had a recovery time."

"I know. I was lucky." I paused. "That was the week I was so…"

"I remember." She glared at me. "You could have lost *everything*. Why?"

I shrugged. "I felt bad that she was so wrapped around the idea of me when nothing could ever really happen between us. I thought that if I gave her a little validation, she might be able to move on."

Alicia rolled her eyes. "You actually thought that doing whatever you did with her would make her *less* obsessed with you instead of more?"

"I thought kissing her just once would be enough to show her that she wasn't crazy and make her feel better about the whole thing. The rest just happened."

She made a noise of disgust and left the room. A few minutes later, she took off and I didn't see her for two days.

***

She came back, though. For a while, I almost wished she hadn't because she seemed to relish punishing me in a million little ways. Getting her the dog she'd always wanted and I never did was one of many concessions I made to appease her during that time. Sort of comical, really, since I can't imagine life without Maggie now.

But for reasons I didn't need to completely understand, Alicia stayed with me. Our relationship survived Lily. We grew back together over time, even became stronger in some ways.

Just in time to face the ultimate test.

Chapter Twenty-Seven

JACKIE | *DAVID*

When I get home from school, Lily's sitting at the kitchen table with her laptop. We decided last night that she'd stay with us through the weekend.

I don't want her to go.

She smiles at me. "Hey, you." I toss my flip phone onto the table. "You don't have a smartphone? I thought that was illegal."

I'm not in the mood to joke. I sit down across from her.

"He didn't answer me."

"Who? David?"

I explain about the phone and hand it to Lily. "I texted him this morning, before I left."

Lily frowns as she reads the message where I pretty much begged him to talk to me. To explain. "Oh, Jackie."

"Please don't be mad," I say hurriedly. "It's just... I couldn't betray him without at least hearing his side."

"I understand." I know she really does. That's the best and worst part of all this.

"I don't know if he even kept his phone." I sigh. "But part of me was hoping he did, in case I ever really needed him."

"That bastard," Lily growls. "I hate him for doing this to you. I'm so sorry, Jackie."

"Why?" I ask in a wannabe tough voice. "He's a bastard, right? Like you said. It's no loss. Why should I care?"

"Well. That's true. And if you were a robot, maybe you could respond with perfect logic to every fact available to you at any given time. But that's not how human hearts work." Lily comes over to sit beside me. "You thought he loved you. Of course you care."

It's a long time before I speak again.

"If I tell the police what happened, is he going to go to jail?"

"I don't know," she replies. "This isn't exactly a gray area. I can't imagine why he wouldn't. But there are never any guarantees."

"I don't want to do that to him."

"I get how hard this is to accept, Jackie, but you wouldn't be doing anything to him. The only thing you'd be doing is making the police aware of what's already true. The rest is up to the legal system, and he broke the law."

"This isn't fair."

"It's not. Nothing about this is fair." Lily lays a hand on my shoulder. "And it has to be your decision. All I can do is tell you that I'll be there if you decide to tell, and I'll still be there if you don't."

"Thank you." The phrase doesn't feel like enough. "I don't think I could do this alone."

"I'm here to make sure you don't have to find that out."

I look up at the ceiling and feel my ponytail fall over my shoulders.

"Will you come with me to talk to Mrs. Connell tomorrow?"

"Of course I will."

I pull in a hard breath and try to steel myself for the first of many times.

"Okay."

"Are you sure? I don't want you to feel any pressure, just because I'm leaving in a couple of days. I can always come back."

"No, this is better," I say. "I need to rip the Band-Aid off. I can't keep living like this." Lily reaches over to squeeze my hand.

"How do you feel about talking to Isabel first?"

Oh God.

"I guess I should," I say slowly. "She should hear this from me."

***

When Gran comes home from work, Lily and I are still at the kitchen table and she comes over immediately to sit down across from us.

"Is everything all right?" she asks us, and I shake my head.

"I need to tell you something."

"I'm listening."

But the only thing she has to listen to for a very awkward five minutes is complete silence. I open my mouth twenty different times, but the words simply won't come.

Finally, I bury my face in my hands and say, "Lily, can you tell her? Please?"

"I will if you want me to," she says. I nod and try to brace myself as she places a hand on my back. "Isabel, David's been having sex with Jackie. It's been going on for months now."

Gran doesn't react audibly, and I peek up. Her hands are laced in front of her as she nods, slowly.

"I thought so."

"I'm sorry," I whisper.

"Why are you sorry? That never should have happened, and it was wrong, but it was *his* wrong. Let this be on David, Jackie." I don't bother arguing. "What do you want to do now?"

I sit up straighter, rubbing my temples fiercely. "I *want* to forget this ever happened. But I'm going to... talk to Mrs. Connell tomorrow. I'll tell the truth. And she can tell the police, if she wants."

"She has no choice, love." Gran sighs. "You understand they'll want to talk with you next, right?" I nod again. "I would like to be there."

"Gran, no. It's going to be horrible." I look at Lily in a panic.

"They're going to ask her very detailed questions, Isabel," Lily adds quietly. "You might not want to hear it all."

"I'm sure I don't, but I still want to be there." She takes one look at my face and accurately interprets it. "Jackie, nothing you say will change my opinion of you. I only want to support you."

"It won't help. Please," I plead.

When Gran speaks again, she sounds resigned.

"Well. I'd much prefer to be there, but I suppose it should be up to you. Are you certain?"

"Yes. It's going to be humiliating."

"You have nothing to feel humiliated about, darling. He's the one at fault here."

"But I'm the one who has to tell what happened," I point out. "And I don't think I can do that if you're listening. I'm sorry."

"Very well," says Gran as she glances at Lily. "I'll respect your decision." I look away, afraid to see the pain in her eyes. Gran has been my rock through so much – and right now I need Lily with me, a girl I barely know. Not her. I don't know how to make that hurt Gran's feelings any less.

She leaves soon after, claiming she's meeting a friend for dinner. But as with last night, I know she's giving me space to be with Lily.

Relief and guilt take hold of me. One hand each.

When I ask Lily how she knows what the police are going to ask me, she grimly replies that she's been visiting a message board for rape survivors over the past year.

"I never post," she adds. "I just lurk, although that could change after this week. But I've read a *lot* of posts by people who reported their assaults to the police. You said the detective who came before was nice to you?"

"Yeah. She was okay."

"That's good, because it's not always like that. We'll ask Mrs. Connell to make sure she comes again this time."

Wanting to prepare myself, I ask Lily exactly what the detective's questions will be and she tries to answer. But after about ten minutes, I cut her off and run into the bathroom to escape. Preparing isn't going to work here.

"Sorry," I say as I return to the couch a few minutes later.

"Let's stop," she replies. "Try to relax for a while, okay?"

We spend the next couple of hours binge-watching *Friends* but I'm too distracted to pay attention. After a while, I notice that Lily's not laughing either.

That's when I realize tomorrow is going to be really hard for her too.

***

I didn't even know that the school had a conference room. It's tucked behind a door in the counseling office.

"We're going to go in here because it's a little more comfortable," Mrs. Connell explains. No one says so, but it's also further away from Alicia's office.

I wonder who's going to tell her about this one. And when.

The room isn't cold at all but my teeth are chattering so hard that I'm not sure how I'm going to form words. Lily doesn't look much better than I feel.

"Is it all right if I stay?" Mrs. Connell asks me.

"I don't care," I manage.

"Jackie, let's take this one step at a time, okay?" Detective Keller says as she takes out her familiar notepad. "I can see you're very nervous. There's no rush here, all right?"

"Okay," I reply.

"I understand you want to tell me more about what happened with you and Mr. Harrison?"

I nod stiffly.

"Where would you like to begin?"

"I, um, I lied to you. When you came before."

"I had a feeling that might be the case." Keller opens her notebook to a fresh page. "So what really happened?"

"Well. Me and… I guess I can call him David now…" I'm gripping Lily's hand so hard I have to be hurting her, but she says nothing. "We've been having sex." The words hit the table like a brick.

"Thank you for telling me the truth," Keller says kindly. She doesn't look at all surprised. "I know that wasn't easy to say. Is it okay if I ask you some more questions?"

I nod.

"When and how did this start?"

"About a month into the school year." I try to explain why we went out for coffee that first day, how he kissed me in the car. "We started…" My voice sounds choked. "We started fooling around in his car after school. Usually like once or twice a week." From the corner of my eye, I spot Mrs. Connell. She looks furious. I'm not sure I want her to hear this after all, but it's too late now.

"And when you say you were fooling around, can you tell me what you mean by that?"

"Normally he would… touch me, and stuff."

"I'm sorry, Jackie, but I need to ask you to be more specific, okay?"

Lily said she'd say that. I am *so glad* Gran isn't here. I close my eyes and try to somehow speak without listening to myself. "He would… um… he'd touch me under my clothes. All over. With his hands at first, and then later he used his mouth."

"So he would have oral sex with you?"

"Yes."

"And did he ask you to touch him?"

"Yeah." I can feel my face burning as I force myself to continue. "I mean, I don't know if he asked exactly, but I would do the same things to him."

"So you would perform oral sex on him as well." Keller's voice is steady, as though she does this every day. I guess she probably does.

"Yeah."

"You're doing fine," she adds. "When did he first have intercourse with you?"

"November second." The date is branded painfully in my brain.

"Can you tell me about that?"

"Alicia was out of town. At a conference in Seattle," I mutter guiltily.

"Alicia is his wife?" Keller glances at Mrs. Connell, who nods.

"He asked me if I wanted to come over while she was gone. I told my grandma I was staying with a friend." I hear Lily's breathing change. "I walked to his house from school. And I spent the night with him." I take a drink of water and the glass rattles when I set it back down.

"Okay. So you slept overnight at his house. And he had intercourse with you there."

"Yes."

"To be clear, we're talking vaginal intercourse?"

I look up at the ceiling and try to decide if it's possible to die from mortification. It feels like a legitimate possibility.

"Yup."

"Any other kind?"

"Nothing we hadn't already done."

"Did he use any kind of protection?"

"Condoms." I feel like I'm signing David's death warrant.

"Do you remember the brand?" I do, only because he asked me to get one at some point. I tell her. "Okay. And what happened next?"

"He took me home," I say. "Then we just kept going. Except after that it was almost always in his car. Once at my house, but mostly in his car. Like before."

"Tell me about the time at your house."

"He drove over after school one day. He was upset because…" I trail off, finally looking at Lily.

"You're doing great, Jackie," Lily manages to say, even though she looks like she just witnessed a murder.

"You are," says Keller. "Hang in there. Why was he upset?"

"Because I didn't want to see him anymore. I was feeling too guilty."

"Then what happened?"

"He said he understood. We talked for a while longer, and then we had sex again. It was supposed to be the last time."

"Where did you have sex?"

"In my bed."

"Have you washed your sheets since then?"

"Yeah," I answer. "The next day, I did." I'd been so paranoid that Gran might be able to detect his scent when she came in my room, because I still could.

"Okay. And was that the last time?"

"No. The last time was the afternoon that Mr. Mintz saw us."

"Okay, is this when you and he drove out to that spot in the woods? When you told me you were talking?"

"Yeah." I bite my lip. "That was our usual place. I'm sorry I lied."

Keller shrugs. "You're not the first to do that. Now, Jackie, everything you've been describing to me is illegal whether you were a willing participant or not. But I do need to ask, because this would change some of the charges. Did David ever force you into any of this?"

"No," I say fervently. "He never hurt me and he never pressured me. I love him. And he said he loved me." My breath starts to come in little gasps. Mrs. Connell pushes a box of tissues across the table to me, but my old instincts are kicking in again and I have no intention of crying. "I'm sorry. I just can't believe I'm saying all these things about him." I take another gulp of water, and Lily does the same.

"Don't be sorry," Keller says. "I know this is rough." She gives me a minute to compose myself before moving on. "Do you have anything that can help corroborate what you've told me? Text messages, photos, anything like that?"

"He gave me a cell phone that I could use to text him. One of those cheap flip phones."

"That's good," she says. "Do you still have that phone?"

"Yeah, but I deleted all the messages that were on it. They weren't from his real number anyway. He had another phone for himself." Keller looks disappointed. "I'm sorry. He asked me to delete them and I… didn't know, yet. I didn't know about Lily."

"And you're Lily?" Keller says, looking at her.

"Yes," Lily answers. "I came down here when I heard about the classroom thing." She runs through her own history with him as the detective writes note after note.

"Would you be willing to testify against him?" Keller asks.

"Um. Sure," says Lily, looking startled. "I didn't think I could, though. Isn't it too late?"

"Not necessarily. Not if you're testifying to pattern." Lily and I look at each other. "But let's not get ahead of ourselves. This is unlikely to ever see the inside of a courtroom."

"What usually happens in cases like this?" Mrs. Connell asks.

"No promises, but he'll probably end up pleading to some form of misdemeanor sexual abuse. Depending on his lawyer and which judge he gets, he could end up serving a year or two. Maybe less." She looks at me and totally misreads whatever she sees. "He'll definitely lose his teaching license, though, because he'll have to register as a sex offender. That's something, right?"

I don't reply. David could lose *everything* because of what I'm saying right now. How am I supposed to live with that?

"Do you have anything else from him? Like a note, maybe?"

"I have one note he gave me. He left it on my doorstep with a birthday present. A necklace." I take it out from under my shirt to show her. I don't know why I'm still wearing it.

"What does the note say?"

"Happy birthday. I miss you. And a quote from a poem."

"That's all?"

"Yes. It's typed and he didn't sign it. He was always really careful." I sigh. "No one is going to believe me."

"I believe you," Mrs. Connell says darkly. "I did send Alicia to a conference in early November. I believe Lily, too."

"So do I," Keller adds. "Can you tell me if David has any distinguishing marks, Jackie? Tattoos, anything like that?" I describe the same birthmark Lily did, and the scar on his back.

"And where is his house? Do you remember?"

"It's on Sycamore. A townhouse." Random details start pouring from me like water. "There's a picture of him and Alicia on the dresser in his room, it was taken in San Francisco when they were dating. His bed has blue sheets on it. He has a dog named Maggie and he sings in the shower." I'm talking way too fast now, my words tumbling over each other. I almost sound drunk.

"It's okay, Jackie," says Lily, although she's fighting tears.

"Do you need anything else right now?" Mrs. Connell asks the detective.

"No. This is enough to get started."

"Lily, can you take Jackie home?" Lily nods, swiping at her face.

"What's going to happen?" I can't leave without knowing.

"I'm going to go back to the police station and make a report," Keller replies. "And then I'm going to get a warrant. For David's arrest."

Chapter Twenty-Eight

JACKIE | **DAVID**

I didn't think anything of it when I saw a police car in the lot this morning. Police and resource officers are constantly passing through for various reasons.

But as my fifth period class is ending, right before lunch, I see two uniformed officers turn up outside my classroom. They stare at me through the glass, and one checks his watch. They wait until the bell rings and the students start filing out.

My heart drops like a rock and I know.

This is it.

When they come in at last, Kathryn is with them, her face set in a series of severe lines. I've almost forgotten she has any other expression.

"Kathryn, what is this?" I demand. She says nothing.

"David Harrison?" one of the officers asks.

"Yes, that's me." My mouth has turned to cotton. This must be what a heart attack feels like five minutes before you have it.

"You're under arrest for third degree rape of a minor."

"You've got to be kidding me."

"Place your hands behind your back, sir."

"Wait a minute," I say, taking a step back. The male officer moves toward me, and I realize that for the first time in my life, these cops are not on my side. "You… you don't need the handcuffs. I'll come with you."

"It's policy, Mr. Harrison," the female officer says coolly. "We've parked in the back, so if you come quietly, hopefully not many people will see you."

Is she out of her mind? Everyone will see this.

The male officer turns me around and clicks a pair of handcuffs into place. *Handcuffs.* I am going to be escorted from the school in chains. Like a criminal.

Kathryn stares at me and the smallest hint of triumph seeps through.

"You did this," I whisper, genuinely shocked.

"I didn't do anything. Jackie turned on you. She told us everything this morning."

"What?" My brain can't process anything. "That doesn't make any sense. There's nothing to tell!"

"Spare me, David."

"Let's go." The female officer puts one hand on my upper arm.

"Does Alicia know about this?"

Kathryn nods. "I told her."

"And?"

"Mr. Harrison, your wife is meeting you down at the station," the officer says. "Now, I need you to come with us. The quicker you cooperate, the sooner we can get this moving."

I stand up straighter. "This is a mistake. I want to contact my attorney as soon as we get to… wherever you're taking me."

"We'll make sure you get a chance to do that. Come along."

As we're walking to the parking lot, I feel a sense of surrealism grip me so hard that for a moment I'm relieved. It's only a dream, thank God.

But as we get to the police car and one of the officers holds the door open for me, that soothing thought dissipates as quickly as it came. There's no room in my brain for anything but reality.

Jackie turned on you. She told us everything.

There's only one person who could have convinced her to do that.

***

It takes over an hour to process me, and only then am I allowed to make a call.

"I've been arrested," I say to Marshall, who answers right away when I finally get to the phone.

"Where are they holding you?" I tell him. "I'll be there in twenty minutes. Don't say a single word to anyone."

It's another hour before a guard unlocks the door to my cell and brings me to a small windowless room, about the size of a walk-in closet. Marshall is sitting across from me.

"I'm afraid you're in it pretty deep here, David."

"I don't understand what's happened."

"What's happened is what I warned you about from the beginning. The girl told the whole story to the police."

"Jackie wouldn't do that."

Marshall pulls a sheaf of paper from his briefcase. "She would, and she did." He squints at the paper. "She said that you two have been together for almost six months, that you started seeing each other in September." He glances up at me. "You would meet at a bookstore after school to avoid detection, and then drive to a remote location. You began having oral sex with her not long after that. Full intercourse started in November, when your wife was–"

"Stop, stop," I say, holding up my hands. "I don't want to hear any more. I get the idea." I place my palms flat on the table. I have no idea what to say to this revelation, the information they could only have gotten from Jackie. "This doesn't make sense. Jackie protected me before, you said it yourself. What would make her do this now?" I already know, but I can't accept it.

Marshall flips to another page. "Do you know someone named

Lily O'Neill?"

I cover my mouth, seized by an insane urge to giggle. "She used to be one of my students, years ago."

"And you had sex with her also?"

I sit back in my chair and cover my eyes.

"I'll take that as a yes."

"You've got to be kidding," I say, almost to myself.

"I'm not so much in the comedy business, David. You really should have told me about this."

I vaguely recall him asking me if I'd ever done anything like this before, but Lily was never supposed to count. I don't reply, and Marshall grunts in disapproval.

"Well. Fortunately for you, the statute is up on Lily."

"What's a statute?"

"A time limit on how long the state pursues certain crimes. It means they can't get you for what happened with Lily. But for Jackie, they absolutely can. And they will."

"This can't be happening."

"It is. Take the evening to absorb the shock. You're not going to be arraigned until Monday anyway."

"What does that mean?"

"Arraignment just means that you're brought before a judge to hear the official charges against you and enter a plea. Also where we talk about the possibility of you getting bail."

"So I have to stay here all weekend?" I can't believe what I'm hearing.

"Yes. Sorry."

"But then I'll get bail, right?"

"Most likely. I have no idea how much it will be, though. Do you own your house?" I nod. "If your wife agrees, you can use the equity in it to post your bail."

The blacked-out feeling is returning. "Is Alicia here?"

Marshall nods. "I met her when I came in. She's in the visitor's center, waiting to see you. You can talk to her after we're done."

"How did she look?"

He shrugs. "Shocked. Angry. Pretty much what you'd expect."

"If I get convicted here..." I trail off. "I mean... well... what's the sentence?"

"Five years is the maximum for Class C felonies. You're lucky Jackie was fifteen. If she'd been fourteen, you'd be looking at ten years."

"Five *years?*" I feel my chest constrict. "For a consensual relationship?"

"Were you not listening before? It *wasn't* consensual, David. Get that through your head." I can't find a response to this, and Marshall continues. "My goal is to get you a plea bargain, which means you plead guilty to the crime in exchange for a lighter sentence. Given that it's your first offense, legally speaking, I have a good shot at getting most of your sentence suspended. You won't actually serve it unless you later get convicted of the same crime. You'll be on probation for the rest of what your sentence would have been, and obviously you'll have a record. It will definitely mean the end of your teaching career but in my professional opinion, this is probably the best result we're going to get."

"What if I plead not guilty?"

"That means a trial, at which you'll most likely be convicted. I can still argue for a lighter sentence but at that point, it's up to the judge instead of the prosecutor. I have a much better shot with the district attorney. We make these deals all the time."

"So I'm going to be convicted. Of rape. That's what you're telling me here."

"Unfortunately, we're in the middle of a huge societal upheaval right now when it comes to this kind of thing. People aren't too kindly disposed toward predators, especially ones who target teenagers."

"I'm not a predator!" The mischaracterization in his words

makes me furious. "I have never touched a woman against her will in my life."

Marshall places his pen on the page in front of him. "Jackie's not a woman, David. She's a girl. A minor. And you admitted to me that you had sex with her – multiple times, it sounds like. Having sex with someone who's too young to consent is inherently coercive."

"This is ridiculous," I say. "Jackie *loves* me. She would never be doing this if Lily hadn't talked her into it. There's no way she will ever testify against me in court."

"I think it would be in your best interest to stop making up your mind about what Jackie would or would not do here. If this goes to trial and she does testify against you, my opinion is that you will be convicted. I can't let *you* testify, so there's nothing to refute her story."

"What do you mean, I can't testify?"

"What would you say, that she wanted it? That will get you a conviction even quicker."

"I could just deny the whole thing."

Marshall shakes his head. "No good. You've already told me you're guilty of the crime. I can't advise or allow you to take the stand and commit perjury."

My head feels like there's an ice pick through it.

"Okay, look," I say at last. "I don't think they're going to find any proof of what Jackie told them. Physical proof, I mean." Marshall is already shaking his head long before I reach the end of my statement.

"I disagree. DNA evidence is –"

"There is no DNA evidence, Marshall. That's what I'm telling you. I used a condom every time. I always threw them away in a garbage can on the street somewhere. Unless they want to go through every trash dump in the city, they're never going to find one."

"What about the time she was at your house?"

"I got rid of everything from that night," I reply. "I put an old set of sheets on my bed, and after she left, I threw them all away. And that was back in November, so they're long gone now. That's the only time we were ever together there."

"David, there's always something, no matter how thoroughly you think you cleaned. A hair, a skin cell… and we haven't even talked about your car yet."

"After I came to see you that first time, I had the car detailed. Twice. First I did it myself, then I had a professional do it."

"What about the cell phone you used to contact her?"

"I threw it away. Even if she kept hers, we never used names and it was a prepaid cell phone. They could never trace it back to me, at least not now that mine is gone."

"Sounds to me like you've had some practice with this, David." Marshall's been nothing but professional so far, but for the first time I detect a note of contempt in his voice. He stands up. "I'm going to see what kind of deal I can make with the prosecutor. And then I'm going to seriously advise that you take it."

"But I really don't think Jackie will testify. She'll change her mind."

"We can argue about that later." Marshall gathers up his papers and stands. "Do you want me to send your wife in?"

I'm not sure I do, but I nod anyway. While I'm waiting for her, I start biting at my forearm like some crazed animal.

How can this be happening to me?

Chapter Twenty-Nine

JACKIE | *DAVID*

When we get back to the house, Gran's car is there. She told us this morning that she was calling out of work, something she's *maybe* done twice in the years I've lived here.

"How did it go?" she asks as soon as we walk through the door. I shake my head and run past her to the bathroom. Seconds later, I'm slumped against the toilet, dry-heaving. The only reason I'm not puking is because I was too nauseated from tension to eat breakfast. At least I got my period a few days ago, so I don't have to freak out about *that* horrifying possibility.

What have I done?

I picture David being arrested. Handcuffs circling his thin wrists. Hearing that I destroyed him in the worst possible way. The way I swore I never would, no matter what.

He's never going to love me again. I'll always be the one who ruined everything.

I hear Lily's voice from the living room.

"Do you think it would be okay if I left, for a little bit? I'll come back. I just kind of… need to be alone for a while."

"Of course," Gran snaps. "I will take care of Jackie. I am her grandmother, after all, I think I can manage that much." I wince at her tone. Gran has a terrible ability to sting people with very few

195

words, but she rarely uses it. Especially against someone as nice as Lily.

"Oh, yeah. I know you can, Isabel." Lily sounds embarrassed. "I don't want her to think I'm abandoning her, that's all I meant."

"Do what you need to do." I hear the door open and close, and pluck a towel from the rack, crumpling it under my head so I can lay down on the floor.

A moment later, Gran calls me.

"Jackie? I've made tea." Gran loves tea and I've learned to at least tolerate it. "Will you come and talk to me?"

"Uh huh." I get up from the floor, feeling like my body weighs a thousand pounds.

When I emerge from the bathroom, I see Gran's tiny frame bent over the counter, which makes her look even shorter than usual.

"Gran?"

She turns toward me.

"Are you mad at me?"

She shakes her head. Before I can think about it, I race over and almost knock us both down trying to hug her like I'm five years old again. Her arms circle around me.

"I'm sorry," I say in a rush. "I'm so sorry I didn't want you there this morning. I'm sorry I asked Lily to go instead. I didn't mean to hurt your feelings."

"Oh, Jackie," she says. "I'm – well, it's true that I was a bit hurt, but I'm not upset with you." Gran pulls away, looks up at me and places both hands on my shoulders. "I'm glad Lily could be there. Whatever you need right now is what I want you to have. I just wish I could do something for you. I don't know how to help you through this the way she can."

"It's not that I don't want your help," I try to explain.

"I know, darling, I know. Come sit down, all right?" Gran leads me to the table. I feel a small measure of comfort in the familiarity of our tea ritual.

"Jackie, listen to me. The anger you see is partially directed at myself. I should have known. I should have done something."

"There's nothing you could have –"

She holds up a hand. "Perhaps that's true, but it's not really the point. I want to explain this."

"Okay."

"When you moved in with me, I promised myself that I would protect you. Granted, I couldn't change your situation. I couldn't convince my own son to stop acting like a child and put you first, not that I didn't try. But I could, at least, make sure that you were always safe here with me." Gran's voice ices over. "I've known David for a very long time. Of all people, for him to come into my house and take you into his world, hurt you this way…"

I clasp my mug. It's too hot and hurts my hand, but I've been shaking all morning so it feels kind of good.

I almost forgot the fact that she and David were friends.

"And then, for me not to have realized that this was going on… it makes me feel like I failed you, in the most basic way I could have." Gran puts a hand over mine. "I suppose that's why it's difficult for me to see Lily being the person you need."

"But you did see it, Gran." I don't pull my hand away. "When he was in my room that night. You saw something."

"I suspected. That's all. There was something about how comfortable he looked with you that troubled me. But I didn't push hard enough to find out if my suspicions had merit. I accepted your explanation far too easily."

"It was way too late by then, anyway," I reply quietly. "There's no way you could have known. You trusted me, and I lied to you." I lift my other hand from the mug. It's bright red from the heat. "I'm sorry. I know you thought we were past all that."

"Darling, I know you lied to me, and that's unfortunate. But I can understand why you didn't want David to get in trouble."

I lean back in my chair. "There's another reason I would have hidden it from you anyway."

"Which is?"

"He's married." I keep my eyes fastened to the table. "To one of your friends, even. I knew you'd be ashamed of me. I know you are."

"Jackie, look at me." Gran waits until I do. "I am *not* ashamed of you."

"How could you not be?"

"Because this isn't a situation between equals, dear. If you were older – say, Lily's age – and having an affair with a married man, you're right to think I would be disappointed. But that's not what this is. David took advantage of your youth, your trust, his position of authority over you, and the instability in your past. Not to mention his relationship with me." Gran motions to her laptop. "I've been reading about this all morning. Being a trusted family friend is a time-honored way for predators to slide past the front door."

"Why would you blame yourself then?"

"That's a good question," she says. "I suppose it's hard for conscientious people not to look for their own role in these situations. I've tried to teach you how important it is to take responsibility for your actions, and that's a good rule for life in general. But it doesn't apply to sexual assault."

"He didn't assault me, Gran." I stare into my tea, feeling the guilt take hold of me like it does every single time someone uses that word. "I know you think he did, but he didn't. He never hurt me."

Gran nods. "I'm glad of that. But whether he physically hurt you or not, David very much assaulted you. And he did damage. I can see it in your eyes."

"I don't get it. Doesn't assault mean hurting someone on purpose?"

"It might take you years to understand. It did for Lily. We

were talking about it the first night she came here, after you fell asleep." I nod as though I hadn't been eavesdropping on half of that conversation. "But maybe it won't take that long for you. After all, you have her to help you. She did us a great service, coming back. I would rather have you working through this now than carrying the shame around for years the way she did."

"I know. I – I'm glad Lily's here too."

Gran takes a sip of her tea. "Will you tell me how it went this morning? Please."

I run my hands back and forth over the grain in the wood of the table my grandpa built. "It was all right, I guess. Not as bad as it could have been. There was only one detective there, the same one from before. She was very… straightforward. I don't know. She didn't make me feel any worse than I already did."

"Good. What's going to happen now?"

"She said she was going to get an arrest warrant for David," I answer miserably.

Gran shakes her head, looking as stunned as I feel.

"She said that mostly in these cases people end up taking a plea. So maybe I won't have to go to court." I can't stand the idea of facing David down in a courtroom, telling the whole world everything we did. It would be like this morning, except a million times worse. "I don't want to go to court, Gran. I don't want to testify against him." I rest my forehead against my hands.

"I don't want that either."

My phone vibrates on the table and I glance at it to see a new text alert. "It's Lily." I place my thumb on the sensor and read the message.

Keller got the warrant. She's going to arrest him at lunch.

I hand my phone to Gran, whose hand immediately closes over her mouth.

Me? I crumple like I've been shot.

Chapter Thirty

JACKIE | **DAVID**

I thought Marshall was going to send Alicia right in but for whatever reason, it takes her almost another hour to turn up in my tiny cage. When she does, it's obvious that she's been crying, and she doesn't sit down so much as fling herself into the chair.

"You told me nothing happened," she says, and starts to cry again. They're not normal tears, more like her anger is leaching out through her eyes.

For a split second, I consider telling her the truth but then I discard that idea. The only thing I can do is double down. "Alicia, nothing did."

"Then why would Jackie say it did?"

"I'd like to know that myself! Maybe Lily got to her. I don't know."

"Speaking of Lily, she told the police your relationship was ongoing." She stares at me coldly. "Was it?"

"No, it wasn't." It's not like she can prove otherwise. "I made a mistake with her, and I owned that when you found out about it, but we did *not* have a relationship. I fooled around with her once, and only once."

"I can't keep your stories straight anymore." She glares at me. "All I know is you don't exactly have an unblemished track record when it comes to honesty."

"Alicia, you were still with Scott when we got together."

"Fuck you!" She shoves the table in rage, but when the guard appears at the door, she waves him away and makes a visible effort to lower her voice. "Are you seriously throwing that in my face right now?"

"No! I'm just saying, neither one of us have a perfect history of fidelity. Yes, I cheated on you with Lily, which I immediately regretted. I didn't tell you about it because I didn't want you to get hurt over something that meant nothing to me in the first place. But when you found out on your own, I didn't deny it. I wouldn't deny this either, if something had really happened. You know I would tell you the truth."

She sits back in her chair. "Explain to me why Jackie would lie about this."

I shake my head. "I can't. I don't get it either. Maybe she's more damaged than we ever imagined. Didn't Isabel tell you that she used to lie all the time?"

"Over stupid, small stuff. It's hard for me to believe she would tell *this* lie. I think you did it."

"Listen to me," I say, reaching across the table. She pulls her hand back before I can take it and glares at me.

"Don't touch me, David."

"I'm not saying I didn't screw up. I clearly let Jackie get way too close to me. But what she's saying now... what *is* she saying, exactly? My lawyer didn't tell me much."

"That you two have been having sex for months. After school, mostly. Which, conveniently, is when you tend to leave school and I don't. Now, how would she know that?"

"I probably mentioned to her at some point that you usually stay later than I do. Or maybe you did, even. I'm sure we've both told her a lot of things. She remembers everything." I sigh. "I just can't believe that Jackie would hurt me on purpose, especially if she thinks she loves me. Something else is going on here."

To my horror, I hear my voice break and for the first time I realize how emotional I am. I'm not just scared, or angry. I'm hurt.

Jackie was never supposed to have that much power over me.

Alicia covers her face with her hands. "What are we going to do, David?" Miserable as I am, I note the "we" and allow myself the tiniest sliver of optimism.

"I guess I have to stay here through the weekend. Marshall said I'd be arraigned on Monday morning and then I can probably get out on bail."

"We don't have any money for bail."

"He said we could put up our house," I say quietly.

She scowls. "I don't know about that."

"It's not like I'm going to skip town." She doesn't reply, and I wonder if she'd actually consider leaving me in here to punish me. "There's one other thing," I say hesitantly. "A few weeks ago, I transferred money out of our savings account. To cover Marshall's fees."

"How much?"

"Five thousand. That's how much of a retainer he wanted. At the time, I thought maybe I was going to be arrested. He told me to be ready. I was going to transfer the money back into our savings account but I never got around to it. Which is good, because he's going to want that retainer now."

"You already transferred it," she says slowly.

"Yes, back when I thought I might be arrested."

"So you knew this could happen."

"I thought I was going to be arrested if the police thought I was *kissing* her. It never occurred to me that she would tell them I had sex with her."

"What happens if you need more than five thousand?"

"I don't know. I hadn't gotten that far yet. Maybe I can take out a loan against my pension."

"Are you kidding? Kathryn already started the paperwork to terminate you. She's out for blood and the board will be too. I doubt I'll be able to keep my own job – thanks for that, by the way."

My career suddenly feels like the least of my worries. Marshall had a point about that. But I never wanted Alicia's to be collateral damage.

I run a hand through my hair. "Marshall wants me to take some kind of plea bargain. You know, a reduced sentence."

"You said you didn't do anything. How can you plead guilty to something you didn't do?"

"I have no plans to do that. I'm just telling you what he told me. He thinks that Jackie's accusation is all a jury would need to convict me."

"Bullshit," she says. "If you really didn't do anything, then don't say you did. If you *did,* then some kind of evidence will turn up."

"That's what I said." More or less.

"If that happens, David, we're done."

"It won't."

"Yeah, you said that already. But if you're lying to me, and the police find something that proves you've been sleeping with her, I'm going straight to a lawyer myself. You've been with a student before, you're caught kissing another one –"

"She kissed *me. "*

"… and now she's saying you two had sex. At what point do I become an idiot for continuing to take your word here?"

"What do you want me to do, take a lie detector test?" I ask, realizing even as I say it that's a terrible idea. "I don't know how I go about proving I *didn't* do something."

"I don't either." She stands up. "I'm going home."

"Will you come back and see me tomorrow?"

She shrugs. "I don't know."

I decide to try a little vulnerability. "Alicia… I'm really scared."

She doesn't take the bait. She turns to the door without glancing backward.

"You should be."

***

Here's a news flash: Jail mattresses are not the height of comfort. I spend the night shifting my weight from one side to the other, trying not to think about whatever else might have taken place on this mattress.

I try to organize my thoughts but it's hopeless. I still can't accept the fact that Jackie turned me in. I'm desperate to talk to her. There has to be some explanation.

But as much as I want to reject it, I already know what it is.

Lily never had Jackie's maturity or poise, and while I recognize now that was probably because of her neurotic and judgmental religion, at the time it drove me nuts. Getting involved with her was a definite low point in my youthful stupidity. She didn't bring out my best side, that's for sure.

Even so, she never acted like she hated *me*. Only herself. I wasn't sure how that worked in her mind but I also didn't really care, as long as she didn't consider me to blame for anything.

After she sent that note to Alicia, I realized that somewhere along the line she'd recast me in her head as the villain and herself as the innocent victim. That's the point at which I lost any remaining respect I had for her. At least before, she took responsibility for her choices.

And as with Jackie, I still maintain that they *were her choices.*

Even if no one else is ever going to believe that now.

Chapter Thirty-One

JACKIE | *DAVID*

By the time we get home from a meeting with Detective Keller, my shock has morphed into a full-blown lethargy so powerful it's all I can do to stumble to my room. I don't want to see or talk to anyone, even Lily. I want to hide my entire being under a hard shell like a broken bone inside a cast.

All I took from that meeting is that David's in custody for the weekend. I can't see anything right now except that jail cell and the man I love inside it.

Lily comes in to say goodbye. I've been dreading this moment, but I feel nothing now that it's here. I manage to sit up and hug her, but when I thank her for coming it sounds as automatic and meaningless as something I might say to Nicki after a sleepover.

"You were amazing, Jackie," Lily replies. "Text me or call me anytime you need to talk. And I'll be back soon, I promise."

"Okay. Have a good drive." I turn away from her and a moment later, she leaves my room.

The door is still open so I can hear Gran talking to her in the hallway.

"Lily, I'm sorry," she says. I feel a distant flash of anger, thinking for a moment that Gran is apologizing for me. But I realize pretty quickly that I'm mistaken. "I truly regret speaking to you so rudely yesterday. I was angry with David, not you."

"Don't worry about it, Isabel," Lily replies. "It's fine. I really do get it. It's been a hell of a week for both of you."

"And you."

"Yeah."

"Don't forget to look after yourself somewhere in there. And thank you again for coming down to be with her. With us."

"Of course." Her voice grows indistinct. I grind my fists against each other, wanting her to leave but not wanting to hear her go.

A few minutes later, I sense Gran walking back to my room but instead of trying to join me, she closes my door.

"Thank you," I whisper. To the extent that I can feel anything, I'm grateful that Gran understands how badly I need privacy right now.

***

The following Monday, I get up for school and dress in all black. Feels appropriate. Gran is sitting at the table, but gets up when she sees me and retrieves a basket of warm cinnamon buns from the kitchen. I can smell them from across the room.

"Thanks," I say, taking one from the basket. I hadn't been planning to eat breakfast but these are pretty much my favorite thing on earth. "Are you trying to make me feel better, or just make sure I eat?" Gran only makes cinnamon buns when she wants to reward me or cheer me up.

"Perhaps a bit of both," she says. "Have a seat, dear."

I point to the door. "I need to get going or I'll miss the bus."

"Sit. Please."

"What is it?" I ask, but I'm already sitting down. "I'll be okay. I don't even hear what people say about me anymore. It doesn't matter."

"Mrs. Connell called last night," Gran says. "We both feel strongly that under the circumstances, going to school is not a good idea for you right now."

"Why not?" I don't actually want to go to school, but I do want to talk to Nicki. She texted me on Friday – **WTF is going on???** – but I couldn't tell her over text. My best friend deserves to hear the truth from me face to face, especially after I lied to her.

"Things were already bad for you even before David was arrested. The graffiti and so forth."

I didn't even tell her about that note I got.

"Maybe they'll be better now that people know something happened," I suggest lamely.

Gran shakes her head. "I don't think so, love."

"So what am I supposed to do about school?"

"Mrs. Connell said she could have you enrolled in an online curriculum for the remainder of the year, so you won't fall behind."

"I have to do this the rest of the *year?*"

"Jackie, I know how popular David is with his students. Alicia, I have no doubt, will be pushing some version of events onto her staff that favors him. It's hard for me to imagine any scenario that doesn't have a lot of people blaming you for this, and it's not worth the risk that someone might retaliate against you more directly."

I sigh, unrolling part of the cinnamon roll I no longer feel like eating. She's not wrong, and the idea of not going is a relief in a lot of ways. Some stupid part of me thought that going to school would make things feel more normal, but I know I'm kidding myself. I'm a long, long way from normal life now, even further than I was before.

It's better this way.

"Okay."

Gran nods. "Mrs. Connell will have someone gather your things from your locker and I'll drive to the school this morning to pick them up. While I'm there, she can fill me in on what we do next."

"Right." I leave the cinnamon bun on my plate – I never even took a bite — and go to the bathroom to wash icing off my hands before I get back in bed to sleep half the morning away.

***

I texted Nicki before school to let her know I wouldn't be there, but that I wanted to talk to her. She shows up at my house after school, around the same time I usually do.

"Your bus sucks," she announces as she comes through the door. "I'm glad I don't have to do that every day." She deposits her backpack near the door and tosses her phone on top. "Forget that, though. What the hell happened? You didn't text me back all weekend. Everyone's losing their shit because Mr. Harrison got arrested on Friday for sleeping with you."

"Yeah. I might have heard something about that." I've moved from my bed to the couch, which is about all the progress I can see myself making today, and she sits on the opposite end from me.

"Is it true?"

I nod reluctantly. "It's true." Nicki's face flashes with an emotion I don't see from her very often. She's hurt. "I'm sorry I didn't tell you sooner."

"So he was the guy."

"Yeah."

"You've been sleeping with our *teacher* all this time and you never told me?"

"I didn't tell *anyone*. The only reason I made up that story on my birthday is because I'd just broken things off and I really wanted to talk about him. And because I was drunk," I add as an afterthought.

She sits back on the couch. I can hear her phone blowing up with one Snapchat notification after another, which she ignores. They're probably all asking her about me.

"I wondered," she says finally. "After the whole kissing thing. It didn't make any sense that you would have done that out of nowhere. And I couldn't understand why you'd be hooking up with a guy who had a girlfriend. That totally didn't seem like you. Everything makes a lot more sense now. You've always had a thing for him."

"Not always. Mostly just this year."

"Jackie. I saw the way you looked at him in class last year. Your whole face would change when he said your name. I know how much he meant to you." She snickers suddenly, which seems out of context.

"What's so funny?"

"Sorry. It's not funny. It's just, you mentioned your birthday and it made me realize that I know *way* too much about him now," she says. "Total TMI."

"You're the one who asked." I'm way too depressed to find any part of this funny right now. "What are they saying about me at school?"

Nicki rolls her eyes. "I don't know. Nothing that matters. People suck."

"You can tell me. I know you hear everything. Do they think I'm making it all up?"

"Not really. Mostly they're saying the same shit as before." So I'm still a slut. Perfect. "When are you coming back to school?"

"I'm not. At least not anytime soon. Gran's afraid the other kids are going to take it out on me."

"I can see that," she says quietly. "I mean, you did get the guy arrested. What's going to happen to him?"

"I don't know."

"Will he go to jail?"

"He might."

"Wow. I can't even wrap my mind around this. The oldest guy I've been with was like, twenty."

"Which was illegal," I point out.

"Technically, maybe. But it's not like I would have turned him in." For the first time, Nicki looks a little judgy. "Why did you do that, anyway? I thought you loved him."

"I do."

"But you told the cops…"

"It's complicated." I can't even begin to explain Lily to Nicki. I'm starting to realize that most people aren't interested in understanding the nuance of our situation. They want it to be someone's fault, either his or mine, and there's no middle ground once they pick a side.

Nicki doesn't reply.

"He didn't ever… try anything with you, did he?" I hold my breath waiting for her answer. I can't imagine David touching Nicki, and I feel like this conversation would be going really differently if he had, but how can I be sure now?

She looks taken aback. "No, of course not. Why?"

"Just had to ask."

"You think he was doing other girls at school too?"

"I don't know what I think anymore. Listen. All that stuff I told you about him…"

"Yeah?"

"Can you do me a favor and swear you won't tell anyone else? Ever?"

"I don't tell things like that. You know me." Nicki knows a lot of my secrets. In fact, she's the only person in the world who knows most of the things I told either David or Gran, but not both. And as far as I know, she's never repeated them to anyone. "Anyway, I'd forget them myself if I could." She raises her eyebrows slightly, shakes her head. "For an old guy…"

"Stop. Seriously. I don't want to think about any of that right now."

"Okay. Sorry." She goes across the room to retrieve her phone and starts texting someone. "I should probably get going. I have a ton of homework."

"No problem," I said. Her brother comes over to pick her up about twenty minutes later, and we don't say much in the meantime. I feel kind of hollow as I watch her go.

Something tells me nothing is going to be the same between us after this.

Chapter Thirty-Two

The arraignment, though quick, is far from painless. They read the charges, I plead not guilty, and I'm given a fifty-thousand dollar bail. Using our home equity for that involves a lien on our house, which enrages Alicia to the point where I'm not sure she'll do it. My brother and I haven't spoken in years, and I'm trying to decide if there's any point in begging him for help when Marshall comes to see me and tells me that it's in the works.

"She finally agreed. There's a lot of paperwork. I'll try to help her push it through today but it might be tomorrow."

"Okay." Surprisingly, jail isn't as bad as I thought it would be. It's very quiet. The worst problem is too much time to think.

"All right, let's talk about your situation. You're being charged with three separate crimes," Marshall explains. "Two felonies and one misdemeanor. The felonies are rape in the third degree and second degree sexual abuse. The misdemeanor is third degree sexual abuse." He explains what those charges mean. No surprise, they all reference some kind of sexual act between Jackie and me.

"So what's going to happen?"

"I'm having a drink with the prosecutor later this evening. His name is Rick Sable. That's where I'm going to try and work out a plea bargain for you."

"Would I have to say I'm guilty of something?"

"That's where the 'plea' part of the bargain comes in, yes."

"I'm not pleading guilty to rape, Marshall. I want to fight this."

"David, listen. Assuming a conviction, the felony counts are worth five years apiece and the misdemeanor is one. I'd certainly try to get the sentences run concurrently, which means you'd serve five years, but in the end it's up to the judge. This particular judge goes for contrition, which I can't say I've seen from you yet. If he doesn't like your attitude, it's within his discretion to have the sentences run consecutively. That's eleven years."

Well over half of Jackie's life. Almost a third of mine.

"If you did make a deal with the prosecutor, what would I get instead?"

"I'm going to try to get you between twelve and eighteen months."

A year and a half of sitting in that same cell. I know I said it hasn't been that bad but I'm acutely aware that it's only been two days.

I try to imagine sitting there doing nothing for five hundred and forty six, and having nothing to look forward to on the other side. My career and my marriage would be distant memories.

"No."

"Eighteen months isn't bad at all. You'd probably even be allowed to serve your sentence in here, given the space demands of the prison at the moment. That would be an excellent result."

"Yeah, maybe for you." I want to walk around, but this room is so small. "I'm not accepting any deal that involves me having a record."

"Would you rather have one *after* being locked up for five years?"

"If I can't teach anymore, you might as well lock me up!"

"That's something people say when they've never done time before," Marshall says. "I know a lot of men who have been incarcerated. Eighteen months in county jail is so much better than years, plural, in state prison. If you never listen to anything else I say, hear that."

"I want to go to trial," I repeat. I don't care if it's irrational.

"David. We have *no* defense here. The girl's testimony aside, you don't know what else they're going to find in the way of physical evidence. And given that you did do it, I can't let you get on the stand and say otherwise."

"I get it. The odds are bad."

"More like nonexistent. This is basically a done deal."

"But what if Jackie doesn't testify?"

"Why wouldn't she?"

"She won't go through with it in the end. You watch."

"What does that mean? Are you going to do something to stop her if you get out of here on bail?"

"What? No!" I'm legitimately stunned at his implication. "God, no. I'd never hurt Jackie. I didn't mean it like that at all."

Marshall regards me carefully. "So what makes you think she won't testify?"

"I know her. I know her better than anyone. Maybe Lily talked her into going to the cops but there is no chance she's going to get up in a courtroom and say I raped her. None."

"Did she know about Lily before all this?"

"Of course she didn't."

"So Jackie just found out that you were involved with another student. She's met that student and whatever they talked about was so compelling to her that she decided to go to the police. But in your mind, there's just no chance whatsoever that she's now convinced you belong in jail?"

Well. When he puts it that way.

"Look. Take the night and think it over. If we're going to trial, I have a lot of prep work to do. And in the meantime, I'm going to meet with the prosecutor and try to talk him into this deal. Then

I'm going to recommend again that you take it."

"I won't."

"It's up to you in the end, obviously. But I've cracked tougher nuts than you before."

He gets his things and leaves, and I'm escorted back to my cell where I end up waiting not one but two more days.

***

When I get home, the house is quiet. Not a big shock there, since Alicia didn't even pick me up from jail. I had to take an Uber home. She left me a note that she and Maggie were staying with a friend. I don't even know which friend.

I don't blame her, but I wish she hadn't taken Maggie. I was looking forward to at least one friendly face.

I go for a long run, cherishing the freedom to go wherever I want. When I get back to the house, I log into my computer and search for Lily's name on Facebook.

I never go on Facebook, but it has its useful moments. Her face pops up right away, and I click on it. I'm not sure what I'm looking for, exactly. Maybe something in the way of a clue.

Her profile is restricted so I can't see much, but I do figure out that she's still living in Portland and dating some guy. His is more open and contains several pictures of him and Lily together. She looks happy and settled in a way that she never was when I knew her. Also quite a bit prettier. Of course, it has been eight years.

I shut my laptop and go into the kitchen to make some coffee, wondering for the millionth time what Lily might have told Jackie. Or vice versa.

Jackie never seemed overly interested in my past, or maybe she didn't want to know. One more way she wasn't like Lily, who asked me all kinds of questions about every aspect of my life. I've never liked being interrogated about personal things and it was off-putting most of the time, but a part of me was flattered by her desire to crawl into my head and figure me out. I would carefully dole out little pieces of information here and there, never anything too important.

I ended up sharing a lot more with Jackie because she never pushed me like that. Which makes me realize that if they're talking now, Jackie can tell Lily almost anything she wanted to know back then. Fantastic.

I text Alicia to let her know I'm home. Predictably, she doesn't respond.

Chapter Thirty-Three

JACKIE | *DAVID*

Gran made a few rules about homeschooling. She insists I do all of my schoolwork first thing in the morning and stay out of bed when it's not normal sleeping hours. I think she's trying to hold off my depression, but there's only so much either one of us can do about that.

Now that I've caught up on the work from all the days I blew off, school only takes me a few hours. At one point, it would have been nice to have so much free time but my favorite hobbies, cooking and reading, are inextricably tied to David. I haven't felt much like doing either one.

Lily's been checking in frequently, but I don't want to bother her by texting too often. It was easier when she was here in person.

At first, Gran tried to take me on our normal errands to get me out of the house but the second time we tried that, it became clear that my new reputation had spread all over town. We were standing in line when a heavyset junior from another school came over with a few of his friends. I recognized him from one of Nicki's parties.

"What's up, Jackie?" he asked me, not quietly at all. "Did your grandma hear about you sucking off Mr. H. in the science lab?"

I closed my eyes, wanting to sink through the floor. I couldn't speak, even to deny it, but Gran turned to him and said in a perfect flat tone, "Young man, you are incredibly crude." She looked him up and down, raising an eyebrow. "What a pity you don't run your body as well as you run your mouth."

The boy turned red. Several people in line snickered, including one of his friends, but I was too busy feeling degraded to appreciate Gran's grace under pressure.

"Thanks for handling that," I muttered to her as we escaped to the parking lot.

"Darling, I've dealt with worse than teenage boys in my time."

Gran doesn't seem to blame me for any of this, even though she should. She's made a lot of friends in the thirty years she's lived here, but lately she's been going out a lot less than usual and I wonder if it's because they're pulling away.

Anyway, that trip to the store was the last time Gran asked me to go with her. So now it just feels like I'm in prison. Or at least quarantine.

***

It's midmorning on a Saturday and I'm still in bed since Gran hasn't made me get up yet. Eventually, though, I hear a tap on my door.

"Yeah, Gran?"

She comes in, dressed in her work clothes. "Good morning, dear. I'm heading to the restaurant early. Someone called in sick."

"Okay."

"And you have a visitor."

I look up from my phone. "Who?"

Gran opens the door a little wider and Lily peeks in.

"Hey!" I grin at her, and she comes over to give me a hug. "I didn't know you were coming!" I'm so relieved to see her, I don't even care that I'm in my pajamas.

"It's just for today. I have to leave by four, but I wanted to come see you." Gran smiles at us from the doorway.

"You two have a good time, okay?"

"Thanks, Isabel." Lily sits cross legged on my comforter, her hair tumbling all over her shoulders. "How are you doing?"

I shrug. "Not that great. How come you have to leave so soon?"

"Oh, my boyfriend and I are having dinner at his parents' house tonight."

"You have a boyfriend?" I ask in shock. Lily laughs.

"Yeah. His name is Ben."

"I didn't know that."

"Well, you and I haven't known each other that long. It didn't come up."

"Is he in grad school too?"

"No, he's a web designer. He works for a startup."

"Does he know about…?"

Lily nods. "Not the details, but I told him why I was coming down here before. And I told him about David and me way before that. So yes, he knows the broad strokes."

"Oh." Suddenly I feel like Lily's visiting me in the hospital, which makes me uncomfortable. I get up and go to my closet. "Let me put on some real clothes, okay?"

"Of course." She gets up. "When you're done, I have something to show you."

I come out a few minutes later to find Lily sitting on the couch with her laptop open and a cup of tea in front of her. She drinks tea as religiously as Gran does.

"What's up?" I ask, sitting next to her.

"Remember I was telling you about that message board I lurk on?"

"Yeah."

"So here's the thing." Lily shifts toward me. "The last couple weeks have sucked. Which you totally didn't know already."

I laugh. Only a little but it still feels good.

"So I thought I might post here, and ask for some advice on getting through this. Mainly for you. But I wanted to give you a chance to read what I was going to post first. And if you're not okay with it, then I won't do it at all. I just think it could help. This is a private board, you have to be invited to join it by a current member. So we don't get trolls or anything. The people who post here are really supportive."

"That sounds good," I say. "I'm sure it's fine, what you wrote."

"Yeah?" She looks surprised. Actually, I am too.

"Thanks for checking with me, but I trust you. I'll read the responses later." I start running a brush through my hair. "You know, I feel kind of bad. Sometimes I forget that this is really tough for you too."

"I've had better months," she agrees. "That being said, I don't want you to feel like it's your job to take care of me. You're the one who needs taking care of here. At least in Portland I can escape from it sometimes. You can't even go to school right now." I nod. "My goal hasn't changed. I want to be there for you however I can."

"I know, and you have been. But it would be nice to help you, after everything you've done for me."

"Knowing I can make a difference for you while you're going through this is huge for me. It *is* helping me. I feel like we're in this together, and that's something I didn't have when I was in high school. Someone who understood."

Hearing that makes me feel better. "Go ahead and post it."

Lily opens her browser and taps a few keys. "Okay. Done."

"So what now?" I ask, wondering how we're going to fill the next few hours.

"Well. Since you ask. And as long as we're on the subject of helping *me* out…" Lily pulls her phone off the table and consults it. "I don't suppose you've ever made something called caramel apple blondie pie?"

I laugh again. "What the hell is that?"

"I don't even know! It's apparently this dessert that Ben's mom loves, and I stupidly offered to bring one with me. Only I can't find it anywhere, and I don't really cook. But then I thought, hey, I'm coming down here anyway and *you* can cook…"

I take Lily's phone from her and scan the recipe. "I can make this."

"Seriously?"

"Yeah," I say, still giggling. "But I don't think we have any of the ingredients."

"They're in the car. The shopping I can do."

I stand up. This is the first time in weeks I've found anything humorous, and I love her for it. "Come on. We have an apple corer somewhere."

***

"So does Ben know you can't cook?" I ask as I sort through spice jars.

"What are you talking about?" Lily holds up the paring knife. "I'm totally peeling apples for you right now, in case you hadn't noticed."

Lily's pretty funny. I haven't really noticed that before.

"My mistake."

"Damn right." She grins at me.

"Is this the first time you've met his parents?"

"Yes. That's why it's so important I make a good impression."

"Isn't it *me* making the good impression?" Lily laughs and throws a towel at me. "I wish you lived closer, Lily."

"Me too."

"If you did, you could come over more often. I could pretend you were my sister. We even look a little bit alike."

"Yeah, we do."

"David must have a type. Except we don't look anything like Alicia." I pull the silverware drawer open and pause. "Sorry. I shouldn't keep bringing him up."

"Jackie, it's fine. We can talk about him as much as you want."

I turn on the burner.

"Do you think he's okay?"

"Probably better than you, all things considered."

"I keep thinking about how long he'll be in jail, if he gets convicted."

"Me too. But he brought this on himself."

We work in silence for a few minutes.

"What's Ben like?" I ask finally, to change the subject.

"Oh, he's great. He's kind of this crazy athlete, he's always doing some marathon or another. Which is annoying because it makes me feel lazy. But I've made peace with it, more or less." Lily wipes her hands and pulls up a photo on her phone. "This is him."

I study the photo. Ben is black and his dark, friendly eyes are highlighted by the fact that he's completely bald.

He couldn't look less like David.

"He's really cute," I say. "And he looks nice."

"Yeah, he is. It's going good."

"Have you dated a lot?" I wonder if I'm getting too personal, but Lily answers easily.

"Not tons," she says. "I had one other serious relationship, in college. Besides that, there was no one special. I definitely wasn't ready right away."

"I'm not either," I confess.

"I'd be surprised if you were."

"Was it hard to be with someone else? After him?"

Lily considers the question. "It was and it wasn't. It had been a long time – I was eighteen – but I hadn't dealt with it yet. It was a few more years before I understood what happened. That was actually when it got really tough."

I try to imagine feeling the way I do right now for five more years, and my heart breaks for Lily.

"I was pretty screwed up for a while," she continues. "I grew up super religious, and I was raised to believe that sleeping with *anyone* outside marriage is wrong. So committing adultery on top of that was a really bad way to start out for me. I was afraid that sex would make me feel guilty forever, no matter who I was with."

I measure out sugar, listening intently. That sounds awful. I wonder if it'll be the same way for me, even though I'm not religious. "Did it?"

"I won't lie to you, Jackie. It did at first. But it got better, and until all of this started getting stirred up again it hadn't been an issue for me in a long time. It's different with other people. You'll start to forget eventually, but it takes the right person. Someone who can be patient." She pats my arm. "I wouldn't want you to start sleeping with random people, trying to escape what you feel for David. In the long run, that's probably going to make you pretty miserable."

I shrug. "It's not like anyone's going to want me anyway. I'm a skank, remember?" I'd told her what happened at the grocery store.

Lily shakes her head vigorously. "You are *not* a skank. And any guy who makes you feel like you are is definitely not the right guy to work though this with."

"I guess." I start spooning apple mixture into the crust.

"That smells amazing, by the way."

"It has to rest for twenty minutes." I pre-heat the oven. "Think your post got any replies yet?"

"Want me to check?"

"Sure." Lily goes into the living room. A moment later, I hear her gasp.

"Oh my God. Jackie, you have to see this. There's over forty responses already."

"What?" I run over and sit next to Lily. She tilts the screen toward me, and I read her post first.

Content note: statutory rape trial

When I was in high school, I had a sexual relationship with one of my married teachers. When my parents found out, we moved out of town and never discussed it again. Until fairly recently, I still believed it was my fault since it was "consensual."

Then about a month ago, I found out he was doing it to another student of his. J is sixteen, the same age I was, and like me she's struggling with guilt. We both believed he loved us.

I've gotten to know J in the past few weeks, because I went to talk to her. And somehow this amazing girl found the courage to tell the police what happened. He has been arrested, but he's currently out on bail. She might have to testify against him.

Obviously this has been devastating for J (and me). I was hoping this forum could help us come up with some coping strategies for the next few months. As rough as it's been so far, I have a feeling it's going to get even worse during the trial.

I'm kind of impressed by Lily's ability to summarize the situation so neatly. The term statutory rape still doesn't sit well with me, but I don't challenge it. We skim the responses together, and then read them more carefully. Most of them contain fairly generic words of encouragement, but some are longer and surprisingly insightful.

Lily, it's amazing that you were able to reach out and connect with J. I'm sure it helped her find the strength to come forward. It's funny, we often recommend writing a letter to your younger self while you're processing this kind of thing – and here you have been given the opportunity to actually talk to a version of your younger self, in a way. It gives me chills. Blessings to you for being there, and to her for doing something that I'm sure felt impossible…

J, sweetie, you and Lily will both get lots of advice on how to get through this but in the here and now I want you to know that you did a PHENOMENAL thing. I am in awe of your courage. By having the wherewithal to come forward, you have regained control of your own narrative and you are part of a movement on which an entire nation is turning. Because of you, fewer girls will be abused in the future. I see you, I honor you, and most of all, I BELIEVE you…

Ah, the United States of Sexual Assault Never Happens Here! Lily, my heart goes out to you. I often feel that the type of secondary trauma you described, being taken out of the situation as though YOU were the poison, is in some ways worse than the abuse itself. I love that you and J can be there for each other now. He might be going on trial for what he did to her, but at long last he's also being held accountable for what he did to you. Expect the next few months to be triggering for you as well as J – don't neglect your own self-care…

Is J's family supportive of her? Is yours? It will be key for you both to have your own support systems over the next few months. Don't rely completely on each other – as tempting as that might be, it's critical not to shut out the rest of your people right now...

I've been a teacher for twenty years and I am BEYOND furious at this man for putting you two, and who knows how many others, through this. I have to believe that justice is coming for him in some form or another. I hope that you and J can be at the forefront of it...

"This is incredible," I say quietly.

"See? These are good people."

"They don't blame us at *all.*" After so much judgment from other people, this is hard for me to process.

"Of course they don't. They get it."

The oven buzzes and I rise slowly, still hypnotized by the words of strangers on the Internet. As I place the pie in the oven, Lily comes up behind me.

"I can't believe so many people responded to you."

"They're responding to *us.*"

"Thank you, Lily." I hug her hard.

"I didn't do anything."

"Yes you did. All those people said so, and they were right. I could never do this without you."

"You know, even though I'm not religious anymore, I still believe that people come into our lives at certain times for a reason," Lily says. "I never thought I would see David on trial. I promise you, I need you with me to get through it, just like you need me."

In one way, I know nothing has changed. Anonymous words of support don't make it safe for me to go back to school or easier to stop loving David. The people who wrote those nice things can't save me from the hell of testifying against him, which I still can't bring myself to imagine.

It's hard to picture myself at Lily's age with a regular boyfriend and a normal life, all of this solidly in my past instead of my present.

But something feels different. Reading those words from people who are on my side makes me feel a tiny bit less broken.

I'm not alone in this anymore. I haven't been since I met Lily.

***

She texts me later to tell me that the pie was delicious.

part two

summer

Chapter One

JACKIE | *DAVID*

It's almost eleven o'clock in the morning and I'm sitting by the window waiting for Lily to arrive. She should be here soon.

David's trial starts tomorrow.

Attempting a distraction, I try to decide if she'll be bringing Ben and Archie, their brown and white cocker spaniel. He's the sweetest dog in the entire world and I'm completely in love with him.

Ben's okay too.

But when Lily turns up an hour later, she only has Archie with her.

"Ben's downtown," she explains. "He's going to stay with one of our friends for the next few days." Ben and Lily have visited together several times, and they usually share the sofa bed while Archie sleeps in my room. Which suits me perfectly.

"Why?" I'm on the floor with Archie, laughing as he tickles my face with his tongue.

"Archie, buddy, have some dignity." Lily shakes her head as Archie whines in ecstasy. "He's happier to see you than me these days." But she's smiling.

"Not true," I reply.

"To answer your question, Ben didn't want to get in the way.

He thought the three of us could use some privacy."

"That's a good man you have, Lily," Gran remarks.

"Yeah. He offered to take us out to dinner tonight, though."

"What do you think, Jackie?"

"I don't know," I say, sitting up. The idea of leaving the house is still not really working for me.

"I told Ben that you might rather have him bring some takeout over." I shoot Lily a grateful look. I feel like a coward, but I can't handle the extra stress of being in public tonight.

Even if I won't be here much longer.

***

The day we got word from the district attorney that David's case was going to trial, Lily asked Gran to go for a walk with her. When they came back, they sat me down on the couch.

"Jackie, Lily has a suggestion she wanted to run by us. And I'm…" Gran clasped her hands together. "I have to admit that it would solve a problem to which I've been unable to come up with a solution on my own so far."

"What is it?" I asked. I hadn't really cared, to be honest. I was still trying to absorb the news that I would see David next in a courtroom.

"One of our roommates is moving out next month," Lily said. "Ben and I wondered if you might want to come up to Portland and stay with us for a while, after the trial is over. Like for the rest of the summer. Or longer, if it's working out."

"You want me to come and *live* with you?" That pulled me out of my head in a big way. I wasn't sure what I felt. Flattered, intrigued, uneasy? All of the above?

"The thing is," Gran said, "we can't keep going on like this. You know that, right?"

I nodded slowly.

"You've barely left the house for months because every time

you do, you get harassed. If David gets convicted, it could very well get worse for you even if you change schools. And that's a long time from now anyway, with nothing in between for you to do and nowhere you can go. It's not a healthy way to live."

"Oh, yeah. I know," I said. I would never have believed that my life could be so psychologically punishing and so unbelievably boring at the same time. I'm safe here at home but there is literally nothing to do now that school's out. I've even started helping Gran with her gardening, that's how desperate I am. For that reason alone, going to Portland sounded great, and I'd been wondering what would happen when the trial was over too. "But, live with you… Ben's okay with that?"

"Completely on board," Lily said. I knew she wouldn't say so if it wasn't true, and it didn't really surprise me after I thought about it for a minute.

Lily has good taste. Ben is as nice as he looked in the picture, and he's also super generous and funny. He knows a lot of things about me, so I expected to feel weird when I met him, but it was never a problem. I like him, even feel comfortable with him. Mostly.

"We live in a pretty big house," Lily went on. "It belongs to his parents but they let Ben live there and handle the mortgage however he likes. And he likes having people around, so we usually have a few roommates. When one of them gave us his notice last week, I came up with the idea to try this and Ben thought it was great. He adores you, Jackie."

"What are your other roommates like?" Ben and Lily were one thing, but I wasn't so sure about strangers.

"We have two more at the moment. One is a coworker of Ben's and the other is my old college roommate." She sensed my dilemma. "We've known both of them for years. I'm a hundred percent sure they are safe people for you."

"I don't know. I mean, it sounds okay, but…" I looked at Gran.

"What about you?"

"Jackie, I've thought about moving us somewhere else, but –"

"Gran, no. You can't do that for me. You've lived here forever and you have your friends and your job and this house…"

"I appreciate your understanding of why that would be less than ideal," she said with a small smile. "And you're right, this is where I always planned to stay. Now, you're more important to me than all of that, and I would and will do anything to keep you safe. But if there's perhaps a less drastic measure that would be equally good for you, I feel like I need to be open to that as well."

"But you'd be alone. I don't want to leave you alone." We don't have much in the way of family, me and Gran. I stopped counting my dad a long time ago.

"Darling, there's no question that I'd miss you terribly. But I also never expected you to live with me forever. After all, I didn't know when you moved in here if you might go back to your father–" I shook my head hard. "Well, but we didn't know that then. Anyway, I'll be fine living here by myself, just as I was before you came to stay." Gran pressed her lips together slightly, the only visible sign of emotion. "Of course, I'd expect you to drive down here for frequent visits, now that you have your license." That was about the only thing I managed to accomplish all summer.

"I don't know."

"Well, we don't need to decide anything right now," Lily said. "I know this would be a big change for both of you. The nice thing about it being summer is that we wouldn't need to worry about school. If you come up for a few weeks and it's not working out, no big deal. You can come back here and we'll think of something else."

"It *would* be nice to start over somewhere no one knows me," I said. Then something occurred to me. "Huh. This is strange, right? I'd be moving away to Portland because of David, just like Lily did."

"The irony isn't lost on us," Gran said dryly.

"But Jackie, you have to remember that I never had to deal with anything like this," Lily added. "No one knew what had gone on between us. The main issue in my case was that my parents didn't think I would stay away from David if we still lived here. Whereas he's totally wrecked things for you." Lily paused. "And there's another big difference too. This is *your* choice."

"It's really nice of you guys to offer, Lily," I said, pulling at a loose thread on the couch. "I know I would be a big responsibility for you."

"In some ways, but mostly not so much. It's not like you're a little kid. I already know you're responsible about school and you're not going to run off and start doing meth your first week there. I mean, if you do, trust me – I have no problem bringing you right back to Isabel."

Gran and I both laughed.

"Seriously, we'd be glad to have you, Jackie. Especially me and Ben. And don't forget Archie."

"Oh yeah, Archie." A grin spread over my face. "Okay, you've convinced me."

"I should have opened with that," Lily said.

I went and sat next to Gran. "Are you sure this is okay, Gran?"

Gran put her arm around my shoulders. "Is it the way I would have wanted things to work out? No. Do I occasionally fantasize about throwing David off a building? Possibly." I smiled. "But, do I think this could be the right thing for you? I think we're all in agreement that we have nothing to lose by trying. Sometimes unconventional problems call for creative solutions."

I turned toward Lily. "What about rent?"

Lily shrugged. "You're getting the smallest bedroom. We only charge three hundred for it anyway. Most of Ben's rental income is from the other two rooms."

"I offered to cover the rent," Gran added. "But Lily felt it would be more prudent to send that money directly to you so that you could cover your own expenses while you're there. School, gas, food, that kind of thing."

I felt funny when she said that. Like I was suddenly going to be a grownup.

I went back with Lily that time to see how I liked it, and by the time I got home it didn't feel like much of a decision anymore. My new room was definitely small, but that didn't bother me. I loved the idea of having Lily right down the hall. Her roommates seemed okay, and I was fascinated by the energy of a house filled with people in their twenties. I liked Portland, too. It was fun to be in a bigger, faster city. Best of all, no one gave me a second look when I left the house.

Lily took me everywhere. She showed me her university, the huge bookstore where she works, her favorite place to go for tea. We even visited Ben's office. It was really cool to see her world and feel like maybe there was a place in it for me full-time.

"I like it there, Gran," I said when I got back, almost timidly. "I think it could work." There was a part of me that had been hoping it wouldn't, and I figured Gran probably felt the same way, but outwardly she only expressed support for my decision.

Starting fresh feels more and more like something I'm going to need to do after all this is over, but it's hard for me to accept that I won't live with Gran anymore. I've been packing my things slowly, sending a box or two up with Lily every time she leaves. It feels a little less sudden that way.

"It's not fair," I said one night when I was taping up a box of books and Gran came in to help. "This is the first place that really felt like home to me."

"It's still your home, darling. It always will be." But I could hear the needles of pain in her voice, and I remembered her saying how hard it was to see Lily give me what I needed when she couldn't.

I didn't like it much either.

***

Ben brings over Thai food later that afternoon, and for a change I'm actually hungry. It's a nice feeling, sitting around Gran's table with all three of them.

"Are you all going to be testifying?" Ben asks at one point when Lily mentions the trial.

"Lily's on the list," Gran explains. "But it's unlikely that she'll be called."

"Why?" Ben asks, then glances at me. "Sorry, Jackie. I wasn't thinking. You probably don't want to talk about this right now."

"It's okay," I reply. "It's not like I can think about anything else."

Lily answers his question. "I can only be called as a rebuttal witness if David testifies, which he won't. His entire defense is going to be that there's not enough evidence to know for sure one way or the other. Tie goes to the runner." Lily scowls. I take a small bite of my spring roll, but my appetite is doing its disappearing act again.

"Why is he doing this?" asks Ben impatiently. "I don't get why the guy doesn't take a plea."

"We're guessing he thinks I'll chicken out," I say. "If I don't testify, there's no case. Since Lily can't back me up."

"In other words, David's an arrogant son of a bitch," Lily adds. "Sorry, Isabel."

"I don't care about your language choice, Lily. Call him what he is."

I get up to grab a soda.

"You seem so calm, Jackie," Ben remarks. "You taking 'ludes or something?"

I laugh and glance at Gran and Lily, who both smile. "He thinks I'm calm?" I look back at Ben. "I have full-blown panic attacks about this multiple times a day. You're catching me in between two of them, that's all."

"Don't listen to her," Lily says. "She's been amazing." That won't last when I'm on the stand describing my first time to a roomful of random people, but whatever.

"Are Lily and Isabel going to be allowed in the courtroom for your testimony?" Ben asks.

"I think so." They better be.

"Because if the judge won't let them be there, I'll go in with you," he offers. "I'll even bring some gum for the back of David's chair."

This time, I can't quite laugh.

"Thanks, Ben," I reply, not looking at him. "I appreciate that." And I do, but I'm not sure I want him there. It's hard for me to imagine him still liking me after hearing the details of my testimony.

"You'll do fine," he adds in a rare note of sincerity. "You're ready for this."

Sometimes I still feel uneasy with Ben, especially when he's being nice. It's not his fault. I know he won't ever try anything with me – or at least I mostly know it. He's crazy about Lily and he's a really good guy.

But that's what I thought about David.

The familiar dynamic bothers me a little, and I'm nervous about moving into his house, but it helps that he's not trying to get any closer to me. I've never even been alone with him.

"Well," Gran says after an awkward pause. "I'm ready to switch to a new subject, if no one objects." I nod gratefully. As the conversation takes on a less serious direction, Lily reaches down and squeezes my hand. We don't need to talk about this. She gets it.

***

Ben leaves shortly after dinner is over, like he said he would. Lily walks him to the car, and she's out there a while. The idea of him comforting her makes me feel kind of lonely. I'm relieved when she returns.

"You okay?" Lily asks me, sitting down.

"It's kind of hitting me all at once, I think. That it starts tomorrow."

"Me too."

She goes to take a shower and comes out to find me exactly where she left me, stroking a sleeping Archie on the sofa bed while I stare into space.

"How about we share him tonight?" she suggests, pushing back the blanket.

"Yeah. That'd be good."

I manage to fall asleep, but several hours before dawn I bolt awake like someone fired a gun next to my ear. I'm not all that surprised to find Gran and Lily seated at the kitchen table, their faces dimly visible by the light above the oven. Both are drinking tea in silence.

"I'm sorry, love. Did we wake you?" Gran asks when I walk over.

"Nope," I say, sitting across from Lily as though the three of us are about to play cards.

"Would you like some tea?"

"Sure." Gran gets up to heat more water, and I run my finger over the faded scar on my palm from dinner all those months ago.

None of us speak again until morning.

In fact, after the whistle of the teakettle stops, there's no noise in the room at all apart from Archie's little sleepy sounds and the occasional clink of our mugs on the table.

Chapter Two

JACKIE | **DAVID**

Alicia only recently agreed to help me during my trial. Prior to that, I hadn't seen much of her since I got home from jail. Officially we're still living together, but I have no idea where she is most of the time.

When Marshall finally persuaded her to sit down with us a week ago, he explained how a show of support from her could improve my chances with the jury.

"I'm not going to pretend I can understand how hard this must be for you, Alicia," he said.

"Very wise," she replied. Kathryn forced her to resign soon after I was arrested. I still feel guilty about that.

"But here's the thing. David needs your help if he's going to avoid a prison sentence. I've been working on his defense for months, and I think we have a shot because the state's case is fairly weak, but it's a huge risk. He knows this. I still think his best option is a plea bargain, but David has made it clear that he wants to run the risk of a trial, and that is his right."

Alicia looked at me for the first time. "Maybe you should listen to him, David."

"I'm not going to say I raped Jackie," I repeated for the hundredth time. "Because I didn't." I stared at Marshall, wondering if the man ever gets tired of arguing with stubborn clients.

It's not like he doesn't have a point. The way the law is written, I'm guilty of the crimes and of course, I knew that our relationship was technically illegal. But that's all it is, a technicality. If I were nineteen to her sixteen, we probably wouldn't be here right now.

More importantly, I'll go to my grave knowing that everything we did was consensual.

Marshall continued. "If I'm going to prevail here, everything has to be going our way. Legally, it makes no difference whether or not you believe your husband. But juries are human. If they think you do, it carries some weight. That's all I can tell you. It might be enough to tip the scales in his favor."

Alicia sat back in her chair, considering my plight and her power over it. Visibly deriving some satisfaction from the latter.

"Alicia. Please." I didn't mind feeding into her game a little. I figured she had earned it.

She'd shrugged. "I'll think about it." She stood up and left, but when I returned home from that meeting an hour or so later, she was waiting for me.

"You're home," I said. Maggie was all but dancing around me, so happy to have both of her parents back.

"I've decided to help you," she announced. I was almost as surprised by her outright concession as I was that she'd made it at all. I thought at a minimum she'd want to drag it out longer.

"That's great. Thank you." I glanced at her hand. She was still wearing her ring. I went over to the couch and sat a few feet from her, fully expecting her to bolt. Instead, she regarded me evenly.

"What changed your mind?" I asked carefully.

"Marshall says the state really has no case against you."

"They don't." I took a deep breath. "They're calling Matt to say what he saw in the classroom, but he's not going to help them much. The only other witnesses are the detective and Jackie."

"She's really going through with this, huh?"

I shrugged. I was still having trouble believing that.

"What about Lily?"

"She can't testify unless I do." I explained what Marshall had told me. "Lily's not allowed to get on the stand and say what happened between us unless I deny it, under oath."

"Lucky break for you, I guess."

"The only downside is it basically prevents me from testifying in my own defense. There's no way I can do that without the prosecutor asking me about Lily, and then I'd be trapped. I can't risk the jury finding out about her, because then they would definitely think something happened with Jackie."

"Yep. I can relate to that." Her voice was chilly.

"You still don't believe me, do you?"

"Not sure what to believe. I go back and forth. Part of me thinks that if you were guilty, they would have found something to support that. Also…" She paused. "I know you really cared about Jackie. The reason I never tried to get in the way of your relationship with her is because it seemed so good for both of you. You were different after she came along. You were excited about teaching again, more engaged in everything."

"I was?" I hadn't known that.

She nodded. "The thing with Lily made sense to me, after I thought about it. I know how you like to be adored and she clearly gave you that. With Jackie, it always seemed more like there was a mutual respect in play. It's a little harder for me to imagine you doing anything to wreck that, especially after being scared straight."

"I wouldn't."

"At the same time, I have enough sense to know that I could be kidding myself." She sighed. "So I've decided to pretend I'm the jury. Innocent until proven guilty. I doubt you're as innocent as you claim to be, but I'm not *positive* you belong in prison either."

"Fair enough."

"I'm only agreeing to see you through the trial. After that, I don't know what's going to happen to us. Even if I do still love you." The last sentence sounded more like a bitter confession than anything.

"I understand." I was determined not to push her into any hasty decisions. I wasn't sure enough that they would cut in my favor. I didn't say anything else, and a moment later she left the house again, Maggie at her heels.

***

Now, on the morning of the trial, we arrive at the courthouse first thing. Despite her warning that this could be temporary, it makes me feel better to have her at my side. She knows me well enough to see how scared I am. There are so few witnesses that this will probably be over by tomorrow. This one day will decide the rest of my life.

"Where are we supposed to be meeting Marshall?" Alicia asks.

"Courtroom five," I reply. "Let's get some coffee first, okay?" She nods. It goes without saying, I didn't sleep well last night. I doubt she did either but I can't swear to it, since she was elsewhere again.

There's a coffee shop in the atrium of the courthouse and I head for it. We're barely through the door when my brain registers Jackie half a beat behind the sight of her. The delay is because she looks *really* different than she did the last time I saw her. As our eyes meet, I see Lily standing there with her.

The sight of them together turns my stomach. I have no trouble recognizing Lily from her Facebook photos, though I'm not certain I would have otherwise. She's really undergone an incredible transformation since high school. She actually looks a damn sight better than Jackie, who appears to have spent the last few months in a concentration camp.

You did that to her, my brain reports without my permission. I shove the thought away.

Isabel is with them, and so is the boyfriend I found on Lily's profile. I could have figured out who he was from context, by the protective way he moves toward Lily when he sees the look on her face.

"David, we should go," Alicia whispers in my ear. "We'll find somewhere else."

"Yeah. Okay." We move toward the door and I look back once more. Lily's turned away, but Jackie is still watching me. I'm going to be haunted by that look all through the trial, I know, and not only because she appears to be a phantom of her former self.

***

The courtroom doesn't look exactly like it does on television, mainly because it's smaller. But it's easy to identify a witness stand next to the higher judge's table and a small area for the jury.

It's crowded in here, which doesn't make me feel any better. I can feel people looking at me. Marshall told me to look my best, so I'm in my wedding/funeral suit and trying to keep my head high.

He's waiting for us at the door and quickly escorts us to the front. Alicia sits directly behind me in the first row, and Marshall and I sit down at the defense table.

"Make sure you don't move around too much," he reminds me in a low voice. "It's distracting. And it could make you look shifty. Look at the jury as much as you want, try to make eye contact with at least a couple of them. But keep your body still." I nod stiffly, my heart pounding.

It feels like an entire day passes before things get started.

"All rise," I hear at last. "The honorable Judge Clark presiding." I stand with everyone else.

"You may be seated," the judge says. "Before we begin, I'm aware that this case is of an especially sensitive nature in that it involves a minor. As such, I am putting every single person in this room on notice. Anyone who disrupts the process in any way will leave and they will not come back. The only voices I want to hear are those of the witnesses and the lawyers. Are the parties ready to proceed?"

"Ready for trial, Your Honor," the prosecutor says.

"We're ready as well, Your Honor," Marshall adds.

The judge calls for opening statements, and the prosecutor goes first. He's talking kind of fast, or maybe I'm too nervous to listen properly. Either way, he's on his feet for two or three minutes and I only hear him say Jackie's name once. I glance around when he's finished, then remember that she isn't allowed to be in the courtroom until her testimony. I don't see Lily or Isabel either, but I do see Kathryn. She's seated in the third row, glowering at me.

On the day she hired me, she told me I'd be an asset to the school.

Marshall gets up next and starts to speak. As soon as he does, I'm glad I stuck with him instead of switching to a public defender. The money we spent is nothing to me so long as it gets me out of this, and Marshall is good at what he does.

With the jury, he has an easy and relaxed way about him that almost seems too casual for the situation, but I can see that it's effective. He seems approachable, like a guy you want to trust. The way I hope I look.

"A lot of kids have crushes on their teachers," he begins after introducing himself. "Heck, I'll never forget my own gym teacher back in high school. She was attractive and sweet – well, sweet for a gym teacher, anyway – and I definitely had a thing for her. I'm sure more than a few of you can relate to that feeling as well. There's something about a teacher, especially a young and good looking one, that inspires kids in more ways than academic. That's a pretty normal thing to some extent.

"But sometimes it goes too far. And that's what's happened here. Now, is it my intent to disparage Jackie Culver? Not in any way. Let me tell you something kind of surprising about my client, David Harrison. He doesn't hold this against her. For the last two years, he's been a dedicated teacher to her. In fact, his mentoring Jackie was a big factor in her winning a prestigious state essay contest last September. Now because of these accusations, his career is all but over. He's in court, fighting for his freedom and trying to clear his name of one of the worst things a teacher can be accused of nowadays. Can you imagine what that must feel like?

"Personally, I wouldn't blame him for being angry. But that's not David Harrison. He cares about Jackie – and that was where he became vulnerable. When I talk to you again at the end of all this, I'm going to tell you the same thing I'm about to say now. The evidence will *not* prove that they had a sexual affair. The evidence will prove only that David Harrison is guilty of poor judgment. He could and should have kept his distance from her a little more, given more thought to protecting himself, and it's for that reason he is no longer teaching.

"He should have kept better boundaries with her, no question, because their closeness ultimately led to a very regrettable result." Marshall sighs. "Jackie tried to kiss him during school, in a classroom. Not a good situation, no one disputes that. But on the other hand, can we blame him for *not* anticipating that this student he had known for over a year, guided and encouraged and even respected, would try to do something like that? I don't think so.

"I already told you that my client feels no anger toward Jackie Culver. He feels compassion for her, and I won't ask any of you to deny that compassion in yourselves either. I only ask that you not be blinded by it. Because the sad truth is, she's not the one whose life is being destroyed over this. David Harrison will likely never teach again. His wife, Alicia, has even had to resign from her own position in the school as vice principal." He motions to Alicia, and she looks at the jury. Marshall wanted them to see her and know who she was. "Their reputations are ruined because once the stain of an accusation like this smears you, it never goes away.

"You can question David's judgment all you want, and I'll agree with you, but in this room all that matters is the evidence that you'll hear. After you hear that evidence, I know that you will find this man not guilty. The prosecution cannot and will not prove anything more than what I just told you." As he finishes his speech, he makes his way back to me and rests a meaty hand on my shoulder.

He told me beforehand that he would have to word his speech very carefully. Since he does in fact have knowledge of my guilt, he can't directly lie to the jury and tell them I didn't do it. And I have to admire the way he pulled it off.

He made me sound innocent even though he never actually said so.

Chapter Three

JACKIE | *DAVID*

"I don't know how much longer I can sit here like this," Lily mutters. We've been in a courthouse conference room for almost an hour. Rick arranged for us to wait in here so we could have privacy.

Technically I don't *need* to be here until it's my turn to testify, which will probably be tomorrow. I just wanted to be close enough to hear about what was going on as it happened and of course, everyone wanted to be here with me. But as I'm looking at Lily's face, I'm rethinking the whole idea.

This morning was the first time Lily had seen him in eight years. She's taking it hard, and I'm not doing so great myself. He looks different in that suit but not different enough to prevent a swarm of memories from attacking me like bees the moment I saw him. Knowing he's only a couple of rooms away from me right now is messing with my head.

I'm about to suggest that we go home after all when Ben speaks up.

"Hey, Jackie, can you help me with something?" He's hunched over his laptop. The Wi-Fi connection in the courthouse isn't the best but Ben was able to make it work. He knew he wouldn't be able to sit still for hours doing nothing, so he brought his job with him. "We're branding this section of our website specifically for teenagers. I could use your opinion."

"Sure," I say, going to sit down next to him. He spends the better part of the next hour walking me through his design and asking for my ideas and input. I'm surprised to find that I'm genuinely interested, and kind of flattered that he asked me. He's even taking notes. At some point, I notice Lily watching him and her face is filled with so much tenderness that it goes straight through my heart.

I don't understand at first, but it clicks a moment later when I realize that Ben probably doesn't really need my help. He's trying to distract me from what's happening.

Part of me wants to take offense – I'm not a baby, after all – but I can't quite get there. Mostly all I can feel is how much these two care about me. How important it is to them that I feel secure, and the way they work together to make it happen.

I'm not sure there's an exact word for this, but I like it.

***

By the time Rick returns, it's almost noon and he announces that the judge has broken for lunch.

"We're done with Matt Mintz's testimony," he adds. "It went okay."

"Just okay?" Gran asks.

"Yeah. I knew he wouldn't be a big advocate for us, since he and David are friends, but it could have been worse."

"Did he say it looked like they were kissing?" Lily asks.

"He said he couldn't be sure. But that's fine. We're talking about a two-second glance through a window. I didn't expect him to be our smoking gun. That's going to be up to you, Jackie."

"When do I go?" I ask.

"I want to put Detective Keller up next, and then I'll probably ask that we break for the day."

"Why?"

"Because I want your testimony to be as close to the end as possible. The defense isn't putting up any witnesses, so as soon as you're done we go to closing arguments, and then they'll deliberate. I want your voice to be ringing in their ears when they do." He takes a step toward me. "I know you're anxious to get this over with but like I told you, we don't have the greatest case here. Our best chance is making the jury focus on you as much as they possibly can."

"Are you sure I can't testify?" Lily asks.

Rick sits down and folds his hands in front of him. "We talked about this, Lily. If we had corroboration, it would be one thing, but–"

"We don't," she finishes. "I know. It's totally useless. *I'm* totally useless."

"Don't say that!" I exclaim. "It's not your fault."

Lily looks at me, shaking her head. Then she turns to Ben. "Can we get out of here? I can't be here anymore right now."

"Yeah, of course," he says, closing his laptop and getting quickly to his feet.

Lily looks back at me, tears in her eyes. "Are you going to be okay?"

"I'll go too," I say.

"No, it's all right. You stay here with Isabel." Before I can say anything, Lily leaves the room with Ben right on her heels, and a moment later we can hear her sobbing in the hallway. I make a move to go out there, but Gran takes hold of my arm.

"Let her go, dear. Ben will look after her." I open my mouth to protest, but Gran shakes her head. "Jackie, please, trust me. Give her a little time." I sit down, stung.

So much for my warm fuzzy feeling earlier.

***

Gran and I sit in the room alone for the next couple of hours, not talking. She reads a book while I alternate between playing games on my phone and replying to messages on the rape survivor message board. Lily and I have both become regular posters.

She started another thread after she left earlier, but I can't make myself read it right now.

I'm kind of glad I can't hear what Detective Keller is saying about me in her testimony. I know she has to tell the jury all about how I lied at first. I talked to her a couple of days ago, and she told me that she was on my side and intended to tell the jury that she always thought something had happened between me and David. She said it's really common for people in my situation to hide the truth at first, and it doesn't mean anything.

But they're probably going to think I'm a liar anyway.

Every time I think about testifying tomorrow, my stomach does a triple somersault and I feel so dizzy I have to close my eyes and lean against the wall. I've been trying to push it from my mind but that's not going well, because I keep thinking instead about the first time David kissed me.

It wasn't my first kiss, but it might as well have been. Nobody ever kissed me like David did that day. He started off super light like he always does but once he got going, he sealed his lips against mine and exhaled into my mouth so slowly and deliberately that I felt his breath travel into my own lungs. When I had to breathe out again, he didn't move away. He breathed me back into himself.

It's a classic David maneuver. But I didn't know that then.

Having him literally take my breath away was so intensely intimate that it *almost* made everything we did together later feel superfluous. He did it again when we had sex for the first time, kissed me that same way while he was still inside me. I'll remember that moment for the rest of my life.

But when I think about him kissing Lily like that... getting her off with his hands, his mouth, exactly the way he did with me… those memories I used to treasure start crumbling to pieces.

I'm starting to understand what she meant when she said it felt like he practiced for me on her. He sucked up her love and loyalty like some kind of sponge, then wrung her out over the sink once he was done with her so he could start over on someone else.

On me.

I have to keep thinking about this, because it's the only way I can find the strength to testify against him. When I thought it was just him and me in this forbidden world together, leaving it was absolutely unthinkable. But leaving it behind to join Lily is a whole different thing.

I could never have done this to him before I knew about her. So I keep wondering, is it wrong for me to do it now?

I mean, I still can't think of David as a criminal. I wish I did, but Lily and I both knew what we were doing. Emotionally, it doesn't feel like he assaulted me. It feels like he betrayed me, even though that doesn't make any sense. We didn't know each other back then. Why should Lily's existence bother me more than anyone else in his past?

Do you really think I go around doing this all the time?

I'd never realized how much that mattered to me, believing that I was the only one special enough to make him cheat on Alicia. Not until I knew I wasn't.

Does he really deserve to go to prison just because he hurt me?

***

Lily is waiting on the porch steps when Gran and I get home. As soon as she gets to her feet and folds me into a fierce hug, the ache I've felt ever since she left with Ben starts to disintegrate. It doesn't fade completely, but I can tell it will. If I let it.

"I'm so sorry, Jackie."

"You don't need to be sorry," I manage.

"I promised to stick by you and I left you there."

"That's not why…" I take a deep breath. "Look, it's no big deal. Come inside." I go in the house, but Lily doesn't follow me and I hear her voice through the open door.

"I failed her, Isabel."

"You're too hard on yourself, darling. Come in."

"I might as well not have come at all, if I was going to bail out like that."

"Lily. Listen to me." Gran's voice takes on the steely edge I know so well. "If it weren't for you, Jackie never would have made it this far. You know this. But she doesn't expect it to be easy for you. She never has, and neither do I."

I stick my head back outside. "Do you still want me to come to Portland with you?"

"Of course I do," Lily says, sounding genuinely shocked. "Why would that have changed?"

"Then we're fine." At least I hope we are. "Would you come in the damn house already?"

Once we're in the kitchen, Gran pours a glass of wine for herself and starts to pour one for Lily, who stops her. "No. Don't do that. It's been the wrong kind of day."

"All right," Gran says, corking the bottle and putting it in the fridge. She goes to her room to change, and I try not to stare at her glass. I want some myself, but I know what Lily means. Better not to go there. My dad taught me that much by example.

"You're really not mad at me?" Lily asks quietly.

I pause, wanting to answer truthfully. "I wasn't ever mad."

"I hurt your feelings."

"Maybe a little."

"Because I asked Ben to leave with me instead of you?"

"Yeah." I look down, feeling ashamed for some reason. "Something like that."

"Jackie, I asked him to go with me because I was falling apart and I didn't want you to have to try to be strong for me. The whole point here is that I'm trying to be strong for *you.*"

"But… you said you needed me." I hate always being the one who needs to borrow strength, and I'm going to need every bit I can get from her tomorrow.

Maybe today I could have given her some.

"And I do."

"Then why can't I help you when you're feeling like that?"

"You're right." She nods. "I should have let you. Next time I will, I promise." She puts her arm around me and I hug her back.

"Rick said Detective Keller did really well," I tell her. "I'm up first thing tomorrow."

"Okay. I'm ready now. I'll sit in the back so none of the jurors notice me. But you'll be able to see me."

It still might not be enough to get me through. But nothing else would come close.

***

It's almost time now. I feel like I'm waiting for my own execution. I've had nothing to do for the last ten minutes except pace the room and try to gag down a few bites of a sweet roll Gran insisted on buying for me even though I can't swallow anything.

Lily sits at the table clutching Ben's hand.

"I should have worn makeup," I say to no one in particular, glancing at myself in the mirrored window.

"No, natural is better for this," Rick answers as he comes into the room. "You want to look like yourself."

"I look like a vampire."

"You look nervous. Which is okay. Come sit down." I shake my head, and he shrugs. "Suit yourself, I'm going to sit. We need to go over a few last-minute reminders."

"I'm listening." The others assemble around the table, and I grip the back of a chair.

"You're all going to be in the room?"

"Yes," Gran says. I changed my mind about that in the end. I want all of them there, even Ben.

"Okay, well, it's *critical* that all of you stay quiet. I mean absolutely silent. No matter what happens, no matter what you hear. I can't stress this enough. Any outbursts at all will not only get you banned from the courtroom, they could even get the case dismissed and I know you don't want to do that to Jackie." He looks at Lily. "Is that clear?"

"Yes," she says, sitting ramrod straight in her chair. "I won't say anything."

"I want you all in the back row. If you feel like you might get emotional, slip out as quietly as you possibly can. No distractions. We need to keep the jurors' attention focused completely on Jackie."

"But no pressure or anything." I don't know how I can joke right now. It just comes out.

Rick gives me a thin smile. "Okay. Jackie. When I ask you questions, I want you to talk right into the microphone and speak as slowly as you can, okay?"

"Okay."

"Don't look at David if you can help it. It's going to be hard not to, but do what you can to resist that impulse. You look at me, or your family, or the jury."

I look down at my hands, which are trembling noticeably, and hold them up for Rick to see.

"Yeah, I saw that. It's okay if you're shaking a little. It's even okay if you look scared. Talking in front of a roomful of people is stressful for most adults. They'll understand if you're afraid. What we want to avoid are things like slumping over, turning your shoulders in or crossing your arms, tilting your body away from the jury." Rick demonstrates as he speaks. "Sometimes jurors attach a lot of meaning to silly things, and they pay attention to body language. If you look like you're trying to hide anything, they won't like that. Try to sit up straight."

I nod.

"You remember the questions we went over before?" We practiced in the courtroom a week ago. It was awful. "It'll be the same today. The more detailed you can be when you answer, the better. And be specific, okay?"

"Okay."

"I'm going to ask for a recess after we're done with direct so you can collect yourself. One step at a time, right?" Rick looks at his watch. "I think that's everything. Let's go."

My heart is pounding so hard as we approach the courtroom that I can actually hear my own blood pulsing in my forehead. Lily's hand feels cold around mine.

"You're going to do fine," she says. "Think about all the people who are pulling for you. Pretend they're in the room with us." When we woke up this morning, we found almost a hundred posts and private messages of last-minute encouragement on the message board.

Despite Rick's warning, my eyes find David instantly and refuse to leave him. After all this time, he still draws me like a magnet. He's already seated at his table, deep in conversation with his lawyer, but he glances up at me as I walk in and then looks away again immediately.

It feels like only seconds before I hear Rick speak.

"The prosecution calls Jackie Culver."

I stand.

Chapter Four

JACKIE | **DAVID**

Matt's testimony was harder to listen to than I thought it would be. Even though he was theoretically a prosecution witness, Alicia commented afterward that it was hard to tell whose side he was on, and I had to agree. When Rick Sable asked him what happened, he said he *thought* Jackie was kissing me, but he wasn't certain. In response, Rick got Matt to confess that he'd been friends with me and Alicia for years and pounced on that like a cat. Ultimately, Matt admitted that he was heavily biased in my favor.

Unfortunately, the detective who followed him was a powerful advocate who more than compensated for Matt's tepidity. She tossed me disdainful glances throughout her testimony and sounded almost bored as she described the way predators "groom" their victims, how what I did with Jackie was "practically a textbook case of statutory rape."

Bitch.

"Cops testify all the time," Marshall explained to me once it was over. "They get a lot of practice, so they've got a huge advantage over most witnesses. They also put people in two categories, degenerate criminal or upstanding citizen, and white juries tend to take their word on which one you are." Everyone on my jury is white. Typical for this town.

"Nothing she said proves I did anything." I was fuming.

"True, but she sure made it easier for the jury to believe Jackie when she tells her story."

"Is she next?"

"She is. Jackie's the only one left. She goes tomorrow."

***

Now I'm watching her walk into the courtroom. And she's watching me.

Jackie has incredibly expressive eyes. They've always given away everything she can't say in words. That's how she first told me I was becoming the most important person in her life.

All of that is still there, which makes the pain in her gaze even more upsetting for me now. Marshall told me to pretend she's a random student of mine I don't know very well. To accomplish that, I have to shut down the part of me that still loves her, bury it beneath a sheet of steel.

She does not want to do this. I don't doubt that for a second. I can tell by her very movements how hard it is for her not to turn and run from the room.

Until she actually sits in the chair, part of me fully expects her to do exactly that.

It's troubling to me how young and helpless they've made her look. Her hair is scraped back into a pretty severe ponytail, a hairstyle I happen to know she can't tolerate for more than an hour because it makes her scalp ache.

The bailiff swears her in. At least, I think that's what he's saying. I can't hear a word anyone is saying until she starts to speak. The prosecutor must have asked her name.

"Jaclyn Marie Culver."

"How old are you?"

"Sixteen."

"And where do you go to school?"

"I used to go to South Point High School. I finished last semester online."

"What grade are you in?"

"I'll be a junior next year."

"And Jackie, do you know David Harrison?" Rick points to me. She nods but continues resolutely facing the lawyer.

"Yes, I do."

"How do you know him?"

"He was my English teacher my freshman and sophomore year. And I also… had a relationship with him."

"Okay. Jackie, I'll ask you a few more questions about that but first, can you tell me why you stopped attending South Point High School earlier this year?"

She takes a deep breath and looks over at the jury. "There were a lot of rumors going around about me." Marshall jots down a note, which says only the word *rumors*. "I was starting to get harassed, pretty much on a daily basis. My grandmother and the principal, Mrs. Connell, thought it would be safer for me to finish the year from home."

"And your grandmother is your guardian, correct? You live with her?"

"Yes."

"What were the rumors about, Jackie?"

"They were about David and I being involved with each other. Everyone found out and the kids at school got really vicious. The teachers treated me differently too."

"Okay. Can you tell us about the exact nature of your relationship with David Harrison?"

She stares ahead like she's still determined not to look at me, and I hold my breath. "We, um… we were seeing each other outside of school. And we had been having sex."

My heart sinks. She really said it.

"When did that part of your relationship start?"

"October of last year."

"How old were you then?"

"I was fifteen." She glances at the jury, and I see two of the jurors raise their eyebrows.

"How did it start, Jackie?"

"He took me out one day to get coffee, and drove me home afterward. And he kissed me in his car. Before long he was driving me home pretty often and we started to do more than kiss."

"What else did you do?"

She interlaces her fingers in her lap. "Normally we would have oral sex."

"And by that you mean?"

She bites her lip. "I would put my mouth on him… on his penis… and he would put his mouth on my vagina."

The few times Jackie has managed to shock me usually involved things she said to me *in flagrante delicto*. Things that wouldn't have been extreme from a grown woman took me aback when she said them, mostly because of where she started. At first she spoke with a hesitancy I found charming, but her confidence grew almost as quickly as her repertoire.

She used to *live* for these moments, and the description she just gave is so clinical it almost feels like a lie. I bet the prosecutor told her to say it like that. It makes me want to stand up and start quoting some of the things she's asked me to do to her.

But that would be counterproductive.

Rick lets her statement hang for a torturously long pause, during which I can feel the jury looking at me. I know they're measuring my reaction and I try to keep my face blank but it's impossible to know whether I'm succeeding. It almost doesn't matter if they convict me. Her words alone are burning me to the ground.

"Did it ever go beyond that, Jackie?"

"Yes, in early November. I went to his house and spent the

night there."

"And while you were at his house, what happened?"

"We had sex. Intercourse."

"Vaginal intercourse?"

She nods. "Yes."

"And did he continue to have vaginal intercourse with you after that night?"

"Yes. It went on for another three months or so."

"How many times did Mr. Harrison have either oral or vaginal sex with you, Jackie?"

"I'm not sure. I didn't keep count."

"Was it more than ten?"

"Yes."

"More than twenty?"

"Yes." She makes the mistake of glancing at me then. I can see my own despair in her face like a reflection.

I'm sorry, David.

She doesn't need to say it in words for me to hear it.

"Jackie, do you need a break?"

"No. I'm all right." She looks at the jury again. One of the jurors is writing something down.

"Did Mr. Harrison take any steps to conceal his relationship with you?"

"Yes. He bought both of us prepaid cell phones so we wouldn't have to use our regular phones to contact each other, and whenever we were in his car he would always spread a blanket or a towel over the backseat before we had sex."

For God's sake. I would have done that anyway, I always did before. It feels more hygienic to me, but needless to say it sounds completely sinister coming from her.

"What happened to the cell phone he gave you?"

"The police took it."

"When they took it, did it have any messages from David on it?"

"No." Jackie looks down. "I had deleted all of them."

"Why?"

"Because the last time we talked, he asked me to. In case anyone found out about the phone."

"Did Mr. Harrison ever tell you anything about his feelings for you, Jackie?"

"Objection," Marshall declares, jarring me and Jackie both. "The question calls for hearsay."

"State of mind exception, Your Honor." I don't know what that means, but the judge nods.

"Overruled."

Rick looks at her. "You can answer, Jackie."

"Yes. He said he loved me."

"And how did you feel about him?"

She takes a drink of water and for the first time since she started speaking, her voice shakes a little. "I… I loved him. Very much. Sometimes I think I still do."

"Then it can't be easy for you, testifying against him here today."

"Of course it isn't."

"What made you decide to do that?"

Every muscle in my body tightens in anticipation of her answer. Marshall has assured me that they're not allowed to bring up Lily, that it could even cause a mistrial if they do.

"I wasn't going to, at first. But then I met one of David's former students, and she told me–"

"Objection, Your Honor!" Marshall is on his feet. "This statement is inadmissible hearsay."

"This also goes to Jackie's state of mind, Your Honor, not the truth of the matter."

"Sorry, Mr. Sable. On this, you're shut down. Objection sustained." The judge turns to Jackie. "Miss Culver, you're to tell the jury only about your own experiences. Anything you may or may not have heard from other people about Mr. Harrison is off limits. Do you understand?"

She nods. "Yes."

But they *heard* it! Anyone with a functioning brain could figure out what she was about to say.

In other words, I'm fucked. I try to catch Marshall's eye but he ignores me.

Rick switches gears. "Did you report this to the police on your own?" he asks.

"No. They came to me. After Mr. Mintz, another one of my teachers, saw me and David together in a classroom and the principal reported it."

"What were you doing in the classroom?"

"I was basically kissing him."

"Was he kissing you back?"

"Yes, but then Mr. Mintz came in so we stopped. We didn't think he saw us."

"Jackie, when Detective Keller first asked you about your relationship with David Harrison, what did you tell her?"

She looks at the jury again. "I told her we didn't have a relationship. That he was only my teacher, and when I tried to kiss him in Mr. Mintz's room, he said no."

"So you denied that he had had sex with you?"

"Yes, I did."

"Why did you do that?"

"Because at the time, I was still trying to protect him." She stares at the ceiling for a moment.

"Why were you trying to protect him?"

"Because I loved him and I didn't want to get him in trouble."

"Okay. But at some point you did decide to tell the police the truth."

"Yes. It was a few weeks later."

"Can you tell us a little bit about what your life has been like since then, Jackie?"

"It's been hell, basically. Like I said, everyone found out about it at school. I started getting harassed there, and almost any time I was out in public. My grandmother knows a lot of people in our town and it seems like everyone blames me for what happened. So she got hassled a lot too."

"At this time, do you plan to return to South Point High School?"

"No."

"You'll be going to a different school next year?"

"Yes, in a different city. I'll be moving in with friends." The moment she says this, I know instinctively that she's going to Portland to live with Lily. What other friends does she have? For some reason, this thought is almost intolerable.

"You're going to be leaving your home and your town and your grandmother so you can safely finish high school."

"Yes." Jackie clears her throat. "It's really bad for me here, now. Everyone knows what happened. And I don't want my grandmother to suffer any more because of me than she already has."

"Thank you, Jackie." Rick goes over to his table and consults a piece of paper while Jackie and I both check out the jury again. It's really hard to read anything in their faces. They don't look like they disbelieve her, but they don't look too friendly, either. Only a few are looking at her. The rest of them are watching me.

"That's all I have, Your Honor. I'd like to request that we give Jackie a break before we start on cross-examination."

"Twenty minute recess," the judge says. Rick goes straight to Jackie and escorts her down from the witness stand, hustling her away.

I manage to wait until the jury is out of the room before I let my head sink onto the table. My sense of defeat is total.

"I tried to warn you," Marshall says quietly, placing a hand on my back. "Keep your head up, man. It's not over yet. My turn comes next."

It takes me a good five minutes to recover enough to turn my head and look for Alicia. By the time I manage to do that, she's gone.

Chapter Five

JACKIE | *DAVID*

"Well done," Gran says to me as soon as we're back in the little room. She and Lily take turns hugging me, and Ben gives me a thumbs-up.

"She did great," Rick says. "But it's not time to celebrate yet. She still has to get through cross examination."

"Did I answer the question about Lily okay?" I ask him.

"It was perfect. Even though the judge cut you off, I think you got in enough to suggest that he did it before. Not totally ethical on my part, but..." He shrugs.

"Better than nothing," Lily fills in quietly. I'm still holding onto her.

"All right. We don't have much time, so let's get ready for cross." This time I do sit down. My legs feel like rubber. "Remember, everything he asks you about –"

"He already knows the answer."

"Exactly. But that's not going to be a problem, because all you have to do is tell the truth. Be as open as you can, okay? Try not to get defensive."

"I won't."

"Remember, his job is to keep David out of prison. Everything he asks you, he's asking with that goal in mind. It's not personal."

I nod. "We've come this far. Hang in there. Do you need anything before we go back in?"

"Maybe some juice."

"On it," Ben says, rushing from the room. Lily puts a hand over mine.

"You're almost done."

"Yeah." But Rick's warned me multiple times that this part will be the worst.

***

It's a little bit easier to step up to the witness box the second time, but not to the point of being easy. My entire body feels like it's seizing with every step and I'm glad this blouse Gran bought for me is dark blue because I'm sweating right through it.

David's lawyer gets up and introduces himself to me. He has a warm, friendly voice and comes within five feet of the witness stand. I look over at Lily and she gives me a small, private gesture of encouragement. I sit up a little straighter.

I'm doing this for us, I remind myself firmly. *For both of us.*

"Is it all right if I call you Jackie?" I nod once. "Jackie, you spent quite a bit of time with Mr. Harrison outside of class during your freshman year, correct?"

"Yes."

"As I understand it, he would give you extra assignments and you would come in to discuss them with him, that kind of thing."

"Right."

"And he never touched you, never made any kind of move on you?"

"Not then."

"Did you tell your grandmother, as well as many other people, that David Harrison was the best teacher you ever had?"

"Yes, I did. And he was."

"I apologize if this is a painful subject, Jackie, but your father is not actively in your life, correct?"

"Objection," Rick says before I can respond. "Relevance?"

"Your Honor, the relevance will become clear in a moment."

"Overruled," he says.

"Your dad's not around, right Jackie?"

"No." Rick said he might try to get into this, but I can't imagine what good it's going to do.

"Would you say that David Harrison was something of a father figure in your life?"

"Ew," I can't help answering. "No, I wouldn't."

"You wouldn't? Why the 'ew'? Because you have romantic feelings for him?"

I feel like rolling my eyes, but Rick said not to show exasperation no matter what he asked. Seriously, though? Maybe I should become a lawyer, if all you have to do is stand in a courtroom and ask really fucking obvious questions. "That, and because we've had sex."

"Right. You claim you've had sex with Mr. Harrison."

"It happened!" Rick raises his hand from the table, a wordless reminder to stay calm.

"I don't mean to insult you," Marshall says. "But it's my job to ask the question. You've already admitted lying to the police and to your principal. I imagine you lied to your grandmother as well?"

"Yes, I lied to keep the relationship secret." I reach for the glass of water in front of me, trying to slow my racing heart. "So did David."

Marshall takes on a lecturing, parental tone that I would despise from anyone. "So Jackie, if you admit that you lied to all of these people, how can we be sure that you're telling the truth now?"

"I wasn't under oath when I lied before." I look at the jury again.

"That's important to you, then? Being under oath?"

"Yes. I'd never lie under oath, especially about something this serious."

"I'm glad you recognize how serious it is, Jackie," he says, pacing the stand a little bit in front of me. "Do you fully understand the consequences your teacher is facing because of you?"

"It's not because of me," I say, wishing I could truly believe that. "But yes, I do."

"You realize that if convicted here, David Harrison faces serious prison time and he'll have to register as a sex offender? That means he'll never be able to teach again, and you said yourself he was a great teacher. Can you really live with that?"

Of course I can't live with that. I'm barely surviving this. But I never get a chance to say so.

"Objection, Your Honor. He's badgering the witness."

I can't help it. My eyes fall on David again. I keep expecting him to look pissed, but he doesn't. He looks sad and resigned, and also absurdly young. David turned thirty-five in June and he's never looked anywhere near that, at least not to me, but right now he looks about twenty. It's like he's spent the past months in some kind of time warp.

"Sustained. Take it down a notch, counselor."

"I apologize, Jackie," Marshall says pompously.

"Just move on, Mr. Adler," the judge says.

"All right, let's try this another way." He paces before me again. "You say that you and Mr. Harrison had sex, both oral and vaginal, multiple times – is that correct?"

"Yes." When we were practicing last week, Rick told me to go back to yes and no answers if I got into trouble.

"At any time, did he force you to do anything?"

"No."

"So assuming that what you're telling us here today is in fact true, you're saying that you willingly had sex with him. Do you know Alicia Harrison, Jackie?" He points to where she's sitting, directly behind David, and I feel the familiar gut punch when she scowls at me.

"A little bit," I answer. "Not that well."

"Who is Alicia Harrison?"

I swallow. "She's David's wife."

"She's also a friend of your grandmother's, isn't that right?"

"Well, she was." Gran hasn't said a word to me about Alicia since all this happened.

"Didn't you in fact meet her even before you were in Mr. Harrison's English class?"

"Yes, I did."

"So you not only knew David Harrison was married, you knew his wife. She was a family friend, it sounds like. Would that be fair?"

"Yes."

"And you're saying that you had sex with her husband. Willingly."

I hate this guy. I mumble something.

"Can you speak up, please?"

I lean closer to the microphone. *"Yes."*

"You're telling us that David Harrison chose to have a sexual relationship with you even though he was married to someone else?"

"Not just me. He did it before," I snap before I can stop myself.

"Objection!" Marshall yells. "Your Honor –"

"Sustained. The jury will completely disregard the last remark by this witness." The judge turns to me again. "I already told you not to talk about anyone else, Miss Culver. If I have to say it a third time, I'm going to direct a verdict for the defendant."

"I'm sorry," I say. But I'm not. I don't care anymore. I just want this to be over.

"Ask your question again, Mr. Adler."

"You're asking us to believe that David Harrison would choose to be sexually involved with one of his students, a girl less than half his age, despite being a respected teacher and a married man?"

"That's what happened. So yes."

"But we can't trust your word, can we, Jackie?" This asshole is sounding more condescending with every question.

"I'm not lying."

"You admitted that you lied to the most important people in your life as well as to law enforcement. You have strong feelings for Mr. Harrison. You told the detective that you tried to kiss him and he refused you. Detective Keller told us you were in fact rather insistent that it was your fault and Mr. Harrison did nothing wrong."

"Is there a question here, Your Honor?" Rick asks.

"Here's my question, Jackie. You admit to lying, and you admit to propositioning one of your married teachers – in a classroom, no less. Would you consider either of those actions to be in keeping with the behavior of an ethical person?"

I sigh. "No."

Lily has her face buried in her hands. I know that each of these questions tear at the same raw wounds on her that they do on me.

"Thank you, Jackie. I appreciate your honesty. Can you tell me if you've ever broken the law? For example, have you ever had any alcohol or smoked pot – say, at a party?"

"Yes." He'd have a hard time finding any kid at my school who hasn't.

"And have you ever lied about doing those things?"

"I might have."

"In fact, your grandmother had real problems with your inability to tell the truth when you first moved in with her. She couldn't trust you. Is that true?"

I hesitate and then nod. "Yes. It's true."

"You lied to her quite frequently, I'm told." Gran looks murderous, even through her legendary poker face. She must have told Alicia this stuff at some point, but Gran never holds grudges once we've worked through things and hearing the defense attorney use her own words against me now is clearly making her furious.

"I used to, I don't anymore."

"So apart from the recent occasion when you lied to her about Mr. Harrison, when was the last time you lied to her?"

"I'm *not lying* about David."

"By your own admission, you did."

"In the beginning, yes, but then I told her the truth and I'm telling the truth now!" How many times does he have to hammer this?

"But you have lied to her many times before."

"Objection, Your Honor." Rick's on his feet again. "Asked and answered."

"Sustained. Do you have anything else, counselor?"

"Yes, Your Honor. Jackie, you said one other thing earlier that caught my ear. You said that your peers and teachers treated you differently after the rumor started at school, correct?"

"They did."

"Wasn't the substance of this supposed rumor that you and Mr. Harrison were having a sexual relationship?"

"Yes." I tense again because this feels like a trick.

"So if you claim that was the truth, why would you call it a rumor?" he asks, sounding curious.

"I… I don't know. I mean, it *was* the truth but the things they were saying about me weren't true." Lily insisted that they weren't, anyway. "They were calling me a slut."

"Oh, I understand they were being cruel about it but weren't they saying, in essence, that you had initiated the whole thing? Which, I remind you, is exactly what you told the police?"

"Yes." I understand what he's doing now, and I don't know how to fix this.

"So what part of it was untrue?"

I'm hoping Rick will object again to give me time to think, but apparently he can't. The silence drags out until I answer. "I guess it was true for the most part."

"Do you know the difference between truth and lies, Jackie?"

"Yes," I say, hating the fragility in my voice. "I am not lying." I can't take this anymore.

"Okay," he says almost gently. "That's all I have, Jackie."

"Redirect, Mr. Sable?" the judge asks. Rick gets up and comes over to me.

"Jackie, when you told your grandmother what really happened between you and David Harrison, what was her reaction?"

"She asked me if I was going to tell the police about it."

"Did she ever suggest to you that she didn't believe you?"

"No, not at all. She knew something had happened. She was waiting for me to tell her the truth."

"So even though you had some problems with lying when you first moved in with her, when you told her that David was having a sexual relationship with you, she had no trouble accepting that."

"That's right."

"Okay. Thank you, Jackie. I have nothing further."

It's over. I get down from the witness stand and go in the back where Gran and Lily are sitting. I collapse between them.

"What time is it?" I whisper.

"Half past ten," Gran responds. I feel like I spent a lifetime on that stand but it was actually a little less than an hour.

"Mr. Sable, do you have any more witnesses?" I hear the judge ask.

"No, Your Honor. Prosecution rests."

"Mr. Adler?"

David's lawyer gets up. "Defense rests as well."

"All right. Let's take a quick breather and then go to closing arguments. Ten minutes." The gavel smacks and the courtroom starts buzzing, but I don't make a move. I have no strength left, not even enough to pretend for all the people who are staring at me.

Rick comes up to the row we're sitting in. "You okay, Jackie? You did really well."

I stare blankly at him.

"May we go?" Gran asks.

"I'd like Jackie to stay for closing arguments. And move closer to the front, if she can handle it. That way I can point her out to the jury once more." He looks at Lily. "You need to stay here, though. I don't want the jury reading anything into your presence, because Jackie's comment on cross came really close to getting the whole case thrown out."

"No one looked at me," she says warily.

"It's not worth the risk."

"Can I sit with Jackie?" Ben asks. Rick considers him.

"Yeah, I can live with that. Jackie, what do you think? Ben stays with you up front? All you have to do is stand up when I ask you to."

I nod and get to my feet. Lily stays behind with Gran, who's holding her hand. I feel like we've swapped supporters.

Ben follows me to the front row on Rick's side of the room. We're level with where Alicia was sitting, but she's not there now. She's sitting at David's table, and her hand is on his arm.

Ben deliberately places himself between me and them.

"Thanks," I whisper to him.

"Don't mention it." He doesn't touch me at all, but his presence beside me feels like a having a superhero escort. "It's almost over."

I nod, looking straight ahead.

Almost over.

Chapter Six

JACKIE | **DAVID**

Alicia has barely spoken to me during the trial, except when the jury is watching. She's been giving me performative little hugs or pats here and there, leaning over like she's whispering encouragement in my ear but actually saying nothing. All things Marshall told her to do. I have no idea if it's making any difference or not.

But when the judge calls a recess, Alicia comes over to my table and sits down in the extra chair beside me. Without saying a word, she lays a hand on my arm and I know it's not for the jury this time. It's a genuine gesture of comfort. I look at her gratefully.

"I think Marshall's doing a good job," she says. We both turn toward him.

"Thank you, Alicia. Closing arguments aren't evidence but done right, they can be effective. We'll see how it goes."

I wish I could testify. It feels unnatural to rest our case with not a single word spoken in my defense. I would feel so much better about my chances if the jury could hear from me. I believe in my ability to persuade people.

Lily, though, always Lily. She's the pin in their grenade, but she can't testify unless I do.

Alicia squeezes my hand, then shocks me by kissing me briefly before going back to her seat. Marshall looks almost as surprised as I feel, but there's no time to think about it before the judge calls us back into session.

"All right, Mr. Sable, we'll hear from you first." Rick gets up and straightens his tie, then walks over to the jury.

"I want to thank you all for being here today," he begins. "I know jury duty isn't much fun, and it's never easy to be charged with making a decision when the stakes are so high.

"To me, this case is a good reminder that people aren't divided into black and white as easily as we sometimes like to think. The truth is that David Harrison did do a lot for Jackie in the beginning. By all accounts, including Jackie's, he was an incredibly supportive person to her during a difficult period of transition. It's never easy for a kid to go and live with someone new instead of their parents. Even if it's a much better situation for them.

"Jackie needed all the help and backup she could get and you know what? She got it. She *thrived.* She not only finished her first year of high school with almost straight A's, she was recognized with a statewide award. That's impressive. And David Harrison was a big part of her success. He was her favorite teacher and she was his protégée.

"It's not easy for us to hold a person like that in our head together with the word rapist. I mean, it doesn't fit, right? Rapists are *bad* people, not dedicated teachers. That's part of what makes this kind of crime so difficult to prosecute. It's hard to believe in the first place. Even when people see something that doesn't look right, they try so hard to believe it was something else.

"Matt Mintz is a perfect example. He didn't see a teenager catching a teacher by surprise – he saw a *teenager and a teacher kissing,* period. How do we know? Because he immediately reported it to the principal. Four months after the fact, he's clearly chosen to believe it wasn't what it looked like because he and David Harrison are friends as well as colleagues, and he can't imagine his friend being capable of such a thing. But if that was truly the case, why did he report it?

"Jackie, would you stand up please?" When she does, everyone turns to look at her. Even I do, albeit from the corner of my eye. "This girl is sixteen years old, and she was brave enough to come in here and tell you all the truth about the way this man betrayed her. I can promise you, that wasn't easy for her." He nods at her and she resumes her seat. That boyfriend of Lily's is sitting with her, and he shoots me an evil-looking glance.

"Is she perfect? No. Has she lied before? Yes. But she's not lying about this. Let's remember, she didn't come forward on her own in some misguided ploy for attention. She told the truth eventually, with great reluctance, only after Matt Mintz *saw David Harrison kissing her in a classroom.* At first, she still tried to protect him. She tried to take all the blame on herself because she loved David and she believed he loved her. That's the only reason she lied initially, and it's understandable.

"His manipulation of her was so comprehensive that Jackie *still* believes what happened was her fault. I think that was evident to all of us when she was giving testimony earlier. She feels ashamed of her behavior, and of course, Mr. Adler's questions only underlined her inclination to blame herself. In Jackie's mind, she's the guilty one here, having knowingly slept with a married man.

"You heard this from Detective Keller already, but I'm going to say it again. David Harrison's actions here are practically a how-to guide for becoming a predator. You find a vulnerable victim to groom, make them feel comfortable with you. If you can, let them make the first move, because the real key is to make them believe that everything you do with them is at their own urging. And on top of that, convince them that you love them.

"It takes patience, but if you do this right, that combination is practically a guarantee that they will never tell anyone.

"You know, when I took this case, and Jackie told me what happened to her, she told me she knew she didn't come off too well in the story. And I told her, like I'll tell you now, that isn't the case. I don't think less of Jackie at all. She is a young girl who was seduced by someone she trusted. How can I judge her for believing in him? That's what abusers make you do. And they're good at it. David Harrison is very, very good at it.

"I've seen you all watching him throughout the trial, trying to reconcile the things you've been hearing with the image of the man himself. Let's face it, he doesn't *look* like a criminal. He looks like the nicest guy who ever lived.

"He's been getting away with this for a long time. He went to great lengths to conceal his affair with Jackie, to make sure there would be no physical evidence. He set up his own victim to protest his guilt. It doesn't get much more premeditated or deliberate than that.

"Jackie believed in David Harrison. Me? I believe her. At this point, the only question is whether you believe her too – and whether you will hold him accountable."

He sits down, and Marshall reaches over to pat my shoulder reassuringly before standing up for his turn. He goes and stands exactly where Rick was and assumes the same disarming demeanor he had when he first addressed them yesterday.

"There are times when I don't like my job," he begins. "This would be one of those days. Let me tell you, it's no fun to be the guy who gets up here and tells you not to automatically take a girl like Jackie Culver at her word. As I told you in the beginning, it's not my intent to make her feel any worse about herself." He looks over at Jackie solemnly. "I'm sorry if it seemed like my questions were doing that." He returns his attention to the jury.

"Cards on the table? I have a fifteen year old daughter. And if she told me one of her teachers did something like what David Harrison's been accused of…" He shakes his head. "I'd do what any of you would do. I'd believe her and I'd leap into action to protect her, because I'm her dad." I watch several of the jurors nodding.

I didn't know about Marshall's daughter. He must think I'm a real prick, but I have to admit he hasn't let it get in the way of his job.

"So I'm not surprised Jackie's grandmother believed her, not a bit. And it's understandable if *you* want to believe her. Of course you don't want to blow off the word of a nice girl when she tells you that something terrible happened to her. That's a good impulse, a kind one.

"But we aren't Jackie's parents, are we? We have a different role here. This isn't an opinion poll you're filling out on Facebook. This is a man's life, and you people have the unfortunate but necessary duty of deciding whether or not there is enough *evidence* here to send him to prison.

"And the facts are these: There is *no* physical evidence. None whatsoever. No fluids belonging to Jackie were found anywhere that she claimed to have had intercourse with David. No cell phone records indicate that they ever sent each other messages or photos.

"The evidence we do have essentially amounts to Jackie's word. Yes, Detective Keller believed Jackie. And I fully respect her opinion as a detective. But again, her belief is not based on any physical evidence her team was able to find. At the end of the day, Detective Keller's opinion is not proof. She doesn't know for sure any more than you do.

"Then we have Matt Mintz, who witnessed Jackie kissing David. Well, we don't dispute that happened. But as Jackie herself told you, *she* initiated that kiss. Not David. Does it make sense to you that if they really were having a relationship, and David had taken steps to ensure that it was this immaculate, he would have let her kiss him in a classroom? Does it ring true that he would take a risk like that after going to such lengths to keep himself above suspicion?

"And let's not forget – Matt himself isn't even sure they were kissing. His sworn testimony, *under oath,* was that he couldn't be certain.

"Finally, we have Jackie herself." Marshall pauses for effect. "When she was testifying, it was pretty clear to me that she cares deeply for David. I don't think she wants to hurt him. So yes, we have to ask ourselves why a good kid like this would come into a courtroom and testify against a man we can all see that she loves. I know that makes us want to accept her word.

"But we also heard that she has some issues when it comes to telling the truth, didn't we? She's had some problems with honesty in the past. Again, I've got a daughter. I understand that kids lie sometimes. None of us want to think that she could be lying about this, but are you *sure* she isn't?

"Can you be completely positive, beyond all reasonable doubt? That's the burden that Jackie's testimony has to meet. And that means if there's any suspicion whatsoever in your mind that what she told you is not true, you have no choice but to find my client not guilty. You can feel all the sympathy in the world for her, and whatever turn of events in her life might have predisposed her to this awful situation. But for the purposes of this trial, you *have* to weigh her credibility. Nothing else matters, because that is all the prosecution has offered you in the way of proof.

"And it's not enough." He pans his eyes slowly across the jury, making eye contact with each of them in turn. "No matter how much you might want it to be."

After he lets the words hang for a moment, he comes to sit back down beside me. I marvel again at his ability to make such a good case for me when he knew all along I was guilty.

The judge gives a long instruction to the jury and dismisses them to deliberate. Alicia comes back to the table. Marshall turns towards us, but Rick comes over before he can speak.

"Marshall. A word?"

The two men step away to have a brief, hushed conversation. Marshall returns within a minute.

"Rick is still willing to offer you the deal from before," he informs me. "Fourteen months."

I run my hands through my hair. "What do you think?" I ask him.

"It's close," he says. "Very close."

"You tried a great case."

"I always do my best, David. No matter what hand I'm dealt." He raises his eyebrows at me. "Going to verdict would be the biggest gamble you'd ever take in your entire life. But it might pay off. You could walk away from this." He sighs. "Or you could end up going to prison for the next five years. Or you can accept the middle road, and never know for sure what the outcome would have been."

Silence reigns for at least a minute. How the hell am I supposed to decide something like this?

"Alicia?" I ask. As I turn to her, the last twelve years of marriage open her thoughts to me once more. I know this woman better than anyone else in the world, whether she still wants me to or not.

Before she even speaks, I know what her answer is going to be.

Chapter Seven

JACKIE | *DAVID*

"I want to take it back," I whisper.

We're back at the house, me and Lily. Rick said there was no point in staying. We have no way of knowing how long it will be before the jury has a verdict.

I'm not sure where Gran went, but she's been gone for more than an hour.

"I know," Lily says. We're sitting on the sofa bed and she's brushing my hair.

"I want to call him."

"You don't have his number," she points out.

"I could go over there."

"Alicia."

"Right." I run my hand over Archie's back. "What the hell is wrong with me?"

"Nothing."

"No. Something's wrong with me. How could I even be thinking this way anymore?" I stare at my phone, fighting an urge to bring up the photo of me and David. I would sell my soul to go back to that day.

"Nothing's wrong with you, Jackie. How could you not feel torn up right now? This morning was the literal worst. I hope you never have to do anything harder." She turns my shoulders so I'm looking at her. "I'm still not sure I could have done it, even now. It's unbelievable that you could do it at sixteen. I'm beyond proud of you, and so are Isabel and Ben."

"I'm jealous of you, Lily," I confess when I'm facing forward again. She starts twisting my hair into a complex braid.

"Why?"

"Because you have Ben. And he's so good to you."

"You'll have someone good too, Jackie. I bet you'll have guys beating down our door in Portland. Ben's going to have to buy a shotgun."

The mental image of Ben interrogating one of my dates is almost enough to make me smile. He totally would, too. "I doubt it. I'm not the kind of girl guys like."

"I wasn't either. Trust me, that will change at some point. High school is bullshit for meeting people."

"I can't wait to get out of here," I say. "I want to forget this ever happened. I almost wish I'd never moved here. But then I wouldn't have met you."

"That's what life is about, taking the good with the bad." Lily shifts my head a bit. "I know it's hard to imagine right now, but we *are* going to get through this. A year from now, it'll be in the past. You'll be in a different place where no one is going to know about it except the people *you* choose to tell."

We don't talk for several more minutes. She finishes my hair. I tell her it looks good, and it does. But there doesn't seem to be anything else to say.

I have no idea how long it is before Gran comes back, but she comes straight over to the sofa bed where we're sitting in silence.

"David rejected the plea again."

Lily sighs but I wait for the rest of what Gran has to say. I know there's more.

"And the jury has a verdict."

Lily closes her eyes and clasps my shoulder. My breathing immediately becomes irregular and my thoughts scatter uncontrollably.

Everything is about to change.

"This is it, girls. Let's get going. I've already called Ben, he'll meet us there."

"Oh my God," I keep repeating. "Oh God. Oh my God. I can't breathe, Gran." We drive back to the courthouse, Lily and I curled against each other in the backseat. By the time we arrive, fear has stiffened my muscles to the point where I can barely move.

We maneuver slowly back to the courtroom where Mrs. Connell is waiting there for us. I almost forgot that she's been here the whole time. Watching and waiting.

"How long were they out for?" Ben asks as he comes up to us.

"Rick says about two hours," Gran replies. She and Lily are each holding one of my hands, and Ben is holding Lily's. We must look ridiculous, lined up like first graders.

David comes in about then, and walks right past us on the way back to his table. He looks scared now, and I've never seen him that way. He's always been so perfectly in command of every situation, of me. But even though I can't see his face, the tight set of his shoulders and the rigid way he walks to the front give him away.

What have I done?

I'm seized by a crazy urge to run up there and tell the judge that I was lying about everything. All of it. But I'm anchored in place by Lily and Gran. Their hands feel like cement blocks around my own.

There's no way out of this. If he gets convicted, I'm going to feel like I'm in prison right along with him. And if he gets away with it... if I went through all that for nothing...

"All rise." We're already standing, of course.

The judge looks over. "Madame Forewoman, the jury has reached a unanimous verdict?"

"Yes, Your Honor."

"Read it to the court, please."

The lady bends over the microphone and clears her throat. "In this matter, the State of Oregon versus David Harrison, on the first count of rape in the third degree, we find the defendant, David Harrison, not guilty."

My knees turn to jelly and Lily's breath rushes out of her.

"No," she says, her voice barely audible. I can't speak.

"On the second count, sexual abuse in the second degree, we find the defendant not guilty."

"Jesus Christ," Ben murmurs.

"And on the third and final count, sexual abuse in the third degree, we find the defendant not guilty."

The final verdict echoes across my heart like a gunshot.

For a split second, everything is silent. Then the courtroom explodes into chaos. Everyone starts talking, but my legs have given out and I'm on the floor. Lily sinks down with me, and the two of us are fully beyond words.

"Order!" the judge calls, pounding his gavel. "Members of the jury, we appreciate your service. David Harrison is free to go. Court is adjourned." Just like that, it's all over.

It's pandemonium in here but I can't hear anything except a faint buzzing noise.

"It was all for nothing," I hear someone say. Then I realize it's me.

Reporters are rushing up to me now, getting in my face. I feel two pairs of hands lifting me off the floor and as I rise, I see David. For the first time since the trial started, our eyes lock.

And he grins at me like this was the plan all along.

Like the two of us have gotten away with murder. Together.

"I'm going to throw up," I say. "I need to get out of here, now."

I can hear Ben and Mrs. Connell shouting, trying to clear a path for me. I feel them pulling me from the room into the somewhat less crowded hallway. Mrs. Connell's hand feels gentle but strong around my elbow and before long I'm in the bathroom. I run into the nearest stall and surrender.

When I emerge a few minutes later, Lily is bent over the sink splashing water over her face. Mrs. Connell is standing nearby with her head in her hands. And Gran…

I've never seen my grandmother cry. Not once. Not even on the day of my grandpa's funeral when I was only six years old. That's not Gran. She's a very private person and she doesn't let go like that, no matter the situation.

But she's crying now. And somehow her silent tears are scarier to me than waiting for the verdict was. It makes me start to cry too. Gran holds out her arms and I fling myself into them.

"It was all for nothing, Gran," I wail.

"No, darling," she says, rubbing my back. "You were so brave. It wasn't for nothing. You told the truth. That's worth something, even if the jury couldn't see it."

"Excuse me?" I hear a small, timid voice behind me and turn to find a familiar-looking woman.

"What? What do you want?" I ask, irrationally freaked out.

"I don't know if you recognize me. I was on the jury," she says. "And I wanted to say how sorry I am."

I wipe my eyes and let go of Gran as I turn to face the woman. "Why… why didn't you believe me?" I can barely get the question out before I start sobbing again.

"I did, Jackie. I did. A lot of the others did too. Personally, I voted to convict him. And I wasn't alone."

"So what happened?" I pull a rough paper towel from a cheap-looking dispenser and rub it against my face. Lily comes over to stand next to me.

"Some of the others… they just couldn't quite get there. Not without any kind of evidence apart from what you told us."

"They thought I was a liar, you mean." I twist the paper towel in my hand.

"It was more like they couldn't be sure. I was sure, but some of the others weren't. And it has to be unanimous for a conviction. We tried to compromise, get them to convict him on the least serious charge. But they wouldn't budge." She looks devastated. "I'm so sorry. I know that doesn't help much. Maybe it doesn't help at all. But I believe you. And I'm sorry he hurt you in such a horrible way."

"Thank you," I whisper. I motion to Lily. "He raped her, too. Only you didn't get to hear about it. The judge wouldn't let her testify."

The woman's face comes alive with anger. "I thought there might be someone... because of what you said. But we weren't allowed to discuss that possibility. I'm sure it would have made the difference for the jurors who voted to acquit him."

"Yeah," Lily says thickly. Her eyes are swollen. We all stand there for a few minutes. I can't stop thinking about the way David was smiling at me.

Finally, the woman moves toward the door. "I'll leave you alone now. I just wanted to tell you that. I hope you can find a way to move forward from here."

I can't think of a reply because I don't see that happening. Ever.

When the four of us are alone again, I look over at Lily. She's glancing at her phone.

"We should go," she says. "Ben offered to either get us all drunk or go to their house and set his car on fire, one of the two. He said to let Jackie choose."

A surprising bark of laughter escapes from me as I pull another towel from the dispenser, and even Gran manages to smile.

We start making our way outside. Sometime between the juror's revelation and Ben's attempt at a joke, Gran stopped crying.

I'm glad. I can't stand to see her cry.

part three

fall

three years later

Chapter One

JACKIE | *DAVID*

"You're definitely coming this weekend?"

"Yes, Gran, I promise." I'm late for class, and shove a book in my bag. "I'll be there. Why are you freaking out?"

"Make sure to bring Lily with you," Gran says, ignoring my question.

"I don't think she can come this time. She's swamped with wedding stuff."

"Tell her I insist. And remind her that I'm officiating the ceremony." Gran's voice is light, but I can tell she's serious.

"Okay, Gran, I'll tell her. I've got to go, I'm crazy late."

"Good-bye, darling. Have a good class."

I click off my phone and put it in my pocket.

"I'm leaving, big boy," I say, patting Peanut's head. His name is a joke – my dog is enormous. We think he's some kind of mastiff mix. I found him at the pound last year and immediately fell for him.

The bedroom I still rent from Ben and Lily is ludicrously small for us, and Ben's told me a number of times that he won't increase my rent even if I move to one of the bigger rooms, but I've never seen the need. Peanut and I do fine in here.

I'm doing fine here.

It's ridiculous how fast the last three years have gone. At first I was afraid that the instant bond Lily and I formed in David's wake would somehow wear off after his acquittal. I don't know which of us took that harder, but I can barely remember moving in here a couple of days later. We both went into something like a living coma that took months to wear off.

For my part, I couldn't stop internalizing the verdict. Despite what that one juror said, it felt like they had declared him innocent. Which made me endlessly question whether I should have gone through with it in the first place. Only Lily could pull me out of that rabbit hole.

But she struggled too. She spent countless hours haunted by the difference her testimony could have made, no matter how many times I reminded her that she wasn't given a choice. It's not like she chickened out.

It was a process for both of us, a long one, and we needed each other to survive it. After a while, I actually started to fear the survival itself. By Thanksgiving we were slowly starting to enjoy things again, and I was so scared she wouldn't need me anymore. That I'd be left behind again, this time for good.

I shouldn't have worried. It didn't happen overnight but at this point, my relationship with Lily transcends David. We have our own history now, and Ben is a crucial part of it. That feeling I had during the trial, that we were almost like a family – it wasn't a fluke. Lily and Ben look out for me the way I imagine older siblings would.

The best part is that they *chose* me. I've never doubted Gran's love, but during one of our visits while I was listening to her talk excitedly about a party she was throwing, I realized that I must have been kind of a drag on her when I was younger. It's a good thing that didn't occur to me sooner. When I moved in with Gran, I worried constantly about what I would do if she died. I never

would have been able to relax enough to call her house my home if
I'd also felt like a burden on her.

Living here, though, I have no such worries. This is a house
where I carry my weight. I've even been paying my own rent since
I became legally emancipated two years ago. Lily and Ben say I'm
a great roommate and considering some of the people who have
cycled in and out of here, I'm now in a position to agree with
them. The three of us, plus Archie and Peanut – we're solid. For
once in my life, I'm on the inside of something. It's other people
who come and go.

Ben even let me help him when he proposed to Lily last spring.

Other things got better once I graduated high school. I finished
in the top ten percent of my class, which wasn't hard since I didn't
do much besides work and study. My occasional efforts to make a
friend my own age never ended well. Everyone assumed that living
on my own meant I would be glad to host a never-ending party,
which got old, and my colossal trust issues didn't help either.

The classes themselves were easy, but attending them – not so
much. David clung to me like a persistent ghost, and it didn't take
much to trigger deeply conflicting memories of him.

Never once during my final years in high school did I allow
myself to be alone with a male teacher.

It was a huge relief to put that behind me. I had Lily and Ben
and my job at a local restaurant where the head chef was training
me to be her assistant, and that was basically enough, but it was
a pretty small life. I only enrolled in community college because I
have my eye on culinary school eventually.

I assumed college would be another thing I'd have to survive to
get to the good part, but to my surprise it's actually going okay and
I'm even starting to get out more. Lily always tells me that it's fine
to take things slowly, so I am. But at least I'm finally an adult, and
acting like one doesn't make me feel so freakish anymore.

***

"Why does she want me there so bad?" Lily asks.

"No clue," I reply as I inhale leftover Chinese. I got off work about twenty minutes ago, and I'm starving. "She just said it was important and to make sure you came. Oh, and she threatened the wedding if you didn't."

Ben laughs. "Classic Isabel."

"Speaking of which, did you drop off the deposit check?" Lily asks him.

"Yes. I even went to get measured for my tux. Do I get extra credit for that?"

"It's so unfair," I remark. "Guys can *rent* tuxes."

"Wedding dress rentals are a thing," Lily says. "But my dress was pretty cheap anyway."

"Only because you look disgustingly gorgeous in literally everything." I finish bolting down my meal. "If I ever get married, I'm eloping. Probably in jeans."

"I'm going to be your witness and wear Armani, just to screw with you," Ben says.

"What makes you think I'd even tell you?"

"Like I wouldn't find out. Hey, if you don't want me reading your diary, stop leaving it under your mattress."

"Why do we keep this guy around again?" I ask Lily.

She smiles. "He's good eye candy."

"Plus, you're both hopeless at doing anything around the house more complicated than changing a lightbulb," Ben adds.

"Fine." I shrug. "If that's how you feel, I guess I don't have to make tiramisu for your birthday next week."

"Wait, did you say tiramisu? I take it back. I grovel. Please make tiramisu. I'll do anything."

I nod sternly. "Much better."

"Your cooking is like the ring. It makes you way too powerful. Come to think of it, isn't that why *you* still live here?"

I throw the takeout carton at him. "I'm taking the dogs for a walk. Anyone want to come?"

"I ran fifteen miles today," Ben replies. "I'm good."

"No one needs to hear your bragging, Ben."

"I'll go with you," Lily says. "I've been chained to my desk doing paperwork all day." Lily started working with veterans as a support coordinator last year.

We spend most of the walk talking about wedding plans. I had no idea weddings were so much work, but it's fun too. I love seeing Lily get so excited about it.

"How's Isabel doing?" she asks me.

"She's good. Actually, I think she's seeing someone." I grin. "Hey, I wonder if that's why she wants us to come down this weekend."

"That'd be great if she was," Lily says.

Like I said, Gran seems to have picked up right where she left off without missing a beat. I don't even worry about her being alone anymore, because she seems perfectly content.

I haven't kept in touch with anyone else since I moved. I ended up blocking Nicki on Instagram, which still makes me feel guilty since she never did anything bad to me. In fact, she tried to text me a bunch of times before David's trial started. But I couldn't talk to her about that at the time, and afterward she was too strongly linked in my mind with that whole horrible year. I needed to move on without her and I never did come up with a way to explain that.

"I've been meaning to ask, do you ever hear from your dad anymore?" Lily asks.

"Nope. It seemed to get harder for him to remember who I was with every passing year. He didn't even know I'd moved to Portland until I'd been here for months. I think he's officially out now."

"What an asshole."

"Honestly? I don't even care. There's nothing I need from him anymore," I add as I stoop down to pet the dogs. I'm careful to give them both equal attention, so neither one gets jealous.

***

"Hello!" I call. "We're here, what's the big emergency?" Lily follows me in and sets down her overnight bag.

"Hi, girls." Gran comes out of the kitchen, and I can see immediately that I misjudged the purpose of this visit. She seems weighted down by something.

"What's wrong?" I ask, suddenly worried.

"I have something to tell you two. It wasn't news for the phone." Gran hesitates. "It's about David." I flinch at the sound of his name.

"Great. Hang on a second," Lily says. "I get the feeling I'm going to need a glass of wine for this conversation. Jackie?"

"Sure." I sit down on the worn sofa and pull my legs up under me, wishing Peanut was here. Gran sits across from me, but we don't speak.

Lily returns from the kitchen with two glasses of wine and hands one to me. "All right, Isabel, I'm ready," she says, sitting beside me. "What's going on with David?"

Gran's face is somber. "The short version? He's accepted a plea bargain for possession of child pornography. Twelve years."

"*What?*" Lily cries.

"I don't understand," I say, feeling a cold chill hit in my chest that's going to last for hours. "How?"

"Apparently, David's teaching license was revoked for a year once Kathryn fired him. But it seems after that year was over, he reapplied and somehow managed to charm the commission into giving him a second chance. He and Alicia started working at a new school. She went back to teaching as well." She pauses for a moment to let us absorb everything.

David back in the classroom. I've spent the last three years convincing myself that wasn't a possibility for him anymore.

"So what happened?" Lily whispers.

"Everything was fine for a while. And then a few weeks ago, another student reported him. Her story was almost exactly the same as what happened with the two of you." Neither of us can formulate a response. "With one notable difference. This time, David took photos of the girl."

"You're kidding," I say.

"No. He never did that with you, did he?"

"Definitely not," Lily replies. I shake my head silently.

"I suppose he felt invincible after the trial."

"Can you blame him?" I mutter. I take a drink of wine, even though I already feel sick.

"The photos were apparently rather explicit. This girl eventually told her mother what happened, and when they searched his house they found all of them."

"How many were there?" I ask, wondering where he could have taken them. In the woods?

"Almost forty. Twelve years was actually not a bad deal for him. As I understand it, he could have gotten as long as two years per image. Then of course, there were the sexual assault charges on top of that."

"How did you hear about this?" Lily asks.

"That was another shock," she says. "Alicia turned up on my doorstep two days ago."

"No way."

"She told me what happened. Then…" Gran reaches for an unmarked envelope on the coffee table I hadn't noticed. "She asked me to pass this on to you, Jackie."

"Why didn't she reach out to me herself?"

"If I had to guess, I would say she's too ashamed to face you." Gran hands me the small sealed manila envelope. I feel like I'm accepting a bomb.

"What is it?"

"I don't know. I asked her, but she said it was something only you had a right to see, and I wanted to respect that." She pauses. "I hope I did the right thing."

I nod absently, feeling around the edges of the envelope. My fingers locate hard corners. There's something in here besides a note.

"I don't like this, Lily," I murmur. "There's something bad in here." Did I block this out somehow? Did he actually take pictures of me and I don't remember? What else could this possibly be?

"He's in prison now, darling," Gran says quietly. "He's not going to hurt you or anyone else again."

"You don't have to open it if you don't want to," Lily adds.

"Yes I do," I say, trying to sound braver than I feel. "I need to know." I turn the envelope over in my hands, take a deep breath, and break the seal.

A single sheet of paper falls onto my lap, wrapped around two Polaroid photographs that are facing inward and taped to each other. I'm guessing Alicia did that so I wouldn't see them by mistake, which strikes me as deeply thoughtful under the circumstances.

I unfold the note while Gran and Lily watch me, and read the handwritten words to myself first.

Jackie,

If you're reading this, I assume Isabel told you what happened.

I found these after David was arrested. They were hidden in a place the police missed during their search. I thought that you should be the one to decide what to do with them now.

Alicia

I guess she didn't leave him after the trial. Lily and I spent hours debating that one.

I hand the note to Lily and slowly run a fingernail underneath the tape sealing the two photos together. My heart is pounding at least as hard as it did when I was testifying against him.

I pry the photos apart, tilting them toward me so that Gran won't see them. I set the right on top of the left, wanting to deal with them one at a time, and inhale sharply.

David's bedroom is instantly recognizable by the blue sheets. The lighting isn't great but it's sufficient to leave nothing to the imagination. I'm completely naked in the photo, clearly asleep underneath a sheet that only comes up to my thighs. My arms are crossed over my head.

What the actual fuck?

I quickly swap the photos. The second shows me in his shower, from behind. I thought their open-concept bathroom was so weird at the time, but now I see that there was at least one benefit to it. He could take a picture of me from across the room without me ever knowing.

It's not as sickening as the first one, mostly because it's hazier. But it's bad enough.

"Okay," I say when my voice returns at last. "So. When I said he never took pictures of me… that wasn't a hundred percent accurate." I close my eyes, but it's way too late. Those images are never going away.

"Where?" Gran asks, her face stony. "When?"

"These were taken at his house. The night I slept over there."

"You didn't know?"

"No." Lily's been averting her eyes respectfully, but I pass her the photos now. I don't want anyone else to see them, ever, but we're in this together. "I'm asleep in one of them. And he took the other one when my back was turned. I had no idea."

All I can think about is how differently things would have

ended if I'd known these photos existed during the trial. He would have been convicted, and this other girl wouldn't have gotten hurt. I can hear Lily thinking the same thing next to me as she pulls the photos apart and looks at them.

Now I know exactly how it felt when she found out about me.

"It looks like…" Her voice catches. "This one looks almost like he posed you."

I take the first photo back and examine it again. Shit, she's right. I didn't even notice that, but the way I'm positioned is totally unnatural. I've never slept that way in my life.

He didn't exactly have a hard time talking me into sleeping naked with him. By that point in the evening, I was all about it. The idea excited me.

I'm sure he liked it for the same reasons I did. But apparently I was also posing for his sick little porn collection and I didn't even know it.

He was so adamant that we never do pictures, ever, not even when we were sexting. What the hell did he say to this poor girl to convince her to take *forty* photos? Did she even have a choice?

What has he become in the last three years?

Chapter Two

JACKIE | **DAVID**

The best he can do, Marshall says.

"It's a good result, David." He looks at me wearily. "I seem to recall urging you to get some counseling, after the first time."

"You wouldn't understand."

"I don't especially want to." He sifts through his briefcase. "Questions?"

"How long do I stay here?"

"Until sentencing. The district attorney and I agreed, but the judge still has to sign off." He pauses. "Danielle will probably be making a victim impact statement, so prepare yourself for that."

Of course she will. She's a *victim* now. "And then where do I go?"

"You'll be transferred to Two Rivers. It's in Umatilla, a few hours north of here. Minimum security."

"And you're positive there's no other way out of this?"

"Quite certain, yes. You were lucky the first time. This time there's proof, which means a guaranteed conviction. Twelve years is more than fair. The only reason you avoided federal distribution charges is because there's no proof you intended to share the photos."

"I didn't." They were only for me. And for her.

"Small mercies. Compared to federal facilities, Rivers isn't too bad from what I've heard."

"Any advice?"

He sighs. "You're immediately going to be assimilated into the general population. Forget everything you've ever been to anyone in your life – none of that matters in prison. No one is going to give a damn about you. You're a number now."

Got it. I'm Jean Valjean. Dani would have appreciated the irony.

"Inmates like to cozy up to the newcomers, because they're scared and they tend to say a lot more than they should. Do not trust anyone, no matter how sympathetic they seem. The fewer people who find out what you're there for, the safer you'll be."

"Can they find out if I don't tell them?"

"They have their ways. Yeah."

"So how exactly am I supposed to avoid getting ass-raped my first day there?" I've never been a physically impressive guy, to say the least. I was routinely mistaken for a student until I was almost thirty.

"I can try to get you protective custody, but that's normally meant to be temporary. You're in this for the long haul. My best advice is to make some friends."

Friends? Is he kidding?

"The more people you can get on your side, ideally before they find out what you did, the better your chances. I'm not saying your chances are *good*, mind you. This is not a pleasant experience you're about to embark on here. And don't forget about the first rule. Never trust anyone with more detail than you can get away with."

For the first time in my life, I'm contemplating suicide. It seems preferable in a lot of ways. I'll have to give that one some serious thought tonight.

"Have you heard from Alicia?" I ask.

Marshall nods. "She asked me if I knew any good divorce

attorneys. Can't say that was much of a shock."

"I'm surprised she didn't already file. She moved out months ago." Nothing was ever the same between us after the trial, but she stayed with me until recently. I don't know why.

"Guess you'll need to ask her about that."

"At this point, I doubt I'm ever going to see her again."

"I think you might. She's in the waiting room."

"Here? Now?"

Marshall nods. "Should I send her in?"

"Sure." I don't have a clue what this is about, since I have no intention of contesting the divorce.

Marshall gets up. "I'll be back next week to see how you're doing. And I need you to authorize me to go to your house and find you some clothes for sentencing."

"Fine. Alicia should have the key, if you want to get it from her."

He nods and takes off, giving me the feeling he's relieved to be done with me. A few moments later, my wife strolls in looking profoundly gratified.

"Nice to see you where you belong, David."

"What do you want, Alicia?"

"To savor the moment."

I roll my eyes. "You're the one who believed me the first time."

"Yeah. I guess that was pretty stupid of me, wasn't it?" Her voice is hard. "I chose to believe that my husband of eight years *hadn't* been throat fucking one of my students right under my nose. I thought you were a better person than that. But you know what, David? Deep down, I knew you really weren't. And as soon as Jackie came forward, I was sure."

"Then why did you stay?"

The way she smiles sends a chill through me.

"Because I wanted to take care of you myself."

"Meaning what?"

"I was hoping you'd be convicted the first time, naturally. That's why I told you not to go for the plea bargain. A year wasn't even close to being punishment enough. I thought the jury would have seen what was right in front of their faces. But it didn't work out that way."

"So you decided to take matters into your own hands."

"That's right. I considered a lot of different things. I thought of slipping estrogen into your coffee. I thought of disappearing with Maggie so you'd never know what happened to us. I thought of arranging for you to come home and find *me* screwing someone else in our bed." She shrugs. "But none of that would have been enough. You needed to *pay* for what you did to those girls. And after a while, I realized that if I gave you enough time, you would do the dirty work for me."

"*That's* why you didn't leave me?"

"Well, partly. The rest took longer than I thought it would."

"Enlighten me." I clench my fists.

"I've been systematically draining our assets over the last three years and storing them in various places unconnected to either one of us. In other words, they're no longer marital property. On paper, we have nothing to split except a house that's close to worthless now, because I cashed out most of the home equity line." She giggles. "Oh, and I ran up almost twenty thousand dollars of debt on your old credit card. The one you had before we were married, remember? Then I let you go delinquent on the payments. When you do get out of here, you're going to be broke, and your credit will be trashed."

I can only sit there. Stunned.

I really should have seen this coming. My wife has always had a taste for revenge. When she was a kid, her best friend started some nasty rumor about her. To retaliate, Alicia invited her and a number of other friends to her house for a sleepover. Once her friend had fallen asleep, she surreptitiously planted two cups of fake blood in her sleeping bag. By the time the girl woke up in the morning, she was practically covered in it.

Those were the days before cell phone cameras, but it didn't matter. The story was all over school in a matter of hours, according to Alicia.

I think she was eleven then. She clearly hasn't changed much, except to quietly become even more vindictive. This one must have been only too easy. She's always handled our finances, ever since we first got together.

I gave her everything she needed to bury me.

"I'll hire a lawyer. I'll tell him everything you're telling me now."

"You'll have a real job proving any of it. I made the credit card purchases online, from your laptop. No signatures. The money I took from our joint accounts was all legitimate. The bank doesn't care what you do with it once it's gone." She grins. "Besides, lawyers usually want money. Remember? I'm not even sure how you're going to pay Marshall what you owe him. But that's your problem, not mine."

"Wow." I can't even begin to think how to respond to this.

"I'm not finished. Didn't you ever wonder why Danielle suddenly decided to go to her mom?"

Only every second of every day since my life went to hell a few weeks ago.

"She didn't."

"What's that supposed to mean?"

"I hid a motion-activated camera near the entrance to our bedroom when I moved out," she explains. I cover my face with my hands and groan. "I was pretty sure you were screwing her by then. And based on what Jackie had to say, I figured you'd start using our house as a playground the minute I was gone. Sure enough, within a week you were starting to bring her over. From there, it was pretty simple to set up a dummy email account and send her mother a clip of you two walking into our room." She chuckles again. "I didn't even know *you'd* been taking pictures of her. That was so perfect. Just like I thought you would, you ended up hanging yourself."

"I'm going to prison for *twelve years* because you couldn't just divorce me like a normal person?"

Her tone changes to one of horrible faux-sympathy. "It's awful, isn't it? But the really important thing for you to remember, David, is that you're going to prison because you can't seem to keep your dick out of teenage girls." Then her face turns serious for the first time. "You are scum. I wish I'd never laid eyes on you. Whatever happens to you next, I want you to remember that you deserve it *all.* Every last minute of it."

Chapter Three

JACKIE | DAVID

In the end, it's Lily's suggestion. We've been sitting up together for hours, like we have so many nights before.

"We could go see him."

I get up to watch the rain coursing down the window, my back stiff after sitting in one place for so long. The gears in my brain are grinding together painfully, still attempting to process everything.

"I wish we'd brought Peanut." I know that's not an answer. "He's good at calming me down."

"He gets carsick. Anyway, we didn't know we needed him."

I return to the armchair, sinking into it. My eyes drift toward the photos, which are upside down on the coffee table. Every detail of what happened between me and David moments after he took the shower photo has been playing on a repeat loop in my brain for hours.

"I wonder how many times he looked at those," I say to Lily, who's slumped over on the arm of the couch. "You really want to go see him?"

She shrugs. "All I can think right now is… I'm getting married. And you're in college and you're doing so well. This is supposed to be a *good* time for us. We're supposed to have paid our dues on all this shit, and here we go again." She shakes her head. "I know there's nothing he can say that would change anything, but I still want to know what the hell he *will* say. I need some kind of resolution here."

"You feel like you're ready to see him? I'm not sure I am."

"Oh, it's not a matter of being ready. I'll never be ready for that."

I nod toward the pictures. "Seeing these brought it all back. All my memories of him, of that night. Only they feel completely different now." I take a deep breath. I've never told anyone this, not even Lily. "I know how fucked up this is, but until tonight, a little part of me was glad I had that night with him. I was *glad* it happened before I knew how wrong it was. Am I the sickest person ever?"

"No." Lily sits up. "I know what you mean, Jackie. I went through the same thing. It's hard to think of something as rape when it gave you pleasure at the time."

I nod. We haven't talked about this for at least a year. It feels strange. "I remember this one day, we were driving around and he played me a song by that old band, The Cure. He told me it was his and Alicia's wedding song, which I thought was a little weird. On several levels. But I loved it, though."

Lily covers her mouth with one hand.

"What?"

She holds up a finger, and I wait as she picks up her phone. A few seconds later, a song starts playing and my mouth falls open.

"That sick *fuck*," I whisper.

"You know, for an English teacher, he wasn't very original."

I scratch at a tear on the edge of Gran's couch. "You never told me that."

"I haven't thought about it for years. And he didn't tell me it was their wedding song. Jesus." We listen in silence for about thirty seconds before Lily turns it off, shaking her head in disgust.

"I must have listened to that song two hundred times the first week after he slept with me. I thought it was *romantic,*" I sneer.

"And now?" Lily asks.

"Now…" I shudder and reach for a blanket. "When I saw the pictures, all I could think about was how fucking *young* I looked."

"Same here."

"And that was what he *wanted.* That's what he liked about us. That's what got him…" I groan, pulling the blanket over my head so it covers my mouth and muffles my speech. "God, I can't even say it. It feels so dirty now."

"Well. It was."

My skin is crawling. "I'm not sure I can see him, Lily. I'm scared. What if I feel the same way I did then?"

"You won't," she says confidently. "You're starting to see this for what it was. If you saw him again, you'd feel the same way you did when you saw the photos. The way I felt when I saw him in the café."

"What if I don't?" I ask, my worst fear surfacing. "What if I still *want* him?"

"Here's the thing," Lily says slowly. "I think I need to do this, or at least try. But that doesn't mean you have to do it too. There's no law that says we have to cope with this delightful new information in exactly the same way."

"No, there isn't." Even as I say it, though, I know I can't hide from this forever. "But yeah, I'll go with you. I'll never know for sure unless I see him and besides…"

Lily plays with her ring, sliding it up and down her finger. "Besides?"

I get up from the chair and go over to the couch where she's sitting. I move the photos aside and sit down on the coffee table across from her.

"You showed up for me back then, when I needed you most. I'm not going to let you face him alone now."

"Okay." Despite what she said, Lily looks relieved. "Thank

you."

I reach for my own phone to Google visiting hours at the county jail. Alicia told Gran he would be held there for a few weeks before he was transferred to prison. After a moment, I burst out laughing. Lily looks startled.

"What?"

I hold up my phone. "I wasn't really looking for a sign, but I guess I got one anyway." Lily peers at the screen. "He's allowed to have a maximum of two visitors at a time."

***

We drive there the following morning. At one point, I wrench my hand from the steering wheel and rest it on Lily's.

"Don't forget our rule."

Lily is busy gouging her palms with her fingernails. "Oh, you mean that only one of us gets to freak out at a time?" We made that rule years ago, not long after the trial. One night, Lily wryly noted that we seemed to be taking turns falling apart, and we'd decided that was the way to go. That way, we could always look after each other. "I think we can allow ourselves a one-day exemption on that, under the circumstances." Lily looks out the window. "I'm surprised Isabel didn't try to talk us out of this."

"Me too," I say. "Guess she figures we're both adults now. We can make our own decisions. And/or huge mistakes, should the day take that turn. Which it probably will."

"Loving the optimism."

I pull up to the jail. We applied for a visitation permit in the wee hours of the morning, before we could lose our nerve. What the application couldn't tell us was whether David would agree to see us or not.

I'm not sure which outcome terrifies me more.

We make our way to the visitor center desk and I feel my throat web immediately when I tell the attendant who we're there to see. He tells us to have a seat while he notifies the jailhouse staff that we're here.

It seems like only seconds pass before he stands up and says, "You two can come on back."

"Relaxed security," I mutter to Lily.

"I'm sure it's tighter at the state prison," she says back. Oddly, she now looks much calmer than I feel.

Good.

I surrender my keys and we follow the guard through a long hallway of identical keypad doors. Eventually he swipes his badge to get us into what looks like a cross between an atrium and a school cafeteria. It has round tables and benches bolted to the floor, and a metal staircase leading to a catwalk which circles the room and leads to still more locked doors.

"Have a seat," he says. "A guard will bring the inmate down shortly."

We sit at one of the tables and wait. I keep my hands under the table so David can't see how badly they're shaking, or how many marks they bear from tearing at my own cuticles. He's always been way too observant when it comes to that kind of thing.

I wish again that my dog was with me.

Before long, we hear a loud beep and a clank, and turn to look.

A guard is bringing David over to us.

Chapter Four

JACKIE | **DAVID**

I haven't had the energy to do much in the wake of Alicia's incendiary admission. I've been laying on my prison mattress staring at the ceiling, indulging in elaborate revenge fantasies of my own – when I'm not wondering precisely how and when my life went so far off the rails.

It doesn't seem possible that this is the same woman who loved me so much, she went back on a promise to herself not to ever get married. When we met, Alicia didn't believe in marriage in a big way, and to be honest I didn't either. Obviously, the concept of lifetime monogamy never exactly appealed to me.

She was different. And I was different with her. Something about the two of us fit in a way that we'd never known before, and neither of us wanted to let go. It was the first relationship I'd ever been in that satisfied me, didn't make me want to look elsewhere almost right away. It was years before that happened. And even when it did, I still wanted to go back to Alicia.

I didn't seek out what happened with Dani. I was determined to avoid all that forever after the calamity of Jackie. It was a miracle I got my license back in the first place.

But it turns out it's addictive, being the center of someone's world. I had missed it.

I still can't believe Alicia put in cameras. No one told me there was a video of us in my room, which makes me wonder if Dani's mom even turned it over to the cops. Maybe she didn't see the need, since they had the photos.

I deserve to be fucked, in every sense. I know that. But even so, part of me is relieved that this wasn't Dani's doing. Unlike Jackie, she didn't turn me in on purpose – Alicia forced her hand. Maybe she'll even write to me, when things settle down.

It's not like I'll have a lot else to hold onto in here.

"Harrison. You've got visitors."

I roll over and face the guard. "Who? My lawyer?"

"No." He consults a clipboard. "A Lily O'Neill and Jackie Culver."

The names hit me like a pair of acid burns. There's only one reason those two can possibly have for wanting to see me, and I'm in no mood for a reprise of Alicia's gloats over my misfortune.

So I'm about to tell them to fuck off, but then I have a better idea. I spring to my feet and quickly run my pathetic plastic comb through my hair.

"You want to see them?" the guard asks me.

"Oh yeah. I'll see them, all right."

***

He brings me down to the main visitor's center, not the private cubby where I usually meet with Marshall. On the way down, I ask the guard to remove my handcuffs during the visit. He laughs.

I would have liked to present a more intimidating image, but I suppose I'll need to rely on my knowledge of the girls' hearts to make this worth my while.

They turn toward me when I come in the room and I can see their shock at how disheveled I look. Personally, I'm taken aback in the opposite direction. Granted, they weren't at their best the last time I saw them.

Jackie looks taller. She's cut her hair short in a pixie style that's very flattering, even with dark blue streaks running through it. Never would have expected that look to suit her. She's nineteen now, but as before, her bearing adds quite a few years to her chronological age.

Lily looks exceptionally lovely. I don't know why I'm still surprised by this since she looks much the same as she did three years ago, but it hasn't stopped being bizarre.

"Okay," the guard says. "You get a max of two hours. I'll be standing off to the side here. No touching, no explicit sexual or violent talk, and no passing anything between you." He looks at Jackie. "Please put your hands on the table, miss."

Jackie complies after a beat, crushing them together in front of her chest. The moment she does, I can see the source of her reluctance. She's shaking.

I grin. This will be fun.

"And Harrison, consider this little privilege a one-shot deal. You screw it up, no more visitors the rest of the time you're here."

"No problem," I reply. I watch him back up about ten paces, and then I turn to them.

"Well, well. Jackie Culver. You've grown up," I tell her approvingly. She looks away uneasily, without responding. "And Lily. Always a pleasure. How have you been?" I nod to her hand. "Engagement ring?" I wonder if it's to the guy who was with them at the trial.

"Cut the crap, David, we're not here to catch up." I almost have to admire the derision in her tone. It's all right, though. I can still get to her.

"Why are you here?"

"To see what you have to say for yourself, now that you've finally gotten caught."

"What would you like me to say?"

"How about some kind of explanation?"

"I don't know what there is to explain."

"Start with why you had naked pictures of me hidden in your house," Jackie says softly. Her voice has a lower pitch than I remember.

"What pictures?" I ask, momentarily caught off guard. I know what she means, of course, but how does *she* know about them?

"Like you don't remember," Lily says. "Alicia found them and sent them to Jackie."

It takes considerable willpower to control my reaction to this. My bitch of an ex-wife better watch her back when I get out of here. I'll be used to prison by then.

"You never told me you took them," Jackie adds. "I was in the shower in one and your bed in the other."

"Oh, that's right." I nod as though I had indeed forgotten all about them. "Alicia found those? I can't even remember where I put them." They sure weren't with Dani's pictures. Alicia must have torn the house apart in order to find them.

"You forgot," Lily says scornfully.

"I did, actually. It's been a while."

"And you've been busy," she hisses. "What the hell is wrong with you? First me, then Jackie, now this other girl. How many of us have there been?"

I lift my hands together to scratch my chin. I haven't shaved since I've been in here. I have to get special permission and it hasn't felt worth the effort, even though the itching drives me crazy. "I can't see how that matters now, Lily. In fact, why did it ever matter?"

"It matters because you made us both think that we were the only ones. You swore you never did anything like it before. And all the while, you practically had a rotation going."

"Well, I wasn't expecting the two of you to get together and compare notes, was I?" I respond mildly. "But since you obviously have, you should have also noticed I never forced either of you into anything. You *wanted* to be with me. Isn't that right, Jackie?"

She looks down at her hands.

"It was wrong."

I laugh. "Well, you said that at the time too but it sure didn't stop you from ripping my clothes off every time you were alone with me. You were actually a lot more aggressive than Lily, here." I turn back to Lily and wink at her, enjoying her look of outrage. "Of course, she didn't have the religious baggage you did, so that helped." Lily looks like she wants to punch me. I almost wish she would. It's entertaining to get a rise out of her, and I intend to revel in my last chance to screw with these two. They deserve it. "But I never did anything with either of you that you didn't love."

"You're disgusting," Jackie says, meeting my gaze at last. "You're a fucking sociopath."

"You know, I'm really disappointed in you." For a moment, I feel like my old self again. "I have been ever since the trial. You went to *great* lengths to convince me you could handle a relationship with me in spite of your age. You knew the score from the beginning, but you owned your choices and I respected you for that. Then Lily shows up, gives you a taste of playing the victim, and all of a sudden you can barely look at me? It's a little pathetic, when –" Just in time, I remember where I am and lower my voice. I don't want the guard to take me back until I'm good and ready. "You used to text me during school, telling me how you couldn't wait for me to fuck you. Daily, sometimes. You remember doing that, right?"

Jackie turns red so quickly it makes me fear for her blood pressure.

"She was *fifteen,* David. I was sixteen. It doesn't matter if we wanted it." Lily's voice trembles a little, and I can tell my insults landed exactly as I intended with both of them. It's glorious. "God, Jackie was young enough to be your daughter. Did that register at all, you bastard?"

"Well, I guess you can sleep easy now that the bastard is getting what he deserves at last," I say nonchalantly. "Maybe I'll even find out what it's like to be raped for real – something neither of you would know, by the way – and you can feel like justice was truly served."

It's hard to make light of something that scares me so much.

But they don't need to know that.

"Do you actually expect us to feel sorry for you?" Lily retorts. "Do you have any idea what you put us through? Do you even care?"

I shrug. "Every experience comes down to what you make of it." These two are clearly doing fine despite the *horrible mess* I made of their lives. If anything, I've probably become an anecdote they tell at parties to make themselves sound more interesting.

"I can't believe I thought I was in love with you," Jackie says. "I can't even remember what I thought I loved about you in the first place."

"Enough with the bullshit, Jackie," I reply, letting my impatience show for the first time. She always hated that, they both did. A hint of annoyance from me was usually enough to get them scrambling to make up with me. "You remember everything, I can tell by the look on your face. And I have news for you. You always will." I point to her hands. "I still make you nervous, don't I?"

"Okay. We're done here," Lily says.

I shift slightly to address Lily even though my next words are mostly for Jackie. "She hasn't even had anyone else yet. I'd bet on it. And when she does, it won't be the same. It's going to take her a lot longer than twelve years to forget me." I watch Jackie cringe from my peripheral vision. "And the same goes for you, Lily. That fiancé of yours won't ever be what I was to you. You two are never going to move on from me completely. Even if you could, you wouldn't."

"Is *that* why you did it?" Jackie asks me, dumbfounded. But

I'm done talking to her. I've said enough. I grin at her instead, just like I did after I was acquitted.

Lily stands up to address the guard. "We're leaving." Jackie gets up too, slowly. I'm tempted to tell her that it looks like this didn't go the way she planned, but I don't. The most powerful thing I can do right now is continue withholding.

The guard walks over to me and waves to another one upstairs. "Harrison needs an escort back to his cell."

"Wait. Hang on a second," Lily says. I'm still smiling at Jackie and she's still trying desperately to avoid looking at me. "You're wrong, David. You think that because we're horrified at what you did, we haven't moved on? *That's* bullshit. Jackie and I have great lives now. We're doing better than ever. You're nothing to us anymore."

I look at Lily finally, thinking back to the first time I kissed her. She made it so easy for me.

"Okay, Lily. I'm glad you got that out of your system. But just remember, *you* came to see me."

Lily presses her lips together hard. Jackie puts an arm around her and turns toward the guard. Right before they make it to the door, Lily turns around again. Determined to get the last word, however silly. But she can't make anything come out.

I feel much better now. I may be the one locked up, but that's only temporary. These two will feel my hands on their bodies and hear my words in their minds until the day they die.

Epilogue

JACKIE | *DAVID*

I build the fire log-cabin style, with paper and other kindling in the middle and large sticks layered in a square around them. Gran must have taught me how to do this. I never went camping with my parents.

"Did you tell Ben what happened yet?"

"Parts of it," Lily says. "I told him what he needed to know." I can barely see her in the rapidly fading twilight.

"What did he say?"

"Same thing he's said from the beginning, that we're going to get through this together. All of us."

Ben has proven over and over to be everything Gran said he was from the start. Lily's the only person in the world who can truly sit next to this fire with me, but Ben was the one who taught me how to laugh again. That it's okay to trust someone once in a while, when they earn it.

That at least one man is capable of loving me in a way that adds to my life instead of leaving slash marks in it.

I hope Ben knows how much he means to me, because I'll never be able to say it. I don't know that I'd want to even if I could. I'd rather keep the laughter.

I pull a book of matches from my coat pocket. "Let me see if I can get this thing lit."

It doesn't take too long to get a good strong fire going. We pull the seats we brought from Gran's house a little closer, enjoying the warmth. There's a late-autumn chill in the air. Winter is definitely on the way.

We sit there in silence for over an hour, Lily and me. Until the sky turns black.

"Ready?" I say at last.

"Let's do it."

We stand up and I reach into the back pocket of my jeans to retrieve the Polaroids. I hand one to Lily and pull David's shirt out of the brown paper bag I brought along. Until I saw him again, I'd completely forgotten about his little souvenir from that night. I found it crammed into a corner of my closet at Gran's house, hidden in an old shoebox.

"It still smells like him," I observe. "Count of three?"

Lily nods. "Go ahead."

I count quietly, and we throw the shirt and photos into the fire.

David can't be retried for what he did to me. We didn't have these photos when it could have made a difference. I can't change that. And if that's how it is, I don't want anyone else to ever see them again. Not even me.

I don't want to give him any more of my life than he's already claimed.

By the time he gets out, Lily and I will be in our thirties. She'll be older than David was when I met him. I know my life will be completely different by then. I can even allow for the possibility that it will be good.

As I watch the obscene images of my young body melt and twist in the flames, I picture the last of my childhood burning away with them. Lily's hand closes around mine.

"Do you feel better?"

"No," I admit. "I don't really feel anything. I don't feel like it's over, but I don't feel like it's not over. How about you?"

"I'd say that pretty much nailed it. This one's going to take time."

"He did us a favor, saying the things he did." I sigh. "It helped me see him more clearly."

"Me too."

"Well. Like you said. All we can do now is move forward. Try to be happy."

"We'll get there again," she says firmly.

"Yeah. We will." I look back at the fire. My eyes are smarting a little from the smoke, or at least that's what I prefer to think. "Actually, though, there is one more thing I need to do first."

I don't need to say what that one thing is.

Lily already knows.

***

I glance at my phone to double check the address. It wasn't too hard to find the house.

I get out of my car, walk up to the front door, and ring the bell without hesitating. I expected to feel anxious, but it doesn't seem to be working out that way.

Maybe because I know this is right.

A woman in her late forties answers the door. "Hi there. You must be Jackie?"

"Yes, I am." I hold my hand out and the woman shakes it.

"Please come in. Thank you so much for coming."

"You don't need to thank me."

"Danielle's in the den," she says, leading me down the hall. "She's a little nervous about meeting you."

"Believe me, I know how strange this is for her."

"I really appreciate you doing it. These past weeks have been awful. Well, that really isn't a strong enough word. Our whole family is devastated." She lowers her voice. "Danielle's barely said a word since he accepted the plea. I think she's still in shock. But I'm sure you can understand that."

"I do," I say. "Very much. I hope I can help."

Danielle is sitting in a window seat, looking out into the yard with her knees pulled up against her chest. I feel a pang of recognition so strong I almost wince. This has to be how Lily felt the first time she saw me. But I put my own feelings aside, determined to reveal them only if they serve Danielle.

"Honey? Jackie's here."

The girl doesn't move. "Okay."

"I'll be in the kitchen, if you need me." She pats me on the shoulder and leaves the room.

I go over to the window and sit down on a stool nearby.

"Hi, Danielle." She doesn't respond. "Your mom said she told you I was coming."

"Yeah." She turns her head toward me, looks at me suspiciously. "I know who you are. But I don't get why you wanted to come here."

"Because I understand what you're going through, and I know how much it hurts. So I'd like to help you, if I can."

Danielle rolls her eyes. "My life is ruined. His life is ruined. What can *you* do about that?"

"That depends on what you need right now," I say. "Tell you what. I'll start by telling you what happened between me and David. And then, if you feel like it, you can tell me how it was with you. After that… we'll see what happens. How does that sound?"

Danielle looks out the window again and I wait.

Finally, she looks back at me. And nods.

So I begin to speak.

Acknowledgements

I am deeply indebted to many individuals who not only saw the potential in my writing (for decades, in some cases), but who pushed and strengthened me in ways that exceed my ability to articulate. I am profoundly grateful for their influence and support.

To Brenda Williams, who will always smoke everybody in a "who believes in me most" competition because moms are like that, and I'm lucky enough to have the best one on the planet.

To Catherine Ryan Hyde, for sharing her beautiful stories with the world and encouraging me to do the same.

To Dr. Chris A. Lockwood, whose empathy and humanity set an incredibly high bar for me and anyone else who pays attention.

To Eric Myers, for being the first industry professional to believe in my book as much as I did.

To Kristine Akenson, one of my most tireless supporters and the absolute steadiest rock of a partner in the work we do that I can imagine.

To Matthew Copeland III, whose searing insights played an invaluable role at a crucial time.

To Phaedra Baldwin, for being the face of compassion and strength, and one of the best friends I will ever have.

To Ryan Forsythe, the extremely professional/magical person who was responsible for turning this manuscript into an actual novel.

To Tamie Parker Song, whose lioness heart defies description, for laying the pages of this book in my heart years before I knew I would write it.

To the following individuals who all helped make this book a reality: Amy Beard, Annika Goff, April Lee, Della Baldwin, Grace Nordley, Jessie Roberts, JoAnn McGregor, Kathy Sims, Maggie Knopp, Michaela Barker, Sonja Peterson, Stephen Reynolds, and Taylor Smith.

To my wonderful, goofy family. They are my whole world, and their belief in me is worth the whole world.

Last but not least, to my kitties – who, naturally, couldn't care less whether they're on this list or not, yet their influence simply cannot be overstated.

About the Author

ANDREA WICKBERG is a first-time novelist living in Bend, Oregon. She does most of her writing under the cover of darkness, like a really nerdy superhero. During the daylight hours, she enjoys things that have nothing to do with writing, such as managing projects and volunteering for Saving Grace, a local nonprofit  which supports abuse survivors. She lives with her family and her cats, who frequently compete to see who can cause the most trouble. (The cats, not the family. Usually.)

www.ingramcontent.com/pod-product-compliance
Lightning Source LLC
Chambersburg PA
CBHW071450140726
47997CB00005B/1667